1

Surface Tension

Prose Series 27

Marisa De Franceschi

Surface Tension

Guernica

Toronto/Montreal/New York
1994

Cover conception: Julia Gualtieri

Antonio D'Alfonso, editor
Guernica Editions Inc.
P.O. Box 117, Station P, Toronto (Ontario), Canada M5S 2S6
P.O. Box 633, Station N.D.G., Montreal (Quebec), Canada H4A 3R1
340 Nagel Drive, Cheektowaga, N.Y. 14225-4731 USA

Legal Deposit – Second Quarter
National Library of Canada and Bibliothèque nationale du Québec.

Canadian Cataloguing in Publication Data
De Franceschi, Marisa, 1946–

Surface Tension

(Prose series; 27)
ISBN 0-920717-2

I. Title   II. Series.

PS8557.E36S87 1994   C813'.54   C93-090151-7
PR9199.3.D44S87 1994

For Paolo
and my sister, Nadia

Come back? There is no return, only a coming to, a coming towards. No linearity in experience or identity, only an awareness. The more I look ahead, the more I look inside. This is my geography.

Antonio D'Alfonso,
The Other Shore

1

I can't remember the ocean crossing. I only remember what they have told me about it. I have heard the stories countless times. If that part of my memory which is sealed in the vault of early childhood could resurrect them, they wouldn't be more vivid.

We sailed just after the second great war. That's what my father used to call it. It was great because it managed to annihilate populations, destroy vast cities, and create havoc all over the world. It was not a topical war. It was all encompassing. It showed no prejudice. A democratic war. 'You weren't safe anywhere,' my father used to say as if this was a merit. And then there was the bomb. It was a war full of rage and fury, power and force. That's why it was great.

We are on a Turkish cargo ship sailing from Genoa. It has a strange foreign name. All I am able to say of it are the first words: the Mohammed Ali. Some of the men on the ship have their heads wrapped up in cloth. I am sure they were blown up during the war. All they have left is a face. I pray they won't ever take the bandages off. I don't want to see what's underneath.

The men with the bandaged heads serve us our food. I can't eat. Not because I don't want to. I am hungry. I can't eat because I am afraid the heavy looking bandages will fall off and then I will see the insides of their heads.

Mother can't eat either. She doesn't ever come up to the dining room. She stays in our tiny cabin and throws up all the time. Father and cousin Tino bring her green apples. They're supposed to help the vomiting, but they don't.

'I guess I'm not as tough as I thought,' she says to my father.

It is cousin Tino who notices I am afraid of the men. He laughs and tells me they are just waiters. They are there to serve us and there is nothing wrong with their heads. Those are 'turbans' they are wearing. 'Underneath,' cousin Tino tells me, 'they look just like you and me.'

My father finds a friend on board. A Scandinavian blond. People think she is my mother. This makes me very angry. I am also very angry when my father invites her to eat her meals with us since we have an extra place at our table.

I am told all these things by my cousin Tino. He especially likes the part about the Scandinavian blond. My father smiles boastfully when Tino tells the story. My mother will either shake her head or utter a short reprimand to cousin Tino. 'A good chaperon you turned out to be. While I lay in bed, sick as a dog.'

'Is it my fault you were sick?' my father will say. 'What's a man to do for seventeen days?' That's how long the trip took.

In those days it was unusual for a woman to accompany her husband to America. Most of the men from our village came over alone to pave the way for the wife and family. But my mother and father wouldn't have it any other way.

'And let you loose in America?' my mother would say, her big brown eyes fixed on my father.

'*Vedi,* Tino. See that?' my father used to retaliate with just the hint of a smile on his lips. 'That's trust for you.'

'Come on, uncle Joe,' Tino would joke. 'It's not you she doesn't trust; it's all the women over here, *le americane.*'

This becomes a standing joke. What it really means is this: My father was extremely attractive and quite irresistible, which I do not doubt. He was handsome even in old age. My mother is not really angry about his flirtations. On the contrary, she basks in the glow of her husband's frivolous transgressions. After all, it is she who is married to him.

I find this quite confusing. I vow the man I marry will do no such thing to me.

We have the misfortune of bad weather. But then, what sort of weather can one expect when crossing the north Atlantic in December? My father has chosen to leave during one of the coldest months of the year.

A storm comes upon us a few days past Gibraltar. Our insides roll. Our balance is betrayed. You can feel the pull of the ship deep within the gut. Everything is tied, chained, or bolted to the floor. Few people are in the dining room tonight. They are all being sick in their rooms. I know my mother is. I have heard her throw up. I have seen her, pale and limp, climb back onto the bunk, tears in her eyes, her body trembling. But my father and I, cousin Tino and the Scandinavian blond are seated in our usual places trying to eat.

As the storm intensifies, this becomes impossible. It rages all around us. Tables and chairs break loose and smash to one side of the dining room. We are hustled out and told to go up to the glass enclosed area on the bow of the ship where we usually have afternoon tea. Up there, we are just a few steps away from the deck, where life boats hang in case of an emergency.

We are huddled together and my father thinks it would have been better if they had left us in the dining room. 'Down there, at least, we wouldn't see what we were up against,' he says. Here, the glass windows that protect us from the fierce waves also allow us to see the fury of the ocean.

My father is holding on to me. When he realizes my mother is nowhere to be seen, he wants to go look for her. He tries to hand me over to Tino, but a giant wave hits us and the bow of the ship disappears beneath the water's surface. It comes up again like a gigantic whale surfacing for air. Then it thumps down hard, slapping the waves.

A table crashes on my father and he is pinned beneath it. He loses his grip on me and I am swept away by the roll of the ship.

My father cries out my name. 'Margherita,' he calls. 'Hold on.' But there is nothing to hold on to. It's useless. I am torn from him and he is sure I will be crushed. But I am not. A hand grasps my leg.

'She's okay. I've got her.' I am saved. Tino saves me.

How I wish I could recall this event. To have so much drama submerged is a pity. But it's no use; it will not come up into my mind's screen. For years I was incensed about this non experience, to have crossed the Atlantic and not have the capacity to remember it. Years later, I made the trip again wanting to savor such a voyage for whatever misery or distraction it would offer me. I wanted to know seasickness first hand, to experience what my mother had felt. I wanted to forget Daniel.

Our destination is Canada. We have relatives there: a great aunt and some cousins. They have been in America since the first great war. This is what I hear my parents say. This is how I learn there have been two great wars.

My parents say our relatives are in the hotel business and they are rich. We are going to be staying with them.

It is here my personal memory begins. I find this quite remarkable. To not be able to squeeze out remembrances of that turbulent voyage but to remember events that followed so soon after. From here on, I do not have to rely on the memory of others. I can now accumulate and store events that will surface later, retrieving bits and pieces whenever there is a catalyst. Some, I will notice, remain dormant for decades. But they exist regardless. They are there. And I begin to wonder, what else will I uncover? And when?

2

Cousin Tino washes up in my mind more and more these days. Time passing spotlights the past. I have heard of old women who remember the past as if it happened yesterday but they cannot remember what they had for supper the night before. I am not there yet; I am only in 'middle age' by today's standards. But I wonder if that's where I'm heading. I am already at the stage where I forget the place I left the car in the mall parking lot. And I often find myself driving to I know not where.

Cousin Tino was a part of my life long before I met Steve or Daniel. Cousin Tino came to America with us. He is the first man to enter my conscious life, apart from my father. This is fortunate for me. I know that now. I loved Tino. Unconditionally. Regardless of what he did or had done. We shared a binding trust. A trust one cannot always take for granted.

Steve is the man I married. Am married to, as a matter of fact. Tino and Steve couldn't be more different. Yet I have loved them both. Yes, even Steve. For twenty five years, a quarter of a century, I have been his wife. But I am drifting from him. I am on a slow raft with no means of propulsion. Without oars even. I am simply at the mercy of the current. What to do now? Stay on my raft and see where it will bring me? Or plunge into the frigid water and swim to the other shore?

This penchant for metaphors is something new. Not even to myself can I be straightforward. When I was young, I used to shut my eyes forcefully, squeezing the lids until I could feel my skin crinkle. This was supposed to keep out all my evil thoughts. If that didn't work, I stuck my head under the blankets. But my evil thoughts bombarded me regardless. Now I use metaphors.

I read about another catastrophe. A jumbo jet falls out of the sky. Experts volley arguments using distinct medical vocabulary: 'A massive failure of the fuselage,' 'stress caused by pressurizing and depressurizing.' Some say it is due to 'metal fatigue' while others blame it on 'faulty maintenance'.

This has been happening all too frequently lately. This plane was eighteen years old. After so many years, they speculate, planes can crack and fall apart. Sometimes the cracks are noticed upon routine inspection. Then, something can be done to salvage the situation. But more often, the cracks are not detected or there are no cracks at the time of inspection. Later, something triggers the fault and the metal lets go.

Are human relationships like that, I wonder? Do they have a lifespan too? Is this what is happening to me now? Is it Daniel who is prying me open?

I feel my skin tighten. It is taut. Ready to burst. Like the plane's.

3

My great-aunt's house is a liver-colored brick. My mother says she has never seen such a dark house. Back home, houses are whitewashed, or the stucco is a bright sunset orange, a pale peach, pink, or the blue of the sea when the sun is shining on it. Here, everything is darkness. This is what she says.

A pair of giant trees stand on the front lawn. My mother says they are 'horse chestnut trees'. Not the same as the ones back home. 'We won't be able to eat these,' she warns me and I figure they must only be for horses.

Because it is winter, the trees are bare and spindly looking. There's a nest up at the top but I know there can't be any birds in it now. When I go outside, I like to put my arms around the trees and feel their roughness. I also like the way I can hide behind one if I want to. That's how big they are. Whoever is on the other side can't see me.

A verandah stretches across the front of my great-aunt's house. Two pillars stand like sentinels upon this verandah and reach up to the roof. Their great height and thickness frightens me. I get dizzy when I look up at them.

Inside, there are countless rooms and all sorts of nooks and crannies. The kitchen is painted an egg yolk yellow. It is the first room I see.

An enormous round table sits in the middle of this room. My mother says it is 'oak'. It too is painted yellow. But it is nicked and scratched and I can see the wood peeking through.

This is the strangest table I have ever seen. A rust-colored covering is tucked into it looking as if someone has cut out a circle and filled it with this material. My mother says it is 'leather'.

The yellow oak goes around this circle making it look like a giant frame. It reminds me of a black-eyed Susan.

The chairs are also yellow. And the same leather covers the seats. But these are not the only chairs in the room. There are chairs everywhere. Some are lined up against the walls. Others are stacked in corners. There are chairs made of wood that has not been painted and some are a shiny metal. 'Chrome,' says my mother. These have seats that are split and I can see their insides bulging out like the inside of a fig when someone pulls it open. Those that are really bad have towels draped over them.

There are three doors in and out of the kitchen. Two are used all the time: the one that goes outside and the one that goes to the bathroom. The third door goes to the dining room. It is never used.

Sometimes the door to the bathroom is left open and I can smell pee. I hate using this bathroom, but I often have to. I cover my nose and mouth with my hands whenever I go in. There is another one upstairs, but there are always people in it. And besides, it doesn't smell much better. My great-aunt has boarders. Some live upstairs. They sleep in rooms next to the one we sleep in. Others live downstairs.

These men smell. They smell of beer and pee. I see them come out of the bathroom. I listen to hear if they have washed their hands. They never do. Usually they come out and their hands are still busy with their zippers. Men have zippers in this country; in the old country, my mother says, there were buttons. Four, usually.

Sometimes I will see wet spots on the front of their pants. I know what that is. It isn't water. These men never close the bathroom door. They don't even flush the toilet. My great-aunt has to remind them. 'Shut the bloody door, Sam,' she will yell. Or: 'Can't even flush a goddamned toilet.' And then she will go and do it herself.

When these men come in shaking snow off their clothes, they also smell musty. It reminds me of the mould-covered salami hanging in the cellar. But not exactly. With the cloud of cigarette smoke in the kitchen, the smell is different.

Men come and go at all hours of the day and night. Not only the boarders. These other men come around the side of the house and into the kitchen at the back. They sit at the oak table if there's room. If there isn't, they grab one of the chairs and sit wherever there's space.

Some of these men, the younger ones, sit backwards on the chairs. They twirl the chair around and then lean their elbows on the back of it and sit with their legs apart like that. I have never seen my father sit this way.

My great-aunt and her daughter pop open bottles of beer or they serve the men wine. Sometimes the men say, 'How's about a shot.' Then my great-aunt pulls out a bottle filled with a caramel tinted liquid and she pours some into tiny glasses. I watch them drink it in one gulp. They will often smack their lips afterwards.

My great-aunt and her daughter are bootleggers. That's what I hear. They are also blind pigs. They don't look at all like pigs to me and I am certain they are not blind. I can't understand why my parents would say such things.

Most of the men look dark to me. They wear brown or grey pants and jackets that never match and are always very wrinkled. Their hats tilt to the side, hiding an eye. Their shirts are often threadbare at the collar and their sweaters are tattered. They burn holes in their clothes when cigarette ashes accidentally fall on them. I hear my mother tell my father one man died because of a cigarette burn. He fell asleep in one of the chairs and burned a hole in his shin. The hole wouldn't get better and they had to cut his leg. At the knee, first. Later all the way. Eventually, he died. I never knew people could die from a tiny cigarette burn.

There are those that look clean enough. Now and then I see some with slicked back hair, a grey herringbone coat, a scarf, a hat with a velvet band and a tiny feather sticking out of it. Sometimes there are even women. But not often. If they do come, they are always with a man.

These men do not frighten me, but I don't like them either. I do not yet understand all of what they are saying. And, in fact, they say very little when I do happen by the kitchen. Mostly they just stare at me. I think they see me as a nuisance. They would rather I not be there.

My mother, however, does not like them at all.

4

Mother is squeezing cousin Tino's pimples again. She enjoys this. So does he. He calls to her. '*Zia* Lydia, I've got a batch of pimples on my back.' He lies down on the bare floor, pulls his undershirt up, and gets ready. I have never seen her squeeze pimples on my father. Perhaps he doesn't have any. I have never seen her rub his back either. But she rubs cousin Tino's.

Now I understand her delight in squeezing pimples. The pleasure of seeing pus burst out at you or splash on to the mirror in front of you if it's yourself you're working on. There may even be a bit of blood. All the more exciting. If there isn't, you squeeze until it comes out bright and red. You have to do this, my mother used to say. To make sure all the pus is out. Dull, dark, crimson blood is still pusy blood; it is the bright red kind you are after.

When she runs out of pimples, she hunts for blackheads. She bends her head down close to my cousin's back and searches as if looking for lice.

Blackheads are different. When you squeeze them, they come out wiggly like a worm. A tiny white worm with a tiny pin dot black head. I figure that's why they're called blackheads.

The blackheads around the nose are the most fun. They squiggle out madly as if they have been in hiding and are now running moblike in mass hysteria. They remind me of mother's potato masher, the one with all the little holes on the sides and bottom.

Mother puts whole, hot potatoes into this, then lowers a disk and squeezes the handles together. The potatoes come out just like the blackheads.

I like combing cousin Tino's thick wavy hair. It feels so much softer than my doll's stringy blonde wig. Sometimes I set his hair in pin curls the way mother does mine. I wrap strands of hair around a finger and then stick a bobby pin across the round curl to hold it in place. When I do Tino's hair, my father says, 'And I suppose you're going to be a hairdresser?' And then he likes to tell us we look like chimps grooming one another.

Mother squeezes pimples on herself as well. She sits in front of the mirror prodding and poking, pressing and pulling at her face and whatever other part of her body she can reach. I watch and learn. Later I will do the same.

When I am older, this practice is a topic in health class. At school, they tell us not to squeeze pimples. Just wash your face with soap and water, they say. And never squeeze anything in the nose area. That triangle is dangerous. An infection there could go to your brain.

Mother thinks this is nonsense.

Sometimes I think, what if the teachers were right? Could that be the reason cousin Tino was the way he was?

At night, my parents speak in hushed voices. I pretend to sleep because I want to hear what they are saying. My small bed is in the same room as theirs. Tino is elsewhere.

Their conversations intrigue me. What I can make of them. Mother talks about the men a lot. 'If only I had known,' she says. '*Non sapevo niente.*'

'They're your relatives,' my father will say, because they are. They are not from his side of the family.

I fall asleep with the droning sound of their voices.

During the day, my mother is kept busy. There are glasses to be washed, bottles to be collected, cases to be opened and stored in the ice box. There are beds to be made, rooms to be cleaned, washing to be done. Mother also has us.

Upstairs, there is a small kitchen, where the boarders cook. We have to cook there too. We take turns. Whenever my mother has the chance, I find her scrubbing this tiny kitchen and boiling water to disinfect the plates, the bent forks, and the worn-out spoons. These things we eat with and eat on look older and uglier than the ones we had in the old country, she says. Mother is always afraid we'll catch something from the boarders who are forever coughing and spitting up slimy looking globs. Sometimes we can hear them through the walls. My mother will retch and my father will say something he thinks is funny.

'Maybe he'll choke,' he'll say. This doesn't make mother feel much better.

My great-aunt has a son. He is my cousin too. Just like Tino. But he is not like Tino. This other cousin is big and dark and although I have never seen any monsters, not even pictures of them in books, I think this must be what a monster looks like. His name is Bruno.

When the weather turns warm, Bruno is often shirtless and we can see his hairy chest and his thick muscles. Cousin Tino always wears an undershirt. Even when it is hot.

Bruno wears short pants and he scratches himself all the time. Cousin Tino never wears short pants.

This new cousin has a wife and a daughter who is about my age. Her name is Angela. The name makes me think of angels with wide wings and stars for halos. But when I see Angela, I stop thinking of angels.

Angela is afraid of her father. Whenever she sees him, she stops playing. If she is talking, she stops talking. And if she happens to be laughing, she gets rid of her laugh and puts on a frown. She does this very well. Very quickly. Her father says, 'Get that grin off your face.' And she does.

Whenever her father calls her, his voice is gruff and deep. 'Get me some cigarettes,' he says. Then he will throw some money at her before she has a chance to catch it and when she doesn't catch it he says, 'Clumsy.' She dashes out the back door and lets the screen slam in my face. When she comes back, she is usually gasping for air, red and sweaty.

Sometimes he hits her. My father never hits me. If she takes too long getting the cigarettes, he might hit her. It all depends on his mood. He might hit her across the face with the back of his hand. I have seen him do that. Or he might grab her long blonde hair and lift her up by it. Then he might throw her up against a wall. I run away when I see these things. If I don't run fast enough, he will say, 'What are you gawking at? Get out before I get you too.'

I have seen him kick her with his boots. He lifts her up into the air with each kick. Once, he marched her clear across the backyard and out to the alley like this. She had forgotten to do something. I can't remember what it was.

My mother says, 'He's an animal.'

My father says, 'Mind your own business.'

Angela's mother doesn't say much. She is very quiet when he's around. And she trembles a lot.

My mother says, 'He's going to kill that child one of these days.'

As it turns out, he doesn't have to. Angela will do it herself, later, when she is about eighteen.

Bruno, his wife, and Angela sleep in one of the rooms upstairs. Sometimes I see him as I walk from the tiny kitchen to our bedroom. He is usually lying on the bed. I always feel shaky and weak when I have to pass his room. I try not to look in.

He is not in his room today. At least, I don't see him. I stop and peek in, thinking it is safe. I am curious to see where Angela and her parents sleep.

'Gotcha,' he says popping out from behind the door. I stiffen with fear. 'I knew you were the nosey type,' he says as he tightens his grip. He has me by the shoulders.

I am embarrassed. My face is flushing. I can feel the redness.

I am still too young to know why I feel this way. I am six at the most. But I know I have done something naughty. I think of that line I hear older people say. 'Curiosity killed the cat.' I know little girls aren't supposed to be so curious.

'Where's your mother?' he asks letting go of my shoulders. He doesn't look as mean today as he pours himself some of that caramel-colored liquid my great-aunt gives the men. He swallows it in one gulp then wipes his mouth with the back of his hand and smacks his lips, just like the men. His eyes look glossy and watery. 'Well,' he says. 'I asked you a question. Where's your mother?'

'Downstairs,' I reply. I am polite. My parents have taught me to be polite. Besides, I know enough not to get him angry.

'And your old man?'

I know he means my father, even though he isn't old. 'I don't know,' I tell him. 'He works someplace.'

He walks over to his bed and lies down on it. He folds his arms behind his head and I can see the hair in his armpits. It is very long and it sticks together. He isn't wearing a shirt.

He has dark eyes that gleam like the lumps of coal I see my father shovel into the furnace in the basement and his face is wide and large.

'Get in here,' he says. 'And shut the door.' I go in because I don't know what else to do. Also because I don't know what he'd do if I refused.

'How's about a back rub,' he says.

I pull away.

'Come on,' he says. 'Don't be shy. I'm your cousin. I've seen you and your mother rub your cousin Tino's back. And you even comb his hair, don't you?'

This is true, of course. And so I go to him.

I rub his back for a while and then he turns so that now I am asked to rub his stomach. This feels strange. I have never seen my mother do this. But I continue. I rub and rub because he doesn't tell me to stop. I can feel bristly hairs between my fingers — a new sensation. Cousin Tino doesn't have hair on his chest.

I can feel him staring at me so I keep my eyes away from his. He tells me, 'It feels good. Real good.' He touches my hair and I pull my head back. But I don't stop rubbing.

'That a girl,' he says. 'Don't stop.'

He tells me he likes my long brown hair. 'What soft curls you have,' he says as he runs his hands through it.

Then he asks me to go lower. 'Lower,' he says in his not so nice voice. 'Go down a little lower.' I do as I am told.

I find my hands going over his belly button and I feel stranger still. Then he undoes his zipper. I twitch but I don't know why. I have no idea what it is I am afraid of now. It is a different kind of fear. I am not afraid he is going to hit me the way he hits Angela. It is something else. All I know is what I have seen. And I have never seen my mother do this.

And then it is there. He goes into his pants and pulls it out and he tells me to rub it too. It feels hot and swollen and unsafe. I rub it as I am told to do. This feels wrong. But I don't know why.

This memory lies hidden for decades. I am a grown woman when it finally surfaces.

5

On Sundays we go out to visit my great-uncle who lives on a farm about thirty miles from the city. A bus takes us to a town near my uncle's place, then we walk. Later, when my father buys the old Hudson, we drive out.

My great-uncle and his wife, the great-aunt with all the men, do not live together anymore. 'They don't get along,' I have heard my mother say.

'It's no wonder,' says my father.

My uncle likes to show me his scar. 'See this,' he says, pulling his shirt up. 'That's what your dear great-aunt gave me so I wouldn't ever forget her.'

The scar is a thick white slash on my uncle's belly, just below the heart. It is jagged and ugly. It gives me goose bumps to think a knife was once in my uncle's belly.

My parents like to help my great-uncle out. There are chickens to be fed or tomatoes to hoe and later to pick. My uncle's work is never done and he appreciates all the help he can get.

Mother will cook the Sunday meal while the others work. She also does my uncle's laundry and cleans the house while I play outside. 'That's the least I can do,' she says.

One Sunday, a car pulls into the gravel driveway. Dust flies into my eyes and makes me cough. My great-uncle always warns people not to drive in like that because, in the summer, when it's very dry out here, everything around the farmhouse gets coated with dust. I turn to see who is causing this and when the dust settles, I notice it is my great-aunt and Bruno, Angela's father. They get out of the car and slam the doors. They seem angry. I am standing in front of the barn and they don't notice me.

They go in the back door of the house and I hear the screen squeak and then slam against the frame, squeaking a couple more times before it finally stops. I run up to the house, but I do not go in. That's when I hear my mother scream.

I feel the blood rush into my head as I run inside. Angela's father has caught my mother and pinned her to the wall. He has her hands clasped behind her. My great-aunt is slapping my mother in the face, punching her in the stomach. I scream out and Bruno throws his eyes upon me.

'Get the hell out of here,' he yells. I continue to scream.

'Get rid of her,' my great-aunt says.

My eyes dart about the room looking for a weapon. I spot a broom and grab it. I wave it at Angela's father, but he is too strong. He twists it out of my hands and whips me with it. My mother screams louder.

'Run, Margaret,' she screams. But I don't.

My great-aunt is saying bad things to my mother. I don't understand all of her words, but I know they are not nice words. She is calling my mother a 'bitch'. 'You bitch,' she says. Over and over again, she yells this. She tells my mother she isn't going to live 'the life of Riley.' She tells her, 'Money doesn't grow on trees in America.' Then she hits her again and again.

Chapter 5

I kick Angela's father in the shins, but he just boots me with his foot the way people do when they're trying to get rid of a dog. I tear at my great-aunt's dress but Bruno sends the broom crashing down upon my head. I am afraid they will pull out a knife and stick it into my mother's belly the way they did to my great-uncle. But that doesn't happen. My great-uncle smashes through the door and pulls them off my mother. 'Let her go, you bastard,' he says to Bruno. Blood drips from my mother's nose. When they let go of her, she nearly drops to the floor like a rag doll. 'Get the hell out of here,' my great-uncle yells at the two of them.

I stand there shaking and I watch my great-aunt and Bruno leave. The car spins in the driveway sending more dust into the air.

'Lucky for you I was just coming in from the fields,' says my great-uncle. 'Joe got the tractor going and I'd just jumped up when I noticed the dust.'

My father comes in then. He says, 'What the hell? What did they do this for? *Disgraziati.*'

Sometimes I think, it is just as well some memories have been erased or put in storage for the time being. There is so much I can't forget, it's a good thing there are things I can't remember.

6

The tiny place we move to is full of rats. Mother does not mind mice; she is not the squeamish type. But she has something against rats. As for me, I am afraid of everything.

Father says he is going to kill every last rat so my mother will stop hounding him. He and cousin Tino go out and come back with a bunch of mouse traps, big wooden platforms with deadly springs that are supposed to clamp down on the rats' heads. They cut bits of cheese and gingerly place them in the traps. Then they set the springs, being careful not to get their fingers caught. When the traps are ready, they put them all over the house.

'Don't touch them,' cousin Tino warns me, as if I would.

It does not take long to clean out the rats in the cellar. They are the first to go. Those that did not get their heads snapped, Tino chased out with a broom, whacking them hard as they scampered around in that dark hole under our kitchen. I didn't see Tino do it, but I heard him. 'You little buggers won't be coming up for a midnight snack,' he said to the rats.

When the cellar's cleaned up, my father plugs the holes under the sink and in the bathroom so the rats, if there are any left down there, won't be able to find a way out. But they must be coming in from other places because we always find more. Tino says, '*Porco cane.* They must be sending in the backup troops.'

We don't see them during the day. That's because rats like to come out at night when we are all in bed. Sometimes I can hear them running around the house looking for food. Tino says, 'If we're lucky they'll find some.' He means the cheese. Some even seem to be inside the walls. I can hear them scratching on the other side of the gyproc.

Whenever we hear a spring snap shut, my mother winces. 'There's another one,' she will say and Tino will run to see if it's a rat we've caught or just another false alarm. Sometimes, the rats manage to take the cheese and run away.

Rats are pretty smart.

This morning, cousin Tino comes into the kitchen with two rats. He has the tails gripped between his teeth really tight, so tight he can actually make a big wide grin and not let the rats fall out. He moves his head from side to side and the rats swing one way and then the other. He also makes gruesome noises when he does this. It is supposed to be funny. I know this because my father is laughing. My mother just squeezes her eyes shut and tells Tino to bury the rats out in the garden. That's where all the rats we catch end up. That means they will all be under tomato or cucumber plants next spring. Maybe some will be lucky and end up under flowers.

7

Lately, the house with all the rats keeps rising to the surface for me. It is a vacant lot now, waiting for a developer. There's a sign up saying something to that effect. *Vacant Lot,* it reads. But it is not vacant for me. I can still see Tino with the rat tails in his mouth.

I find myself driving around downtown a lot. I drive over to my great-aunt's place, which is also gone. There is a geared-to-income high rise there instead looking like a beehive with its row upon row of small rectangular windows, each exactly like the other, and a single row of sliding glass doors down the centre of the building. It looks more like a prison than a dwelling. This cold symmetry is not inviting, but beggars can't be choosers, my mother used to say.

Daniel would wince at such architectural folly, although he could explain the rationality behind it: the symmetry is necessary in high rises, he would say; the load bearing walls can not be broken up by irregularly placed windows and doors.

There is only one other house on that street now. The one my great-aunt's daughter moved into when business became more than my aunt could handle on her own. It is only a matter of time before it too will be gobbled up. But, in the meantime, my aunt's daughter, quite old herself now, continues to practice her trade. The men still come and go. And he is still around too. My great-aunt's son, Bruno.

I have to laugh. This street is a short one. It ends just beyond where my great-aunt's house once stood. Then it divides into a horseshoe shape, half going one way half the other. And right in the cradle, where the two streets go their separate ways, stands the police station. It was there then too. The courts were there as well and still are today. And City Hall. The hub of the city.

My great-aunt had guts. I can say that much for her.

Years later, I learned the neatly dressed and dapper gentlemen I used to see were police officers on the take. They used to come regularly to collect their payola, my father used to tell me. As far as I know, my great-aunt was arrested only the one time. And that didn't amount to much. They let her go the same day. For over fifty years that woman stuck her nose up at the law. In consequence she became rich. And they say crime doesn't pay?

I call home to see if Steve is there. 'Where the hell are you?' he shouts over the receiver.

Steve is keeping tabs on me. I know it. He doesn't trust me. I can't blame him. Why should he?

'I'll be a little late,' I tell him in my composed manner.

'How late is late?' he wants to know. He is upset.

'I just stopped off to pick up some groceries.' A lie. I have nothing in the car. I will have to stop somewhere now, and that will take more time.

I drive up the street and follow the right hand curve. The city market is just ahead. Abe's Fish Market is still here. It looks the same. There have been no embellishments.

I walk in to the familiar sound of a tinkling bell and a plump grey haired old man with a serious round face says, 'Hi, Lady. Come on in,' as if I were entering his home.

I walk over to the counter, quickly perusing the fish. 'I'd like some flounder,' I say.

'Sure, Lady. We got flounder.' He still has an accent. I can hear it now. It isn't just the way he says his words; it is the cadence that I remember. The unmistakable Jewishness in him. 'My son will take care of you,' he says.

The son is already cutting a piece of brown waxed paper and going behind the fish counter. This is before I even tell him how much I want.

The father looks back down on a bagel he is cutting in half and spreading with one of his concoctions. This is for a customer who is standing behind the crustacean counter. Must be a regular. I find myself trying to remember if Abe's fish market used to sell lobster and such in the old days. Probably not. For one thing, who could have afforded these luxuries? And the old man was probably more strict then.

I turn to the son. He looks just like the father except he is much skinnier. He has black, curly hair and a protruding nose. Every visible part of his body is covered with the same night black hair: his arms up to his elbows, which I can see because he has rolled up his sleeves, his face which looks like it has a dark shadow on it even though it has been shaved, his neck, visible through the opening at the shirt collar. He could be good-looking if he weren't so miserably thin. His father actually looks better.

So this is the son I used to see when I came with my mother. He would be about my age, if I remember correctly. There's still hope for the skinny son, I catch myself thinking as my eyes dart back and forth, furtively comparing father and son. Yes, I conclude, the father does indeed look better to me.

I blush at my thoughts — vestiges of my tenacious attachment to older men.

'Do you have any fresh flounder?' I ask when he places two frozen fillets on the brown sheet.

'What are you doing with it?' he asks, stopping for a moment.

'I'd like to stuff it.'

'Then this is what you want,' he says matter-of-factly. He looks straight at me and it is as if he is saying, 'I'd like to stuff you, Lady.' I feel more like an intruder than a customer. Maybe it's because I am not a regular, or maybe it's because I am not a Jew, although I could easily pass as one with my dark hair and brown eyes. But my demeanor is all wrong.

'How much would you like?' he asks.

'I guess I'll take six.'

'It's just slightly frozen,' he says, noticing the reticence in my voice. I am, after all, a customer.

He puts four more fillets on the paper and goes to the cash counter.

'Anything else?' he asks.

'I'd like to look a bit, if you don't mind.'

'Sure. Take your time,' he mumbles, his words hollow and insincere.

I turn to the other counter and inspect the three sizes of shrimp. I glance at my watch. I must hurry. I must decide.

Chapter 7

'I'll take a pound of the small shrimp,' I say. 'Small will do since I'm just going to use them to stuff the flounder,' I add. I don't know why I do this sort of thing all the time. I am forever explaining myself to others whenever it comes to trivial matters such as this. I hate myself for it. Why can't I be like those women I see who order what they want the way they want it? No explanation. Period. Hasn't middle age taught me anything? I guess that sort of blatant brassiness comes with old age — still ahead for me. So there is something to look forward to after all.

I feel silly and I want to leave. I can't wait to pay and get out of here. The son weighs the shrimp. It's just over a pound, naturally.

On a small white pad he figures how much I owe him. No calculators here. No fancy stuff. Even if I had had a dozen items, they would have been added up by hand.

The son tosses my purchases into a plastic sack. I thank him. The old man says, 'Come again.' He barely lifts his head when he says this. The son says nothing.

I had every intention of telling them I used to come here when I was a little girl, but it doesn't look as if they're much interested in knowing. And why should they be? They are busy making a living. These mushy recollections of the past must seem trivial indeed.

I trot over to my car laughing to myself. I am so corny. But they are so funny in their intensity. After all, all they do is sell fish. But to look at them, you would think they were manipulating the economic strategy of the entire continent. Perhaps that's why they're so successful. Like Steve. All seriousness. Work is serious business. No levity allowed. I look back for a moment to assure myself they do not see me laughing. They would be offended and I do not wish to offend. But they are paying no attention to me. I can see their heads bent busy at some task. There is work to be done.

When I come out, I find all four tires slashed. The inner city. It's still the same. They may have made pedestrian malls and built skyscrapers, but it is still the same.

I am in a dither. How do I explain this to Steve? Why am I here? Far from my office. What do I say? One day all the lying will catch up to me and that will be the day.

8

A woman named Dorothy used to live in the flat above ours. The one with all the rats.

Whenever I think of Dorothy, I see her sitting or reclining on a blanket which she spread on the front lawn to avoid grass stains on her clothes. Lawn is probably too flamboyant a word for the postage stamp size patch of grass we had in front of the makeshift apartment where we lived, but Dorothy was flamboyant and the word lawn suits her even if it doesn't suit the reality of the environment we lived in.

She was forever filing and painting her nails as she lounged on the blanket. When she did mine in the same flame red as her own, I became her friend forever.

Our place couldn't be called 'a building'. That word conjures up thoughts of a solid structure, a planned environment. Ours was no such thing. I don't know how Daniel would have defined this place and, by the time I met him, it had long since had its rendezvous with the wrecking ball. It was just a jumble of shapes thrown together in a haphazard manner. A small square box of an apartment must have been the original dwelling. Then someone added another box on top of that and they put those ugly steel stairs on the outside of the building — the ones Dorothy's husband climbed everyday. Then they added a few rooms at the back and on to the side and we lived back there. It was a real hodgepodge of a place. But we were glad to have it. At least we were out of my great aunt's house and away from all the men.

Dorothy and her husband don't have any children. She doesn't work as far as we can tell, but he does. He is a garbage man.

Dorothy's husband is very tall. He has the curliest and darkest hair I have ever seen.

Whenever he comes down the steel stairs from their apartment, he stops and gives me a nickel. That's a lot of money.

He goes across the street a lot. That's because there's a hotel over there. A real one. Not like my great-aunt's place.

Dorothy's husband is also very handsome. My mother says he is a 'good-looking man'. She doesn't understand why Dorothy can't see that. My father says, 'I'm sure she does, but maybe one isn't enough for her.'

Dorothy asks me about cousin Tino a lot. She says, 'Where's that cousin of yours?' Or she will say, 'That cousin of your has to loosen up.'

Cousin Tino says if Dorothy doesn't watch herself, she'll be sorry. I don't know what he means.

Dorothy is painting my nails again. We are stretched out on the front lawn. She looks beautiful. Her lips are painted red and they glisten in the sun. Her skin looks warm and soft. It is the color of the chestnuts my mother buys. I want to touch it to see if it feels like my own skin or different. Her hair is pulled back today. She has it tied with a red ribbon. This makes her face look larger and more beautiful. Her eyes stand out. They are black and shiny. So black the whites seem pearly and brighter than anything I have ever seen. She has long dark lashes that fan in front of her eyes. Her lids shimmer. She wears eye shadow on her lids and every time she looks down, I can see a streak of lavender.

Dorothy is not paying attention to my nails. She is letting some of the polish get on my skin. I don't like this. It looks messy and I want my nails perfect, just like hers.

She is looking out back, towards our place, as if she is waiting for something to happen.

Tino appears at the door. Dorothy straightens a bit, but she doesn't get up. She looks at Tino with those lavender eyes. 'Well, well. Look who's here,' she says, as if she didn't know he was inside. Tino doesn't say anything. 'Cat got your tongue?' she says to him. Then she asks him to come over and sit with us.

Tino comes over, but he doesn't sit with us. 'What are you doing to her?' he asks. I find him kind of mean right now.

'Just making the poor kid happy,' says Dorothy. I don't like the way she's calling me 'kid'.

'She's happy,' Tino answers. 'You don't need that shit to be happy,' he says. I know he is talking about the nail polish.

'And what does it take to make you happy?' she says to him. He doesn't answer. So she continues. 'Why don't you take me for a drink sometime?' she says. 'What about right now?'

Tino turns and goes back inside. 'That cousin of yours,' says Dorothy. 'Such a waste.'

That night, I hear Tino tell my mother about Dorothy. My mother laughs and says Dorothy must like

Tino. 'Maybe if her husband didn't spend all his spare time in that hotel across the street, she wouldn't be looking at you,' she says.

My mother doesn't like the hotel. She blames it for a lot of things. But I like the hotel. I like having it there. I like it because it makes collecting bottle caps so easy.

My friend David, who lives in a real apartment building across the street and next to the hotel, picks up bottle caps and brings them over to me. I am not allowed to cross the street because it's a busy one. Besides horses, there are cars, trucks, and buses. In the old country, in our town, we had horses, but not many of the others.

The milkman comes with a horse. Every time he stops in front of our house he has to go. That's what my mother says. Plop. Plop. Plop. What a smell. Neat little shit piles smelling in the street right in front of our place.

There is a cedar hedge around the front yard, then the sidewalk, and then the street. My mother doesn't like it when I take my little chair and sit by the opening in the hedge waiting for David.

'A car might lose control and come right up here and kill you,' she warns me. Crossing the street would have been like asking to go to the moon and I don't even dare try it. I just sit patiently, watching and waiting for David. I like hearing the bottle caps clinking and bouncing around in his pockets when he runs across the street to me. When he comes over, he empties his pockets and we sort the caps into different piles. Then we put the groups into paper bags my mother has given us. I don't know why we do this. I guess it's just for fun because we both enjoy seeing the caps that belong together in their proper piles. When we're done sorting, if we happen to find an intruder in a pile, we pluck it out as if it has some kind of disease.

I liked counting and sorting and trying to keep things in order even then.

It is Dorothy who comes to tell us about David. There is a knock at the door and mother tells me to see who that might be. I am shocked when I see Dorothy standing there. She has never been to our door even though she only lives upstairs. I call out to my mother, 'It's Dorothy, the lady upstairs.'

My mother comes to the door but she doesn't ask Dorothy in. Dorothy asks my mother to come outside. There is something she'd like to tell her. I am not stupid. I know it is something I am not supposed to hear.

David wasn't killed while crossing the street. He was always very careful. I watched him many times from my side. He looked both ways: right then left and right again before coming across.

No, David died as he was standing at the corner waiting for a bus. He had been holding his mother's hand.

It was his birthday and he and his mother were going to Kresge's downtown to get his present. They were standing at the bus stop in front of their apartment building. A large truck went by. David was too close to the curb and the gush of air from the truck sucked him under. That is how my parents describe it.

We get dressed up as if we are going to church. My mother says she just can't come. She can't face it. So it is my father who takes me to the funeral parlor. Tino can't come because he has to work.

We walk quite a way and then my father says, 'There. That's the place.'

It is a very big house, even bigger than my great-aunt's. It has the same kind of brick as hers and it has tall windows which are made up of many little squares.

When we go in the front door, I smell a peculiar odor. It makes me want to sneeze, but I hold on. Everything is quiet in here. I can tell it would not do to sneeze in a place like this.

The floors are covered wall to wall with thick carpets that have large designs on them, all very dark. Browns and greens and blood reds. The wallpaper has gold leaves, trees, and scenes of park-like places.

There are many rooms in this house. We go into one of these where I see rows and rows of chairs. Although the house doesn't look like a church at all, the chairs lined up like this remind me of one. Up ahead, I see flowers. My father tells me David is up there where the flowers are. As we walk towards the flowers, the smell gets worse. I have to put my hand in front of my nose.

I must be walking too quickly because my father tells me to 'slow down'. He doesn't understand I am in a hurry. I want to see David... I want to tell him I'll be waiting for him tomorrow. We only need a few more bottle caps to complete the set we have been working on. When we get to a hundred, we say it is finished.

And then I see him lying upon shiny white cushions. His eyes are closed and it looks as if he is asleep.

'David,' I call out. I am about to give him a shake when my father tells me to be quiet. He catches my hand before I get the chance to touch my friend.

'But, Daddy,' I say. 'David has to get up. We have to go and play.'

I am bewildered. Why is my friend lying there in that shiny whiteness? He is supposed to be with me.

'He's gone, Margherita,' says my father. '*È morto*.'

This is my first encounter with death.

9

Cousin Tino has killed people. I know this. I also know it happened during the war when it was all right to kill people. 'It was either them or us,' Cousin Tino says. Knowing this about cousin Tino does not make me afraid of him. But it does make me afraid of wars.

They are always talking about the war at our house. Every night. They talk about it when I am in bed. When they think I'm asleep. I let them think this. That way, they talk on and on. If I'm around and cousin Tino and my father say something about the war, my mother will say, 'Please, Joe, not now.' Then she'll look over at me and I know she doesn't want me to hear what they are saying.

This only makes me want to go to bed earlier. The earlier I go, the sooner they will start.

These are my bedtime stories.

Tonight it's the Mongol story again. As I turn on my side and curl up comfortably, I listen to hear how the Mongols came into our town killing and taking women and girls away with them. I can't imagine what they would want with a bunch of whining girls and women.

I picture the Mongols as dark people with long mustaches and curly black hair. They are always galloping on horseback, trampling over things and ruining everything. I don't ever see them as regular people.

Cousin Tino always gets excited when he talks about the Mongols. 'Those bastards,' he says. '*Ti ricordi, zio?* The night we caught that bunch?'

'I'll never forget it,' says my father. 'If it weren't for me, he'd have killed them all,' he tells my mother who is still busy cleaning up the kitchen while she listens to them.

'We found them trying to get away,' my father continues. 'Tino and I ambushed their cart and managed to disarm them...'

My favorite part is coming. This is what I have been waiting for. I know exactly what's coming, but I want to hear it again. I lie motionless. That way I won't miss a word.

'.....Tino tied them up hands and feet and shoved them into a corner of the cart while I stood guard.'

'I wanted to kill them then and there,' says Tino. 'But uncle Joe wouldn't let me. *Peccato*.'

'I figured we should take them up to the Americans and let them deal with it,' says my father. 'But, I tell you, Lydia, Tino ground them to a pulp along the way.'

'Filthy swine, *maiali,*' says Tino.

'He bashed their heads in with the butt of his rifle.'

'I wanted to blow their goddamned brains out.'

When the story is over, I roll over on my other side, away from the figures of my father and cousin Tino and my mother, and I try to imagine what it is like to smash someone's skull.

This talk of war lingered in our house like the smell of boiled cabbage. I was fascinated by these stories when I was very young. Later, I was repulsed by them and I grew to almost resent my father and cousin Tino for dwelling on them. Why couldn't they let go? I used to think. Forget it. Be done with it. And then, later still, I finally understood; this would have been impossible, the way it is impossible for me to forget now.

10

My father thinks a little bit of war and misery never killed anybody. He says that sort of thing 'builds character'. Cousin Tino agrees.

'If Dorothy and her husband, and a lot of other people over here, had real important things to worry about, they wouldn't be wasting their time arguing over nonsense.' That's what Tino says. 'Maybe,' he says, 'if Dorothy didn't spend so much time painting her nails, her husband wouldn't be so rough on her.'

My mother repeats what she always says about Dorothy and her husband. 'If he didn't spend so much time at that hotel, she wouldn't waste her time painting her nails.'

Tino says she is defending Dorothy because she is a woman.

This conversation is taking place over dinner on account of the noise that is coming from upstairs.

Dorothy and her husband are having another argument. They get louder and louder while we get quieter and quieter trying to make out what they are saying.

They start throwing things at each other. Every time my mother hears a crash, she tightens her shoulders and squeezes her eyes shut.

This sort of thing can go on for a while, until they tire out or one of them leaves. But tonight it is dragging on and on. Things smash against the floor, which is our ceiling. My mother says, 'One of these days they're going to send the ceiling down on our heads.'

The light fixture begins to sway. We all look up and watch it. There's another crash. Then another, even louder. A thump. As if a body has fallen to the ground. A scream. Something is being dragged across the floor. My mother is getting nervous. 'Tino, *per l'amor di Dio,* do something.' I don't know why she doesn't say this to my father.

'What do you want me to do?' says Tino. Then he looks at me. He knows I like Dorothy.

'We can't just sit here,' says my mother. Then we hear another thump.

My mother practically leaps from the table. 'If you don't go up, I will,' she says bravely. And then the light fixture crashes down upon us. Tiny shards of milk white glass cover the table. Plaster from the ceiling is mixed in with the broken light fixture. Our dinner is ruined.

'*Dio mio,* ' says my mother. 'That could have hurt one of us.'

The noise upstairs stops.

'I can't stand this anymore,' sobs my mother. 'I'm afraid he's going to kill her one of these days.'

It is my father who goes up eventually. We wait expecting to hear the worst. But all is well. Dorothy's husband is asleep on the floor. Dorothy is picking things up.

My father decides it is time to move. He says he is sick and tired of hearing my mother complain about the rats, and about Dorothy and her husband, and my friend David's accident. My mother has a 'litany of complaints'. That's what my father says.

11

I often wonder what makes people turn out the way they do. These days, I spend a lot of time observing, trying to pry everybody open so I can crawl beneath their psyche. That great-aunt of mine, for instance. What would have possessed her to plunge a knife into her husband? I wondered about that for a long time. Why did they hit my mother? Why did Tino have such an obvious distaste for Dorothy?

When I was a teenager, my friend Marion and I used to stumble into this sort of conversation quite regularly. In those days, when she and I were always trying to get at the truth, always trying to divest hypocrisy and pretense, we would come up with all kinds of theories.

'It's in their genes,' I would say, if I happened to be reading an article pointing in that direction. She would always have a smart answer ready, or at least we thought it was smart then.

'I won't argue with you there... That's where it's at,' she would snicker and I'd know she meant jeans, not genes.

I always enjoyed turning people over, turning them inside out. I always hoped to find some lint, some answers.

I remember my father once came home with a smooth, fist-sized stone he had picked up somewhere. He displayed it on my mother's coffee table. She was not amused, but she let it stay for a while. On it he had written the words, 'Please turn me over.' The first time I saw it, I was curious and I proceeded to follow the instructions. When I turned it over, I found the same inscription on the other side. He laughed, but I was furious. I was angry because it was just a joke. When I turned it over, it didn't tell me anything.

Sometimes people are like that. Daniel has been like that for me.

Patience and time answered many of my questions. My great aunt and my great-uncle's squabbles centered around the legitimacy of Bruno, Angela's father, she claiming he was his son, and he disclaiming the accusation. And they hit my mother because she wouldn't be broken in and harnessed. Her hardiness and tenacity, her intelligence, that allowed her to learn the new language and accept the new customs quickly and effortlessly, were testimonials to the rumors that had spread about her own legitimacy.

'What do you mean?' I would ask.

'Well, I wasn't what they expected and so they concluded those old rumors about my mother had to be true.'

'Rumors?'

'Some nonsense about your grandmother and that wealthy Jewish family she used to work for. I guess they though I looked like a Jewess.'

Today, right after work, before heading for Abe's Fish Market, I sat in one of those trendy coffee shops trying to sip a cappuccino — a weak rendition of the real thing. I watched the impromptu performance of strangers. So many of them were wearing jeans and it made me smile and think of Marion.

If I could disrobe these people, I thought, what would I find? Scars, unshaved armpits, dirt behind the ears, painted fingernails hiding enough gook to start a mushroom farm, soiled panties that should have been changed — because you never know when you might be in an accident and will end up on a stretcher — as if the first thing a paramedic would do would be to take your pants off...? Oh, yes, the human body, which can be the source of such immense pleasure, I have learned, can also be disgusting.

And what would they find if they disrobed me? We all have our secrets.

I remember an obstinate old woman my mother used to clean house for. She always refused to obey her daughter's admonishments, threatening to send her to the old age home if she didn't clean up her act. The daughter would shout, 'You smell...Why don't you comb your hair once in a while.' Usually, the old woman said nothing. But once she shocked us. When the daughter — who was not an enticing morsel herself — ended her filibuster and ran out of ammunition, because there was only so much the old woman was guilty of, she turned to her saying, 'Don't you have any mirrors in your house?'

But while time and patience have answered many questions, my docket is still backlogged.

12

A chain-link fence separates our small backyard from a Jewish cemetery. My mother isn't too pleased, but by the time she sees our new house, my father and cousin Tino have already bought it.

Cousin Tino reassures her. 'Shit, aunt Lydia, they can't hurt you now. *Sono morti.* They're all dead. You shouldn't be afraid of dead people. It's the ones who are still alive you should worry about.'

'It was a steal,' says my father.

'Next to a cemetery?' says my mother.

'The owners ran out of money,' he explains. 'They couldn't finish it. That's why we got it so cheap.'

'I think the cemetery had something to do with that,' says my mother.

And so now, instead of rats it is dead people I have to be afraid of.

'Too bad it's a Jewish cemetery,' says my father with a laugh. 'You won't find anything in there,' he says to Tino.

'*Vedremo.* Don't be too sure, uncle Joe. They buried somebody today and they left a shovel in the grass.'

'Stop it, you two,' says my mother. My father and cousin Tino are always picking things up and bringing them home and she wishes they would stop. She calls the stuff 'junk'.

'Well, maybe a shovel, but you know how they are,' says my father. Turning to me he tells me, 'They aren't crazy like us, you know. They don't bury their dead with their Sunday clothes on and rings on their fingers and earrings in their ears. They don't even put makeup on their faces. No, sir. No waste. They're smart people. Very practical. All they do is wrap a shroud around the body — like the one Jesus was buried in — and plunk them into the ground,' he says.

'They use a casket over here,' my mother says.

'Well, whatever,' says my father. 'And I heard they bury them in a sitting position to save space.'

'That's not true,' says my mother. 'Honestly, Joe. *Vergognati*. What are you putting into that girl's head?'

'And they don't bother with flowers either,' he tells me.

'That's because they don't want any sort of ostentation,' says my mother.

I don't know what she means.

My father reminds me Jesus was a Jew before he turned Christian. 'That was a mistake,' he says.

Sometimes I will catch my mother looking at the cemetery out back. 'They don't have the wrought-iron garlands with the beads and the pearls over here,' she will say as if she is talking to herself.

'What do you mean?' I will ask.

'Oh, I'm just thinking about the Jewish cemetery back home. There's one outside town, on the opposite side of our cemetery. We used to go by there on our way to the fields and I always stopped to look in. They had these wonderful wrought-iron garlands on the tombs with strings of bright beads and even pearls entwined in the leaves and curls. I used to wish I could have a few to sew on a dress. And they had magnificent rose bushes. I wanted those too.'

'Did you ever go in and take a rose, Mother?' I ask.

Chapter 12

'No, not ever. But my brother did. Your uncle. He went in one night and dug up an entire bush and brought it home for me.'

'Wasn't he scared?' I ask tingling with fear.

'I suppose he was,' she says. 'But he did it. He planted it in front of the house. It's still there.'

'You mean I can see it if I go?'

'You sure can,' she says.

I learn my grandmother was a '*balia*', a 'wet nurse' for a Jewish family.

'A what?' I ask.

'She used to work for a wealthy Jewish family,' says my mother. 'When the woman had babies, they'd call your grandmother in to nurse them.'

My father would laugh when she said this.

'She wouldn't be able to come home much, but when she did, she always brought us something. They were very good to her,' she tells me.

'Who took care of you?' I ask.

'*La nonna,* my grandmother, poor soul. Sometimes, when I cried, she used to dunk a cloth in sugar water, then twist it so it looked like a nipple and I'd suck on that.'

'You sucked on that?' I say, my eyes widening in disbelief.

'While the Jew had a wet nurse,' my father snickers.

The Jews that used to live in our town are almost all gone now. A lot of them were taken away during the war. My father says my family never hurt any Jew. He says they did their best to hide them. I don't know why my family had to hide Jews.

13

Cousin Tino calls me out back. I look out the window and see him standing by the fence. He is surrounded by tombstones.

'Margherita,' he calls. '*Vieni*. I need you out here.'

I don't like going out there but I go because cousin Tino is calling me.

He is looking into the cemetery. 'See that shovel,' he says. I can barely see it. It's getting dark out. I look over to where he's pointing and then I see it. It is just beyond the fence next to a newly dug grave. I can smell the freshly turned earth, the worms. I can smell the worms. They smell the way they do after a storm, when you find them all over the road. It always frightens me when I see them. They look like tiny snakes and I am afraid of snakes. I am not sure why they all come out after a storm. I think it is because they hear the rain falling and they come to get washed. They must be dirty living deep down under the ground in that brown earth.

But of course this isn't the reason at all.

The smell nauseates me. And the freshly dug grave smells like that.

Cousin Tino wants to toss me over the fence. He has a rope in his hands. He wants me to tie the rope around the shovel and then drag the shovel through the grass over to the fence near him.

I can't understand any of this. Cousin Tino is lifting me over the fence. I am petrified. I am on the other side. I am in the cemetery. I have never been in a cemetery before. Not that I know of. And certainly not in a Jewish cemetery.

'Go on,' he says. '*Dai*. Don't be afraid. There's nothing to be afraid of. Here. Take the rope.' He throws it over the fence to me. 'Tie it around the shovel like I showed you and drag it over to me.' I obey.

I am near the grave and I feel my legs being pulled under. It is the same way I feel when I go to bed at night if I don't hurry and pull my legs up on to the bed. I feel someone is tugging at them from beneath the bed. That is how I feel now. I feel all the dead people in the cemetery, all the Jews, are pulling me down into the ground with them.

But I do get the shovel. I tie the rope to it and I drag it to Tino. Cousin Tino smiles. 'Good girl,' he says. He pulls it under the fence to our side.

I can't remember how he got me out of there, but I know he did. He wouldn't have left me in there. But I simply can't remember. Maybe someday I will. Maybe someday I will be able to fit the final pieces of this scene together.

14

After leaving Abe's Fish Market, I stare dumb-founded at my four slashed tires. I don't know what to do. This is a punishment, I am sure. God is sending signals.

I look around for a phone booth and spot one on the corner just down half a block or so.

Before dialing home again, I hesitate. Can't I get myself out of this predicament without Steve having to come to the rescue? Do I always have to fall back upon him? The answer, of course, is obvious. And so I call Steve for the second time in an hour. Only this time there is no answer. I stand inside the booth listening to the phone ring, not knowing what to do next.

Where could he be? It is unlike him to be out at this time of the day, just before supper. But then it is unlike me to be out here too. I should have been home by now. What am I doing here?

Perhaps this is a new game he is playing. He wants to show me what it would be like without him.

I gingerly place the receiver back in its cradle and stare into space waiting for a solution to present itself. All I can come up with is a cab. I will have to call a cab.

I look up a cab company and dial, then stand outside the booth, fish bag in hand, and wait.

The cab driver is a dark haired young man. I recognize him almost immediately. He is a former client of mine.

Relieved I am still wearing my sunglasses, I hope he will not recognize me. I don't feel like talking to anyone right now. But no such luck. I can tell from the way he is glancing at me in the rearview mirror that he is mulling over who I am and it will come to him in a moment.

'Where to, Madame?' he asks, his eyes fixed on me through the mirror.

I give my address. '606 Summit Drive.'

'That's out in the east end, right?' he inquires.

'Yes. That's right.'

'Nice area,' he adds.

'Yes, very nice.'

In the lull, it suddenly hits him. He knows who I am.

'I remember you now. I knew you looked familiar when I first saw you. You're Mrs. Croff,' he says looking at me through the mirror again. 'You're the lady I saw when I first came here. In the immigration department. Remember me? Joseph. Joseph Habib.'

'Oh, yes, I do recall you now. Sorry, Joseph. But you know how it is. I see so many people every day.'

'Sure, of course,' he adds, not the least bit annoyed, thankfully. 'You still there?' he asks.

'Yes, I am as a matter of fact. I'm still in Immigration.'

'Things as busy as they were a couple of years ago?'

'No, not really. Not right now. You know how it is. Sometimes we get flooded with immigrants, or refugees, actually. It all depends. You know. On the world situation.'

'Yes. Sure does,' he says gloomily.

I know I have probably struck a chord in his memories. Like so many refugees I have helped settle, he had had his share of nightmarish episodes to relate.

'So, you drive a cab, I see.' A silly thing for me to say, but I cannot think of anything else.

'Two years now. It's not bad.'

'What about your family?' And again I am sorry I asked.

'My wife is with me now. She managed to get out. But I lost my brother. And my parents both died during a raid a few years ago. You know how it is with us and the Jews over there.'

I wince. He doesn't know I am married to a Jew. But I am relieved to hear the lack of bitterness in his tone. I find this unusual. Perhaps time has healed his wounds.

'I have a daughter now,' he adds in a much more cheerful manner. 'Born right here in Canada. A Canadian. I have a Canadian daughter,' he repeats proudly.

I smile. I understand his feelings.

'What about you?' he wonders. 'Any children?'

I fight back the trembling sensation that wants to overcome me. I can feel my lips quiver.

'Yes, a son. I have a son. His name is David. He's Canadian too. Just like your daughter. But...' and I stop to swallow, hoping this reflex action will keep down the contents of my stomach which want to surface. 'But he's not going to be here much longer. He'll be leaving for Italy soon... That's where I'm from, you see... He'll be studying architecture in Milan.' I say this as if I had rehearsed it in preparation for the day David leaves, which is quickly approaching.

Joseph must sense the sadness in my tone because he looks back at me and says, 'Sorry... I mean sorry he'll be so far. I can see you'll miss him.'

'Very much,' I manage before tears fill my eyes involuntarily. 'But that's life, isn't it? They grow up and go away. It's to be expected.' I wipe my tears and force a little laugh. 'You know how Italian mothers are. Just like you people.'

'That's true,' he smiles shaking his head from side to side in agreement.

I look out the window and Joseph must sense I do not want to talk right now because he doesn't ask any more questions. We are on an expressway and although we are not over the speed limit, the cars and trucks darting past us and the buildings on the fringe of the highway are dizzying.

We descend the ramp and instantly the pace is altered. A calm, peaceful atmosphere takes over.

'It's nice out here,' Joseph says turning onto a side street. 'Very tranquil... You must make a lot of money working for the government.'

'No, not really,' I say, but I am sure what I make would seem a lot to him. 'I just happen to be married to someone who does. My husband is an accountant. He has his own firm.'

'Well, I guess I won't be meeting him for a while,' Joseph says matter-of-factly.

I am not sure what he means.

'You know. I don't make enough to need an accountant to tell me what to do with my money,' he laughs.

I smile, but inside I feel guilty. I want to tell him I didn't always live like this. I want to tell him I have roomed with rats. But I don't bother.

We near my house and I point it out up ahead. He drives down the street admiring the homes.

'Here we are,' he says as he turns into the driveway. 'Beautiful. This is beautiful,' he continues as he gets out to open my door.

'Thank you, Joseph,' I say as I search in my purse for my wallet. I pay him, extend my hand for a handshake and wish him luck.

'Thanks, Mrs. Croff,' he says looking at my immaculately landscaped surroundings. 'No need to wish you luck,' he adds. 'I can see you've already found it...You're a lucky woman.'

What does he know, I think to myself. A lucky woman? True. I am. Lucky indeed. Too lucky. What he doesn't know is that I am also a dishonest woman.

I watch the cab disappear down the street, then I turn to face my house. It glows golden in this late afternoon sun and I have to admit it is a peaceful oasis. The fluted Doric columns soar to meet an imposing but, I trust, restrained pediment adorned only with a single scrolled relief on the tympanum.

These are words I learned from Daniel.

Palladian windows frame the entrance, all symmetric and in proportion, the way I like it.

I wonder if Daniel would approve? Would he find my composition pleasing? Even if he didn't, it would tell him something; it would tell him he is still with me.

I remember afternoons just like this when David was a youngster and he would be out here shooting baskets while I watched from the front steps. Once he shot thirty-two in a row. How I long for the sounds of the basketball bouncing gleefully on the concrete and the thud of the hoop as the ball makes contact, the swoosh as it slips effortlessly through the net. How I long for the sounds of children playing, the laughter, the squabbles I would often have to referee. And always, in the end, when I had sent the neighborhood children home and called David in, there would be a hug for me. How I ache for those hugs.

Again, tears roll down my cheeks and I know I must not give in. I must carry on. He'll be back. I must think of this.

These sudden nauseous feelings that have been inundating me lately are a concern. It used to be a chronic problem with me. When I was young, before I met Steve.

I have had little to eat today. My appetite is waning. Nothing seems to entice me. At times, I will detect an aroma coming from the cafeteria at work, a pot pie perhaps, and I will order one thinking I'll be able to eat it. But then, after a mouthful or two, I have to push the plate away and wash the taste down with a glass of water.

I once read a person can survive on water alone for almost a year. So I am not going to worry about it. Not yet.

I look down at the bag I am still clutching. Fish. It had momentarily captured my imagination, but I know now I won't be able to stomach it. Not tonight.

Chicken soup is what I need. A hot bowl of my mother's chicken soup. Or cousin Tino's. 'That'll do the trick,' he used to say, mussing my hair with his big hands. And it was true. It always made me feel better no matter the ailment.

I loved the way the soup smell permeated the house as it simmered gently on the stove and I loved watching the steam rise from the bowls as my mother ladled it out for us. Then we would sip carefully in order not to scald our mouths and I could feel the warmth slide down into my stomach and I would begin to sweat. I remember my father would always slurp a few spoonfuls and then he would pull out his handkerchief and blow his nose.

'Joe,' my mother would scold. 'Please! Not at the table.' But he would do it again the next time we had soup.

She used to reprimand cousin Tino as well. He liked to blacken the soup with ground pepper. Turning away from the table, he would sneeze a couple of times and then smack his lips and say, 'Ahh. That felt good.'

Chicken soup. Yes. That's what I need. I don't have the real stuff. Lipton will have to do for now. Chicken soup will make me feel better.

15

My mother is in bed. She has been for days. Sometimes I hear her moan softly. Other times, she talks. I don't know who she is talking to; there is no one in the bedroom. Whatever she is saying, I can't understand it.

When she asks for water, my father or cousin Tino will bring her a glass. If they're busy, I do it.

Cousin Tino thinks we should call a doctor. He says mother is 'hallucinating'. I am afraid to ask what that means.

My father has to go next door to call the doctor because we don't have a phone. When he comes back, his hair is covered with snow and he is rubbing his hands together to warm them up.

'I'd better go out and clear the walk for the doctor,' he says to Tino. 'Get me the broom, Margherita,' and I run to the kitchen for it.

It has been snowing all day and I have been watching the fluffy flakes fall covering last week's dirty snow. The new snow has muffled all sounds around the house.

By the time the doctor comes, the snow has piled up again. When my father opens the door, it pushes the snow back and the doctor stamps his galoshes where the door has scraped away the snow.

The doctor is very old and very fat. He huffs and puffs when he takes his coat off shaking all the snow on our doormat where it melts almost as soon as it hits the floor. Tino takes the coat and hangs it over the kitchen door. The doctor takes his galoshes off. He is wearing shoes inside them. They are shiny black.

'Sorry I took so long, ' he says. 'But the streets are a mess.' Then he laughs, his belly laughing with him, and tells my father and cousin Tino to get used to this. 'You'd better get used to this kind of weather. There's more where this comes from. Not like the old country, is it?'

His glasses are all fogged up and he has to wipe them. When he takes them off, his eyes shrink. They had looked so big before with his glasses on. I wish he would hurry up and go see my mother, but he doesn't seem to be in a rush.

Finally, he goes into the bedroom. My father and cousin Tino do not go in with him. Neither do I, although I want to.

When he comes out, he tells my father it is 'nerves'. 'Just a case of nerves,' he says.

By the end of the week, my mother does not get better the way the doctor promised. At night my father has trouble sleeping because she is always moaning. He decides to sleep on the couch with cousin Tino. It is a couch you can pull out and make into a bed if you have to.

On Saturdays, my father and cousin Tino do not work. My father wonders what we are going to eat. There isn't much left in the house. Tino says he is going to make chicken soup. It'll do my mother good. We go to the chicken place where I always go with mother. It's just down the street.

The chicken place is in an old garage behind someone's house. It is a square building made of grey blocks that have not been painted. To get in, we use a small door that has been cut into the old, large, garage door. I think this is pretty strange: a big door with a little door inside it. As soon as we go in, we can hear the chickens cackling loudly. There are white ones and reddish brown ones, big ones and little ones running around.

Tino and I stand and stare at all the chickens. 'Well,' he asks. 'Which one do you want?'

This is unusual. When I go with my mother, she chooses it herself.

'That one,' I say pointing to a red one.

'That one it is,' he says, tousling my hair with his large rough hands.

The chicken man takes the long hooked pole off the wall. He goes into the wired-off room where the chickens are and they all start cackling even louder and running around flapping their wings. They bump into the man and into each other trying to get away from him. Some flap their wings so hard they actually lift themselves off the ground.

The man pulls our chicken towards him. He grabs her by the legs and holds her wings with his other hand. He ties her scrawny legs together then hangs her upside down from a hook. This is the part I hate. But I look anyway.

He grabs her head and stretches her neck. Then he slits her throat the way I have seen my mother do it whenever we are at my great-uncle's. She told me once they didn't always slit their throats like this; in the old country, they used to stick the sharp end of a pair of scissors into their ear. It was in America she learned to do it this way which was supposed to be easier and more humane. I couldn't see much difference. The end result was always the same.

I watch the dark red blood drip into a pail. It always looks thicker than I think it should. Like paint, really. A lot thicker and darker than the blood that comes out of Tino's pimples or cuts.

The chicken man has to hold her tight. Sometimes, he has a hard time. The chicken wants to get away. I don't blame her. So would I. She doesn't know it's too late.

Once, when my mother killed a chicken at home, she didn't hold tightly and the chicken went flapping all over the basement, blood splattering everywhere. After my mother caught her, she said, 'Now you know why they say "Like a chicken with her head cut off." '

Finally, our chicken stops flapping and twitching. The blood drips less and less. Just a few drops now. The man takes her off the hook and dunks her into a pail of boiling water. Then he plucks the feathers.

'The plucking machine isn't working today,' he says to Tino.

'Plucking machine?' cousin Tino blurts out. '*Ma scherzi?* Just give her to me. I'll show you a plucking machine,' he says showing the man his two big hands.

Tino pulls the feathers off, ripping the skin in places.

'Do you want her dressed?' the man asks.

I can tell Tino doesn't understand what he means. He looks down at me squeezing his eyebrows together and with his finger up towards his head, he makes little circles which means he thinks the chicken man is nuts.

'Hell, no. I want her naked,' he smirks at the man. Looking back at me he says, '*Questo è pazzo.*'

I don't say anything to embarrass Tino. I can tell him later.

On our way home, I start to giggle hoping cousin Tino will ask me why I am giggling. And, of course, that is exactly what he does.

'Why the giggles, young lady?' he asks pretending to be gruff.

'Don't you know what "dressed" means, Tino?' I ask holding my hand in front of my mouth to stop the giggles. 'It means taking the guts out.'

'Sure I knew you had to take the guts out. What do you think? *Che sono scemo?*'

'I mean "dressed". You didn't know what "dressed" meant, did you, Tino?'

He smiles down at me and lifts me up in one big sweeping motion. 'Yup. You're right. I didn't know. You learn something every day.'

'And, know what, Tino?' I add smartly.

'What?'

'It smells when you take the guts out.'

'Is that right? Well, I guess we'll just have to wear nose plugs.'

At home, Tino cuts the chicken open.

'You were right,' he says to me as he pushes himself away from the table. 'It does smell.'

I watch intently, as I always do when my mother does this. The insides of a chicken fascinate me. I can't get over the way everything fits in so neatly. They don't look at all like the insides of animals I have seen crushed in the middle of the road, run over by a truck, guts squished and blood oozing all around. Inside the chicken there is very little blood now since most of it has already dripped out. There is just a bit here and there. Near the liver, maybe, or the heart.

'Do we look like that too, Tino?' I ask.

'Sure do, my dear,' he says matter-of-factly. 'Sure do. We're no different from this old chicken.'

The smell intensifies as he begins to pull out the gizzard. It is all lumpy and bumpy because it is full of corn and other food the chicken ate.

'*L'ultima cena*. The last supper.' Tino makes the sign of the cross over the gizzard and we both suppress our giggles.

'Poor chicken,' I say, afraid God will be angry at what we are saying.

Tino cracks the chicken open a bit more and I spot an egg way down low.

'Look, Tino,' I cry out. 'Look. An egg. A big one. It was almost ready to get laid,' I say.

Tino looks at me and frowns the way he does when he pretends to be serious but I know he isn't. 'You shouldn't talk like that,' he says.

'Like what?' I ask, perplexed. He just laughs.

'Be careful,' I warn him. 'Don't break the egg.'

I guess he figures I know what I am talking about because I see him pull at the intestine carefully in order to get the egg out safely.

'There you go,' he smiles handing me the egg.

'Gee thanks, Tino... I love these eggs... Look,' I say pointing back into the chicken. 'Look at all the other ones. This chicken is full. I've never seen so many eggs inside one chicken before.'

Under this egg we find three more good sized ones, and under those there are more. A dozen or so little round ones. Perfect little circles. They aren't oval yet and they don't have the shell. All they have is a thin covering, like a skin. If we break it, the yellow yolk will ooze out.

The deeper we go, the more we find and the smaller they get.

Even cousin Tino is surprised. '*Madonna*. Look at all the eggs that old chicken would have laid,' he says. 'Too bad. What a waste.'

When we are finished 'dressing' the chicken, Tino puts her into a pot of water with a few carrots, some celery and an onion. Then he goes to see my mother and tells her she'll be having cousin Tino's 'famous chicken soup' in no time.

There is a knock at the door. My father puts his newspaper down and goes to see who it is. It is the neighbor lady.

'I've just come to see how your wife is doing. Sorry I couldn't come sooner, but I've been down with the flu myself.'

'Come in,' says my father. 'She's in the bedroom. Just a case of nerves. That's what the doctor says.'

The neighbor lady walks over to the bedroom. She doesn't go in. 'My God,' she says. 'She's dying. This woman is dying.'

'What are you talking about?' asks my father who is now annoyed. 'The doctor says it's just nerves.'

'She's dying, I tell you. I'd do something if I were you.'

Cousin Tino walks in from the kitchen. He sees the worry on my face.

He goes to the bedroom door and the neighbor lady tells him the same thing she just told my father.

'She's dying. You'd better do something before it's too late.'

My father asks the lady to call an ambulance. Her English is better than his. Soon, two men appear at our door. They have a stretcher. They put my mother on it and take her away. I can hear the siren. Loud, at first. Then weaker and weaker as it goes farther and farther from the house. I stay home with cousin Tino.

'Don't worry, Margherita,' he says. 'She'll be all right.'

I want to believe him.

When my father comes home, he tells cousin Tino my mother has double pneumonia. 'She's critical,' he says.

I hear them talk about me. The neighbor lady is going to come over and take me to her house for the night. They think I'll be able to rest better over there.

My father puts some of my clothes into a brown paper bag when the lady comes.

The hospital calls during the night. The neighbor lady gets dressed quickly and runs over to our house. From the bedroom window, I can see her go up to our front door. I see my father in his pajamas and I listen against the window to catch their words. I hear her tell my father he has to go to the hospital right away if he wants to see my mother. 'She won't last through the night,' I hear her say.

But she is wrong. They are all wrong. Only cousin Tino had been right. He told me she would be all right and she makes it through the night.

The next morning, my father comes to pick me up at the neighbor's and we go home. 'Your mother wants to see you,' he tells me. That's when I know she's going to get better.

Whenever my mother talked about this episode in her life, she would tell me how she only remembers bits and pieces. She remembers being at home in bed and seeing bloody faces on the bedroom walls. She saw devilish figures on the ceiling and she feared they would come and take her away. In the hospital, she remembers the relief she felt when they put an oxygen tent over her. Finally she could breathe. But she does not remember much else. She does not remember seeing my father. And the priest is but a shadow to her. But she does remember the anointing of her feet. When the shadow moved about her and down to her feet, she realized what was happening. It was then she thought of me. She says that's what saved her.

She claimed the experience changed her forever. The fear of death was wiped from her.

'I know what it's like to die,' she used to insist. 'I felt as if I was floating peacefully into the other world, but when your image appeared, I knew then I had to fight back. It wasn't time yet, Margaret.'

Tino gets very excited about my mother's arrival. He's cleaning the house.

'Your mother's coming home today,' he tells me. I jump up and down with joy.

'We have to make some chicken soup,' he says.

16

What was it that had consumed my mother to the point of near death? Sheer physical exhaustion from cleaning people's houses? That was what she used to do then. She was a 'cleaning lady'. Because she was a good one, she was very much in demand and kept constantly busy.

Or could it have been an adverse reaction to the bitter cold of that winter? Unaccustomed to such inhumane temperatures, she might have breathed in too much frigid air on her way home, sweating, no doubt, beneath the clothes from having scrubbed floors and washed walls all day long.

It's hard to say what the catalyst was. My mother was never one to reveal a lot at any particular point in time. A heavy blanket of silence spread over her and it was only occasionally she allowed me to creep beneath it with her. I had to learn to peel away the layers of that woman's personality. She preferred to keep things to herself, to suffer inwardly in many cases. She dished out morsels of her inner workings in controlled doses. She seemed to know instinctively when and what to reveal and I had to grow into these things.

The beating, for instance. Her first responses to my questioning, 'Why did they hit you?' were simple and accurate, but not overly detailed nor very revealing to me then.

'They just didn't like me,' she would say. Or, 'They weren't very nice people, Margaret.'

That would suffice for a while and she would offer nothing else until I questioned again. The time between these inquisitions could be months or even years.

The older I got, the more I wanted to know.

'Why would anyone do such a thing, Mother? I can't imagine a man holding you pinned to the wall so his mother could slap you and punch you. Why, Mother? Why?'

And without bitterness she would reply. 'Because they wanted me to do things, Margaret. Things I didn't want to do.'

'Like what?' I can't imagine.

'What does it matter?'

'They must have had a reason?'

'Actually, what ignited the fuse was when your great-aunt cut off your beautiful curls. Do you remember that?'

'No. Not at all...She cut off my hair?'

'Yes. They'd sent me out to get groceries or something and when I got back she'd cut off your gorgeous curls.'

'But why?'

'She said your long hair was a nuisance and I was wasting my time brushing it. She said I could find better things to do with my time... And so she cut it... I was devastated. You looked like you'd just come out of a concentration camp.'

In time, I learned other things too. But I am sure my mother went to her grave with some well kept secrets.

The passage of time: I used to think it concealed past transgressions with layer upon layer of life's silt. How often have I heard people say, 'Time heals all wounds,' or something to that effect? But I am not too sure anymore. It may instead cause the rotting of memories and then they return to haunt you with their putrid stench; or perhaps it petrifies them and they become more and more precious with time, like diamonds, because, in all honesty, some memories are too precious to forget. Of that I am sure.

Whatever it does, I am now convinced the past does not go away.

I read in the paper about sex crimes committed by a man of the cloth upon young boys. And now, twenty years or so later, when these same boys have had their memories unlocked, the truth comes out.

Reading this makes me think of my son, David, a few years back when he was taking a religious studies course.

'Did you know there's evidence Jesus was five-foot-eleven?' he said.

'Seems reasonable to me,' I had said.

'Do you know why he was five foot eleven?' he asked.

'Genetics?' I quipped.

'...so he could stand out in a crowd,' he informed me.

We both laughed.

'And did you know that when they crucified him the nails went through his wrists and not the palms of his hands?'

'And how did they come to that conclusion? pray tell.'

'Because they've experimented with cadavers.'

'Cadavers?'

'Yeah. They crucified cadavers... Imagine.'

I was glad when David turned to architecture instead.

17

As I approach my front door, I know the house will be empty. I can feel the chill of loneliness already. Something in Steve warned me he would not be here for me. Not that he won't come home eventually. He will. I can depend on that. After what we have been through, I know. Or do I? What if he too abandons me? Why should he be any different from Daniel, or David, my son?

I am being too melodramatic. I tend to do that when I'm alone.

The phone rings and I rush to it anxiously.

'Margaret?'

'Steve. Where are you?'

'I'm at the club. Look, I'm sorry I snapped at you earlier.'

'It's okay. I understand.'

'I thought I'd play a game of squash since you were going to be late and David won't be home till late.'

'David won't be home for dinner? He didn't tell me. I was expecting him.' I feel deceived and angry at my son's lack of concern for me.

'He tried to call you, but you weren't home.'

And so now I am punished for having taken my excursion downtown.

'Look,' says Steve trying to console me. 'He said he won't be too late. I'm just finishing off a drink. I'll be home soon.'

'I'll get dinner started,' I reassure him.

'Just get a salad ready if you can. I picked up some steaks. I'll barbecue when I get home.'

'But I told you I was stopping for something.' I am insulted he didn't trust me to do this.

'Don't get upset, Margaret. Don't overreact like usual. Just get a salad ready and relax. Take a nice warm bath and wait for me. Okay?'

I don't answer right away and I hear him call into the receiver, 'Margaret? Are you still there?'

'I'm here,' I finally respond, to his relief, I am sure.

It is funny how this conversation resembles those we used to have when we were going together. Even then he always attempted to play the tough guy, but in the end he always buckled under. How many times did he hang up on me in sheer torment only to call right back with an apology? He hasn't changed.

'Are you all right?' he asks.

'Yes, I'm fine. I've just had a little problem. I'll tell you about it when you get home.'

'A problem? What kind of problem?' he wants to know. But I don't want to tell him about the slashed tires over the phone.

'No big deal, Steve. Let me get dinner started or we'll never eat tonight.'

When he gets home, Steve finds my stuffed flounder as well as the salad he had ordered. I am trying to make a point, but I tell him it would have been silly to do the steaks with fish on hand. It makes perfect sense, he has to admit. The steaks can wait until tomorrow.

I tell him about the car but I wrap my lies in cotton batting. After all, did I not go to Abe's to surprise him? How can he get angry about that?

18

Steve has me in a ball and chain. I am a prisoner of his own anchored ways. He thinks he has control over me. He doesn't know he is only weighing me down and I will surely die if he doesn't unbind my shackles.

I am at it again. Thinking in metaphors. Why can't I say what I mean?

When I first met Steve, I developed a holy respect for what I saw as his unorthodox ways. His apparent rebellion against the constraints of his religion lit a spark in me. After all, I was the epitome of the 'nice girl'. The kind who would do no wrong, commit no sin knowingly. He would not be harnessed by age-old beliefs and customs and traditions. He would not be restrained by the reins his mother sought to pull. He unleashed his fury upon the old woman. In no uncertain terms he told her, and the world, he would do as he pleased. And he married me.

Was that a façade? Was he then, as now, a conformist to other truths? The truths of business and social prominence? Was he exchanging one God for another?

Then, it was romantic. His sacrifice for an unworthy Christian was rewarding to my personal ego, not to mention my parents. They were absolutely thrilled by the prospect of a Jewish son-in-law. But was it a sacrifice? Could it be that I only made it easier for him to take his chosen path?

I think these thought now. I think about his antagonism towards his mother and other female members of his family. I was so unlike them. I was subservient and unoffensive. Pliable and easily molded. Appreciative and undemanding. Wholly owing to him for daring to let me into his life.

Have I been his doormat all these years? Was this what he meant when he said he loved me?

Tonight, as I get into bed beside him, his body rising and falling to the rhythm of his sleep, I can hardly bear to touch his flesh. I slip under the covers as inconspicuously as possible. I lie still so he won't know I am there.

Instead of the brave warrior, could it be he was the coward? And what does that make me? For I let him go on thinking whatever he pleases. What would he do if I told him he has been duped?

The guilt rises in me and I have to turn away from him. I do owe him. I do. I owe him much. He was the first man I could talk to. The first who cured me of my fears of men, those totally unnatural and oppressive fears which had built up in me over the years, those fears which culminated in a gut wrenching ritual of vomiting whenever a man approached me? How could I forget?

We had so much in common then, or so I thought. Whatever complaints he had about racism or bigotry,

Chapter 18

I tried to match. We used to enumerate our griev-
ances and tally them up for comparison.

'...well, they jailed a lot of Italians during the
war,' I would plead. '...just because, back home, Mussolini was in cahoots with Hitler.'

'Hah!' he would quip. 'What a joke. Have you
heard of Auschwitz and Buchenwald?'

This always made me feel shame and a deep
desire to offer him reparations.

When they started talking about 'visible minori-
ties' using this new terminology to describe existing
problems, he would laugh. 'So what does that make
us? Invisible?'

'Well, look at you now,' I would retort. 'All doctors and lawyers, with rec rooms in the basement,
chandeliers in the dining room, kids off to camp with
monogrammed clothes while the parents holiday in
Cuba' — a popular destination then. '...All we get to
do is dig ditches and lay bricks... And they call us
D.P's and Dagos, grease balls and garlic breath...'

'I won't tell you what they call us,' he would say.

It was a game we enjoyed playing.

At work, the other day, I was listening in on a conversation. It made me think of Steve and me back
then.

They were talking about a chic new restaurant
downtown. 'It positively reeks of garlic,' someone
said. This is now a compliment.

They have even discovered it has medicinal quali-
ties, as if we didn't already know.

19

Steve still buys books on sex and actually reads them. I instead buy books to help me figure him out, among other things.

I can always tell what chapter he is on.

He tells me I am frigid when I can't respond. 'You're frigid,' he says, in that imperious tone of his. Of course, then I am.

'Why do you always have to make fun of me when I want to try something new,' he grovels childishly. 'Here, get rid of that shit you're always reading and look at this,' he says tossing me his book. 'Read what it says. Maybe you'll learn something.'

I once asked Daniel where he had learned all he knew about women. Had he used books? What was his secret?

'No secret,' he had said. 'It comes naturally.'

'To everyone?' I inquired, with Steve in the back of my mind.

'It should, don't you think?'

'But does it?'

'If two people feel part of a whole, it should. Remember Plato? His two halves of a sphere? The unity of lovers completes the sphere.'

If Daniel was right, what does that say about Steve and me? Are we separate entities?

Venn diagrams come to mind. They are separate, yet united. They meet and join and share a common ground. It is true they go off into their own domains, but they are forever entwined. Unified, while maintaining their distinct perimeters.

This is how I see Daniel and me. Even though we are apart.

It's funny how the men in my life are all distant from me now. Tino, living alone in his self-imposed exile as if he had leprosy. When I think of him I think of those Japanese you hear about. The ones who are on an out-island and don't yet know the war is over. He also reminds me of Tarzan, but without Jane; or maybe it's more like Robinson Crusoe.

And Steve is far from me too. Distant is perhaps a better word. He is distant from me, although I am sure he wouldn't think of himself as distant. Nevertheless, he is.

And Daniel? What is he? An M.I.A... Missing-in-action.

20

Steve has had his hair cut. He doesn't go to a regular
barber; he goes to a 'stylist'. His hair is perfect. Well
trimmed and parted on the left side, he has it swept
over and up slightly. The stylist has sprayed it generously and it is staying put.

I know he is up to something. I can always tell.
He is not discreet.

He puts his plan into gear as we are getting ready
for bed. He undresses slowly in front of me saying
nothing. He is too silent. This is a sure giveaway. He
unbuttons his starched white shirt and tosses it on the
armchair. He sits at the foot of the bed and he takes
his socks off making sure I get a good view of his
back. He gets up and faces me and gets ready to unzip
his pants. That's when he tells me he has a surprise.
He unzips his pinstripe pants and lets them fall to the
carpet revealing the surprise: flesh-colored mesh
bikini underwear. I stifle a laugh.

He doesn't say a word. He is waiting for a reaction. I still want to laugh. I think it is ironic that nothing has been able to make me laugh lately and this,
which is meant to excite me, does the trick.

I try to think positively. I try to think about sex.
I tell myself, this is my husband, the man I have been
married to for a quarter of a century. It sounds so
much longer when I think of it in that way.

But it doesn't work... He still looks ridiculous in
those underpants.

I think of Daniel, but that only makes matters
worse. He would never have done such a thing.

If only he would say something. Make a joke. Smile. Wink. Do something. But no, he just stands there waiting for me to react, trying to be nonchalant. As if I didn't know him by now. Who is he trying to kid anyway?

'Nice underwear,' I say to relieve the tension.

He takes this to be a positive reaction and finally smiles the smile of a conqueror. I am relieved. Let him think what he wants.

'Now that we're alone, we can do what we want. You can make all the noise you want,' he says with a smirk.

I look at his crotch only because I don't know where else to look. The fool. He thinks he can fill the void David will bring to my heart. He thinks I will make love with free abandon when I realize I don't have to worry about embarrassing noises and squeaky beds. He doesn't realize that whenever he has had the pleasure of these robust encounters it was thanks to Daniel.

He goes into the bathroom. I can hear him brush his teeth, gargle with mouthwash. That Listerine, no doubt. The one with the medicinal smell that always turns me off. He is so afraid of natural smells. Everything has to be covered up and falsified. I hear him twist off the bottle cap on the cologne. He will splash it all over his torso making matters worse. This scent along with the Listerine and the stuff the stylist plastered on his hair will be quite a concoction.

All of this is turning me cold and I seize up. Literally. When he comes back into the bedroom and slides into bed beside me I am as tight as a drum. It is impossible for him to penetrate me. This has never happened before. Not with Steve, that is, and even I am frightened.

Chapter 20

'What the hell is this?' he blurts out angrily.

'I'm sorry, Steve. I don't know. Really. I'm not feeling well. You know that. It's never happened to me before,' I tell him. But this is a lie. I remember the other times. They flash into my mind as if a high resolution screen has been lit before my eyes. The images terrify me and make me all the more unresponsive to my husband's demands.

'You shithead,' he yells. 'You cold fish.'

That's about as vulgar as he can get.

'Take it easy. I'm sure it'll be all right in the morning,' I try to reassure him and myself as well.

'So this is what I get after all the trouble I went through.'

What a fool, I think to myself. If only he would shut up.

'I come home and plan a lively evening and this is the reception I get.'

'Oh, God, Steve. Stop. Stop. Can't you see what you're doing?'

'No, damn it. All I can see is this padlocked cunt.'

'Stop it,' I scream, startled at his language.

'Well, I'm going to get it one way or another, my darling.'

'Stop it,' I cry as he attempts to penetrate me once again. 'Stop, please, I beg you.'

It is then we hear a car drive up. We see the lights flash across the bedroom window and we know it is David coming home. Steve halts his assault and I breathe a sigh of relief. For now, I am safe.

21

The first time a man tries to take me by force I am eleven or twelve. On Saturdays I babysit my two small cousins who live down the street while my aunt and uncle on my father's side go to work. They have just come over from the old country.

Like my great-aunt, this aunt has boarders too. But there are only two here: Sal and Lucio. Father and son. The house this aunt and uncle live in is very small and they couldn't fit any more boarders in if they wanted.

The father works, but the son doesn't. He doesn't do much of anything, it seems to me, because I always find him hanging around doing nothing. He is nineteen.

The boarders are supposed to live in the basement, but whenever my aunt and uncle are away, Lucio comes up and acts as if he owns the place.

He is very big. A giant. That's what he looks like to me. I hear he is supposed to be good-looking. The girls in my class talk about him all the time, but they don't have to spend their Saturdays with him.

He has big hands. They look almost fat. His face is square and strong looking. He looks like those balloon dolls you can't knock over no matter what because they're round on the bottom.

He also has large feet. I get to see a lot of them because he wears floppy slippers around the house. If the girls in my class saw his feet, I think, they wouldn't think he was so handsome.

He has a large telescope which he always brings with him when he comes up from the basement. He sits at the kitchen window and looks out at something. He snickers and looks at me as I walk about the kitchen ignoring him as much as I can. I wash baby bottles and clean up the sink.

That day, I put the children down for their nap. I am walking by the kitchen on my way to the living room to watch some T.V. He calls me. 'Come and take a peek,' he says. I am curious. I want to know what he is looking at all the time.

The yard behind this house is very small. There is no fence at the back. Where the yard ends, there is an alley and then the backyards of those who live on the street behind this one.

My friend Judy lives in one of those houses whose back yards are parallel to my aunt's. Judy is a 'well-developed' girl; I have heard my uncle say this. She is older than I am, having failed both grade one and grade three, putting her in grade six with me instead of eight where she belongs.

She has bouncy round breasts, the largest I have ever seen on a girl, while I just have two tiny swellings beneath my shirt. Nothing to brag about.

I envy Judy's breasts. Sometimes I prop pillows under my nightshirt to see what I would look like if I had breasts. I would do anything to have breasts like hers, not that I would know what to do with them yet.

I can't say whether Judy was doing it on purpose or not. But she undresses in her bedroom with the curtains open. This was what he was looking at.

I see her do it. I see her take her clothes off right there in the bedroom and I want to scream. I see her lift her arms over her head to pull her sweater off leaving her almost naked. Then she twists her arms back and unhooks her bra and her breasts fall out all bouncy and spring-like. I can't take my eyes off her. When she bends forward to roll her nylons off, her breasts dangle in front of her, changing shape. And then she pulls her panties off. That's when I pull away from the telescope.

He laughs. 'Your girlfriend has some tits,' he says. I blush and run away to the living room where I will be safe. I have never seen him in the living room. It must be out of bounds for him. But he follows me. I hear his great lumbering steps coming in my direction.

His legs are like logs and his feet remind me of a ferocious beast ready to attack.

I am sitting on the couch, trembling. He comes over and sits next to me. I try not to be afraid. I don't know why I should be, but I am. I am very afraid.

He runs his large hands up my skirt saying things to me with words I do not understand.

'Come on,' he says. 'Let me take a look at your pussy. Let me pet your little pussy.'

I think he must be going bonkers because he must surely realize I am not hiding any cat; I don't even own a cat.

I want to scream when his hand slips into my panties, but I can't. My mouth is dry and it refuses to make a sound. I want to get away but his hands are so strong. They are like a vice upon me. His body tries to invade me as he pulls me under him and I think I will surely suffocate. He smiles all the while and looks at me straight in the eye. His big wide face is close to my own and his hot sickeningly sweet breath is a veil suspended above my face.

The hand between my legs rips off my pants with one forceful pull while his heavy body pins me to the sagging couch. I am immobile with terror. I can't imagine what is going to happen next.

I don't know about a man's body yet. I am too young. I don't remember that cousin of mine, Bruno. That won't come to me for years. I don't know anything. Only that this feels wrong and I have never seen anyone do this before.

He tries to spread my legs with his strong hand while I finally begin to struggle to throw him off. He grabs me down there and I manage to bite him. I kick with all my might and he let's go.

'Damn you,' he says. 'You little bitch.'

There is some blood on his arm from my bite. I am glad to see this. Maybe he'll get sick from it. I remember the teacher at school telling us human bites are to be taken very seriously.

He lifts himself up just enough for me to make my getaway. I run out of the house. I run and hide behind the shed and stay there until someone comes home.

I tell no one.

I am scolded for being outside leaving my little cousins crying helplessly.

My aunt is upset. I can't be trusted. I am a silly child who only thinks of playing. I cannot accept responsibility.

I keep my secret for years. I live with it because I don't see what else to do.

22

In those days we ran back and forth to Italy every time there was a crisis in the old country. It was a one-sided affair since it was always someone from here going there; it was never the other way around. These crises came in many forms. Most were related to someone's illness or death: a grandparent, a brother, a sister, a niece or a nephew. It was such a regular occurrence that for a long time I used to think of Italy as one gigantic chronic care hospital of sorts where people were forever suffering dreadful diseases and lingering on death's door.

Once in a while, the crisis would simply be related to the more pleasant cycle of life: a marriage, a birth, which meant someone needed new accommodations, or property had to be divided, sold, or exchanged. But mostly it was the grave sickness and death that dragged us back to the old country.

For a long time, it seemed to me that whatever it was we were doing over here wasn't real living; the real stuff was happening over there and whatever was going on here was like a game, like playing house. The people in the old country must have thought so too because they certainly didn't seem to understand that things happened here as well.

These trips heaped up like rocks in a rock pile for me. They became time markers, delineating events which set themselves into me, outposts from which I could later look out upon the landscape.

Usually, the emissaries of these catastrophes or changes were those flimsy envelopes which were so light and transparent it always amazed me they had made it across the ocean. But if the portent of bad news arrived by telegram, we knew it meant someone over here would have to make the sacrifice and go.

When a telegram arrives telling us my grandfather's leg has to be amputated, my father is in a tither. He went last year when they cut off my grandfather's foot and now it is my uncle's turn to go.

My aunt raises a big fuss because she wants to go too.

'I'm not going on vacation,' my uncle shouts at her.

'Well, I'm not staying here all alone with two kids and two boarders,' she shouts back.

'What's the matter with you?' says my uncle. 'Someone has to take care of the house. And what's this about Sal and Lucio? We'll lose those two if you don't stay home.'

That's when my parents get their bright idea.

'Stop arguing,' says my father. 'I've got a solution. Lydia and I can move into your place and you won't have to worry about the house or Sal and Lucio. We can kill two birds with one stone. We'll be doing you a favour and it'll give us a chance to sell our place.'

'Right,' my mother agrees. 'You know we've been thinking of selling and building a new place. This'll work out fine.'

And so it is settled. They are going and we are staying.

The thought of living in the same house as Lucio terrifies me. I beg my parents to let me go to Italy with my aunt and uncle. I tell them I want to see my grandfather before he dies. And this is true. But it is not the whole truth.

They worry I will be missing too much school. It is early June and I have a few more weeks to go. But I am a good student and they know it. The excuse is weak and in the end I win.

A giant airplane will whisk me away from Lucio. I will be far from his groping hands and his clammy, smelly body. I know I will have to return, but for a while, I will be safe.

The first leg of our journey is short and hectic. None of us has ever been on a plane before, only ships. My father told us what to expect. He knows because he used to fly during the war. But knowing doesn't help. My cousins scream and kick until their little round faces are red and sweaty.

'It's their ears,' my aunt cries as she and my uncle juggle the children from one lap to the other. I am kept busy chasing the stewardess asking her to warm bottles or rinse out facecloths. My ears hurt too, but I don't say anything and no one asks. And then, before we know it, we are descending into Montreal where we will be changing planes.

A thin old man gets on the plane in Montreal. His dark black hair is very shiny and combed straight back. I know that, like my father, he must use a cream to keep it smooth and flat. But my father looks handsome with his hair like that whereas the man does not.

He has a long, skinny, horse face. His eyes, black and sad looking, bulge out from under their lids as if someone has been squeezing his scrawny neck forcing his eyeballs to pop out.

The man, however, is very polite and he has a strange accent when he speaks.

He is talking to my aunt and uncle about the children. 'It's very difficult to travel with children, I presume,' he says. My aunt looks at him and tries to smile. 'Try to get them to suck on their bottle,' he advises. 'That should help the ears.'

The man tells my aunt and uncle they are lucky they have me. I am such a big help. He has seen me follow my aunt's orders without complaint even though I am more interested in looking out the window.

I blush at his compliment. I can't imagine why he is saying these things. He looks at me a lot and I am sure it is because I look funny in the outfit I am wearing.

It is an aqua knit suit: a skirt and matching top. My mother got it for me especially for the trip. She said it wouldn't wrinkle. I don't like it. The skirt is straight and it circles my shapeless hips and thighs like a giant elastic band. I have never had such an outfit before. But I wear what I am given.

I hate the outfit most of all because it shows what I don't have. Breasts, for instance. I think a suit like this deserves something to fill it out. Then it wouldn't look so dumb. All I have are two tiny swellings like two little olives that just barely manage to make a dent in my top.

My little cousins are finally settled. Drops of sweat are streaking down my aunt's face and her eyes are red and puffy. The baby is asleep in her arms. My uncle is holding Anthony. The drone of the plane finally lulls them all to sleep. I guess it's all right for me to look out the window.

I have been sitting in the aisle seat to help my aunt and uncle and I have had to stretch to see out the window, past the man. He notices and insists on giving me his seat, but I say no, thank you.

How impolite I am, says my aunt who opens her eyes when she hears me talking to the man. To be disturbing the gentleman like that.

He tells my aunt he doesn't mind. He insists I take his seat as long as she doesn't mind. And so I move to the window seat.

'You are too kind,' she says. Then she too drops off to sleep.

I look out the window and see a fluffy layer of clouds like giant cotton balls hanging in the sky. I wonder what it's like to float above the earth like this. I wish I could throw myself on to a cloud and ride it.

Some of them are like cotton candy and I bet they feel and taste that way too. I wonder if they would melt in my mouth the way the candy does.

The skinny old man with the horse face asks me if this is my first time flying.

'Yes,' I tell him. 'But my father was in the air force during the war,' I add.

He smiles.

'Pretty soon we'll be out of these clouds,' he tells me. 'Then you'll be able to see the St. Lawrence.'

I wonder how he knows this.

'And if it's clear when we get to the east coast, you'll be able to see icebergs,' he tells me. 'Did your father tell you to look for icebergs?' he asks me.

I blush because my father didn't mention them. I get the feeling he doesn't believe my father used to fly.

'No,' I reply. 'But he told me the land would look like a quilt.'

'Yes, that's a fact,' he admits. 'Just be patient. We'll pass this bank of clouds shortly.'

And in a while, the blanket of clouds begins to break up and I catch glimpses of the land below.

I look to see patches of green the color of my father's wine bottles. There is also a lighter green the color my mother painted our front room: 'chartreuse', she called it. And there are light sandy browns and browns the color of tree bark. The sparkling blue are lakes. It looks as if someone spilled blue paint all over the quilt. The winding string I see are roads and, of course, the blue, curving snake-like through the quilt is the river.

The man says we will soon be over the area where the river turns salty.

'Where?' I blurt out, surprised at this bit of information.

'You can't see where,' he tells me. But if you were down there you'd be able to tell because you'd taste the salt in the water.'

I have never been in salt water — except for the time this summer when I stepped on a nail and I had to put my foot in a pail of hot water and my mother added salt to it. I tell the man about this and he says it doesn't count.

'The salt water in the ocean is different,' he informs me.

When he talks to me, the man is very close. I can smell his stale breath. I turn towards the window and keep as far away from him as I can. His breath reminds me of something. I get flashes of memories when I smell him, but I can't put them all together.

'Soon we'll be over Newfoundland,' he says. 'You'll be able to see the icebergs. They'll look like tiny white spots from here, but believe me, they're big. One of them sank the Titanic, you know,' he tells me. 'And two thirds are beneath the surface,' he adds.

While he talks to me he presses against my elbow with his one arm. With the other he points out the window.

He spots a whole bunch of icebergs and creeps closer to me still. He is leaning into me and pressing against my left breast. It doesn't feel right but I don't know what to do about it. I feel very warm and sweaty. I steal a look across the aisle. My aunt is asleep with the baby in her arms, my uncle with Anthony.

The man is pressing his elbow into me. On the bone below my abdomen and between my legs. He presses hard when he leans over to point out the window.

I can no longer hear what he is saying. I smell his breath and I feel him but I do not understand him.

No one seems to notice. I feel trapped. When a stewardess walks by, he gets up and I can breathe again. Then he turns back to me and presses even harder.

Night is falling and I am more afraid. I see the engine near us spurt out sparks. The man notices I am frightened. He tells me not to worry. 'This is natural,' he says. 'This is normal.' What is, I wonder? What is he talking about? I can't tell.

Everyone on the plane seems to be falling asleep. The stewardesses stop making rounds. I feel very faint. I don't dare fall asleep. I am exhausted, but I am sure terrible things will happen to me if I let myself sleep. I must keep awake. He stays awake too and he keeps touching me. I want to cry, I want to escape but I can't. His elbow is tight into me.

What is God doing to me, I wonder? Why am I being punished? Not even here am I safe? Where is it safe? No matter what I do and where I go, this evil pursues me.

'Morning comes early on eastbound flights,' says the man. 'We'll be there before you know it... What a shame... I'm only going as far as London. What about you and your parents?' he asks.

'They aren't my parents,' I blurt out. 'They're my aunt and uncle.'

'I see,' he adds. 'And where are you going with your aunt and uncle?' he wants to know.

My heart pounds within my chest and I sweat with fear. I must not tell him where we are going. I must keep this a secret. Otherwise he will follow me.

'We're going to France,' I tell him. This is not a total lie. We will be stopping there before going on to Milan.

'Ah, France,' he says. 'It's a shame you are so young,' he adds as he slips and slides my long brown hair through his fingers. 'But I can see it in you, my dear. You will be a lovely woman when you grow up. What a lucky man, the one who wins your heart.'

My hands begin to shake and my mouth is dry with fear. He notices my uneasiness and takes my hands in his. I look over to my aunt and uncle. I can hear them snoring.

'Relax,' he tells me as he strokes my hands and leans over me pretending to be pointing to the fire-breathing motor. That's when he leads my hands to his private parts and I can feel the hardness inside his pants. I keep my eyes glued to the flames darting from the engine.

I can see the light of the new day. The sun is coming up very bright and shiny. It strikes the plane and comes in through our window. The passengers have pulled their shades down but ours has been up all night, just like us. And so we are the first to see the sunrise.

The streak of light coming in our window wakes a few passengers and the stewardesses begin to move about quietly. I can hear the clinking of plates and the smell of coffee drifts through the cabin.

One by one the passengers pull up their shades and in a while the whole plane is full of brightness. The glare is so intense it hurts the eyes to look out.

'Look,' says the man. 'That's Ireland.' I look out and see the outline of the coast. 'Can you see the coast coming up?' he asks. He is pressing against me very hard.

To me, Ireland has always meant rescue and safety. I know London is not far ahead and then the man will go away and I won't have to see him ever again. I feel dirty. I feel sticky and dirty. I do not understand what is happening. I must be a terrible person. I must be a sinner.

We prepare to land and I breathe a sigh of relief. For once I am thankful my aunt and uncle will be needing me. I will get to hold the baby while they take care of Anthony and pull out our bags.

We land with a thud and a thump. I hear the man tell my aunt and uncle to have a pleasant stay in France. I blush, afraid he will discover I lied, but they are too busy to be paying much attention to him.

'Your niece is a wonderful young lady,' I hear him say. 'I've enjoyed her company tremendously.'

'We're so pleased,' says my aunt making an effort to be polite even though she is very tired. 'I hope she hasn't been too much of a bother,' she adds.

'Not at all,' he assures her with a smile.

He extends his hand to each of them then stretches it out for me to shake. I take a step backwards and my aunt notices. 'Give the man your hand, Margaret,' she orders shaking her head with displeasure at my apparent insubordination.

I do as I am told... And then I take the baby from her arms feeling rescued at last.

Still, I do not remember the cousin. Those other times have been sealed. They have been swept away. They are under the rug. Hiding. Becoming moldy and decaying. But the stench of their decay will soon be uncovered.

23

Thinking back, knowing what I know now, it is no wonder my teenage years became laden by these stepping stones of perversity which presented themselves to me at regular intervals. Just when I was entering those years of trial and error, when everyone was experimenting and testing the waters, I began to retreat into a hardened shell of fear. I suspected even then that my feelings towards boys and men were not natural, but I could not escape my fears, let alone understand them. They were just there, like a disease.

It is in high school that the force of my fears erupt. Not immediately, mind you. It is more of a crescendo of impending doom.

When I leave the relatively safe cocoon of elementary school, I discover those my age have blossomed over the summer. In grade eight, you were the exception if you had a boyfriend; now it is almost a given. Everyone either has one or wants one. The former is preferable, but the latter is acceptable. There is always the possibility you are in between boyfriends.

I see girls dance with boys at sock hops, walk home from school with them, the boys usually carrying the girl's load of books, and then they will stand on front porches teasing and touching, male and female hormones conversing.

There are girls who don't have boyfriends. Those that are labeled 'ugly', for instance. 'Put a bag over her head and I might take a look at the rest of her,' I hear them say. Or, 'She doesn't need a mask on Hallowe'en.' And 'browners' don't have them. These are mousey creatures with brains unlike the former who are just plain ugly.

And there are a few even stranger than the 'browners' and the 'uglies', who do not seem to be interested in boys at all.

I soon find myself in a group of sorts. Like water that seeks its own level, those of us from the Catholic grade schools have flowed together. It has been a process of elimination and some of us misfits have inadvertently stuck to one another like flies to sticky paper. None of us has a boyfriend. This is what sets us apart from the other groups. We are definitely not the 'in' crowd.

We all know what we are supposed to say — things like: 'Isn't he cute. He's a living doll. What a hunk.' Something along those lines — but it doesn't get us far.

I go along with all of this because I am very curious to know what secrets boys possess and what it is they can do to bring such squeals of joy from the mouths of so many girls. Girls may be shy around them: awkward, silly, giddy, uncomfortable even, but not afraid. I am afraid. When they get near me I feel nauseous and weak.

The smell of sweat can still make me feel that way.

I have heard things about boys. I have heard they have explosions between their legs and they operate on you with their instrument. I take all of this literally and my fear grows at the sight of so many boys wandering freely through the corridors of our high school while carrying on their person such weapons.

But it is the girls' reaction to all this that puzzles me more.

I also hear girls titter about monthly visitors and asking each other if he came or not; 'Did *he* come?' they ask. 'Did your monthly visitor arrive on time?' There's always such a sigh of relief from the other girl when she says, 'Whew! *He* did. Thank God,' stretching the word God out to display her sense of relief.

One day, someone asks me how it is when my monthly visitor comes. I tell her mother won't allow such nonsense. The girls then snicker and walk away giggling, and I know something is wrong.

It is a girl named Marion who alerts me to the possibility that I am being made fun of.

'Boy, have you got a lot to learn,' she says as she approaches me.

Not much later, and right on the heels of Marion's pronouncements, almost as if the knowledge brought on the reality, my own monthly visitor makes his debut with all his gory, bloodstained entourage. I feel as if a battle is being fought inside my body, as toy soldiers equipped with tiny bayonets jab and poke and pull at my insides seeking to escape. I retch and vomit until there is nothing else to disgorge and finally the soldiers retreat and leave me in peace.

'A woman's fate,' says Marion, and I wonder what I ever did to deserve this. 'Now you know why they call it "the curse",' she says.

I don't like being in this group, but I think it is better than being alone and Marion actually makes it palatable. She always has something shocking to say.

'What's better than tulips on a piano?' she asks us.

The rest of us look at one another and shrug our shoulders. 'I don't know,' we all say in unison. 'What?'

'Tulips on an organ,' she proceeds to inform us.

We look at one another with a stunned expression on our faces.

'Boy, do I have to draw you a picture?' she says. 'Tulips — two lips,' she explains as we stare at her. '...on an organ. Organ, as in that part of the male anatomy which he seeks to hide inside one of several female apertures — in this case, the mouth. Organ, as in orgasm,' she continues.

'Oh,' we say. 'Now we get it.'

'Don't you wish,' she says.

Lunchtime, we spend in the gymnasium as spectators at intramural games. In fact, we are there to watch the boys. It is as close as we can get to them. Or, should I say, as close as they will get to us. Their bare legs show below their gym shorts. Some are hairier than others. Armpits dart out at us as they go for a jump shot directly in front of our bewildered faces. Some are full of long black hairs. If the shorts are too snug we see their bulge.

'That's where they hide their arsenal,' says Marion and we all snicker.

My friends don't seem to mind the stench of male perspiration that hangs about the gym. And later, when the boys come to class, and their smell permeates the classroom, no one minds either. But I find it impossible to concentrate on my Latin.

I am sure to this day I failed Latin because it was first period in the afternoon, following right on the heels of these intramural sessions.

Marion and I get along best. She is close to being a 'browner', but she is too smart to be classified under that label. Everyone knows that. Even the girls in the 'in' crowd.

Pat, short for Patricia, is the only one who really doesn't seem interested in boys and Priscilla is a delicate and fragile flower, while Yvette is the one who seems more normal than any of us. But none of us is as normal as we think we should be. None of us has ever had a date. We don't even get asked to dance at the sock hops. Only Yvette dances, but that doesn't count. She goes out and asks boys on ladies' choices. At least she has the guts, we think. The rest of us wouldn't dare.

I want to be with the cheerleaders or with the girls who attract circles of admirers when they dance the watusi or the twist. Some of these girls are like drops of oil in water: forever floating on top. When these girls dance, everyone moves aside and forms a ring around them. We all watch them gyrate to the music.

I want to be in the circle too. In my daydreams, I am that exciting figure dancing before the adoring gaze of her fellow classmates. But, in reality, I am not even in the ring. I have to stand back and crane my neck to see the stars in the centre.

We go through high school soaking up innumerable disappointments, unable most of the time to decipher what is being presented to us.

We do not measure time in months but rather by events: the monthly dances we sometimes attend as wallflowers, the end of football season, when our heroes are hoisted up on stage before our adoring eyes during our Friday morning assemblies meant to bolster school spirit. And then we have the proms, two each year. One on a winter theme, the other spring.

For all this we are spectators. And we go on daydreaming. We go on hoping.

It isn't until our fourth year that we sense the curtain is coming down. There is even a song that puts our feelings to music: 'It's now or never.'

Many will be graduating after this year. From our group, only Marion and I plan to stay on for grade thirteen. Even so, we feel this is it for us too. The grade twelve prom is our last chance. Our Waterloo. Our last stand. It hovers above us and walks beside us like a taunting evil angel. We don't admit it to one another, but the fear is there, lurking in our teenage minds. How ever are we going to get asked to this grand finale?

To make matters worse, it is the only prom we are having this year. Someone has decided two was too many.

None of us has delusions of grandeur any more. We do not bother dreaming of becoming prom queen or of being the centre of the dance circle. Our aspirations have toned down. We only hope for the bare minimum these days. Please, God, let me be asked to the prom. This is what I pray silently and I am sure the other girls in my group plead with similar versions of this soliloquy.

Miraculously, Pat is asked. She tells us this while we are in the girls change room putting on our gym bloomers. She tells us this with a great deal of pride and a good bit of superiority. We feel the weight of the prom upon us.

Then it's Yvette. She too has a date. And finally Priscilla. Marion and I are the only ones left. I am stunned by this structural change in our group.

I begin to make new allies. I set my eyes upon groups of girls who are closer to the top notch levels, a few strata above our own, but not quite up there with the real powers. I stay away from Marion — a loser just like me. The others in our old group, I don't have to worry about; they are staying away from me anyway. They are busy discussing prom dresses and shoes and gloves.

What have I got to lose? I figure. I begin hanging around a girl named Lucy and her troop of followers. I tag along like a stray dog when they walk home. I sit by their tables in the cafeteria and try to walk from class to class with them. Finally, I dare suggest they come into the corner diner with me for a cherry coke. 'My treat,' I say imploringly. I am surprised when they say yes.

And so I find myself sipping cherry coke with my new friends. I am exhilarated. I have done it. I have managed to extricate myself from the old group and graft myself onto Lucy's.

Lucy talks about the prom. She has a steady. She is pinned. She seems the nicest of the bunch. I feel I can trust her. When all the others are gone, I reveal my secret longing. I want to go to the prom.

I am surprised at how nice she is about it. She doesn't say, 'Don't you have a date?' or anything like that. No putdown. In fact, she looks at me straight in the eye for a moment and then tells me not to worry. She will fix it.

I am not too sure what she means. All I had hoped for was a word to one of the boys she and the others in her gang always seem to have buzzing around them. But she is going to do better than that. 'I'll get you a date,' she says. 'A blind date. Have you ever been on a blind date before? I know just the guy. He's perfect for you. Don't you worry about a thing. I'll take care of everything.'

I like her a lot because she has taken me under her wing. And she doesn't tell anyone about me or our plan. She seems genuinely interested in me. I can't figure out why.

She begins inviting me to her house and a whole new world opens up before me.

Lucy looks like the older sister she lives with. The same red hair, the ice blue eyes, the aquiline nose and the heavily madeup face. They both wear eye shadow and rouge and their lips are a rich berry red that matches their hair. Their skin has a translucent quality. It is fair and flawless. Like a canvass waiting to be painted. There is a sprinkling of freckles across the bridge of the nose.

I have pimples which my mother and I still can't resist squeezing. I often end up with splotches on my face. Sometimes I have to spread gobs of Clearasil on my forehead. Lucy never has pimples.

Lucy and her sister paint their long nails the same color as their lips. My own nails are jagged and badly bitten. I chew them to the very edge of my finger until blood appears. I also bite down the sides tearing bits of skin away.

Lucy and her sister are both very shapely. They have tiny waists they cinch in with wide belts. This makes their waists look even smaller and their bosoms bigger.

Lucy talks like her sister too. I realize this the first time I meet the woman.

'Come in, dear,' her sister says, sucking on a peach. 'Make yourself at home.' She has that same languid sort of style.

Lucy has parents but she doesn't live with them. And Lucy's sister is married but she doesn't live with her husband. Instead she has a boyfriend who is now on the couch in the living room. A stout, broad shouldered man wearing a dark suit, a white shirt and a red tie. He says, 'Hi, honey,' to me as if he has known me all his life.

One of the man's hands lies flat, palms turned upwards on the couch. He doesn't move it when Lucy's sister slithers back to the couch and sits next to him.

The idea of Lucy's sister sitting on this man's hand sends shivers up and down my spine. The whole time I am there, he keeps his hand under her and she is as nonchalant as can be. All I can think about while I am there is Lucy's sister's rear end and the man's hand.

Lucy takes me to her room. I know her own boyfriend spends a lot of time at her place but I didn't expect to find him sleeping on her bed.

He is shirtless, wearing only jeans. She walks over to him and tousles his hair. Then she falls on top of him. He wakes up and nuzzles into her. 'Come here, doll, ' he says as he pulls her up against him. They kiss. I stand there and stare.

The boyfriend finally gets up and pulls on a t-shirt. He rolls a pack of cigarettes into the arm of his sleeve. 'Gotta get movin,' he says.

'He pumps gas on the corner,' Lucy offers as explanation.

'Doesn't your sister mind?' I ask dumbfounded.

'Not at all,' says Lucy. 'Just as long as I use these,' she says dangling something that looks like an elastic before my eyes. Lucy laughs when she realizes I haven't got a clue.

'You poor thing,' she says. 'It's a condom. A safe.' This isn't said in a mean way. Not at all. She just thinks I am funny.

At Lucy's I never know what to expect. I could go in and find Lucy on the bed naked, her big breasts in full view. I myself still have tiny ones. Or she will be coming out of the shower, a towel wrapped provocatively around her. She will go into her room giggling. 'Ooh, it's soooo cold.' Then she may close the door and I will wait and wonder what is happening in there with the boyfriend.

My mother knows none of this. I wouldn't dare tell her.

For a while, I think Lucy has forgotten her promise. But I don't say anything. Most of the time I am too mesmerized by what I see and hear to think about much else. I am still frightened of boys deep down. I am frightened when I see the man and I think of his hand. Frightened of the condoms. Frightened of the boyfriend.

And yet I still want to go to the prom. I want to be like everyone else.

One day at school, Lucy runs up to me. 'Come on over tonight, Margaret. I've got that blind date I promised you,' she whispers discreetly. 'I want to tell you all about him. It's all set.'

My heart thumps loudly and I am sure Lucy can hear it. I can actually feel the weight of it against my puny chest. My throat seems to swell. I feel as if I am choking. I am dizzy and faint but I know I should be happy.

I tell the girls in my old gang about the date. I don't mention it is a blind date and that Lucy set it up.

Only Marion is left out now.

24

I tell my mother about Bruce, my blind date. 'My new friend, Lucy, knows someone who really wants to take me to the prom.' That's what I say. 'It'll be a blind date,' I continue sheepishly as I watch my mother's reaction out of the corner of my eye. I am hoping she'll believe it's a blind date from my point of view only. I have implied he has seen me and that's why he wants to take me to the prom. Surprisingly, she goes along with it.

She prepares me for the big day. I wear a floor length, gold velvet gown with a deep 'V' of satin on the bodice whose apex ends at my midriff. It makes it look as if I have a doll's waist while visually expanding my upper bodice. I guess she wants to create an optical illusion: make it look as if there is something in my chest besides bones. It reminds me of those Elizabethan dresses I have read about, the ones women wore over whalebone corsets so they'd look like an hourglass.

Gold pumps and a gold sequined purse are added to harmonize. She sends me to the hairdresser and he does my hair in the latest style. It is teased, backcombed, pulled, and tugged until I have an enormous, round, nest-shaped structure sitting on the top of my long pointed head. It is called a beehive. To me, it looks like a pile of steel wool. I know the wiry concoction is my own hair but it feels heavy and foreign. I think it gives me a horse face. Long and narrow to begin with, the additional height doesn't do much for me. But who am I to complain?

The hairdresser must see it too as he nears the end of his stylistic creation because he decides to pull out a few wisps of hair to cover my naked forehead. After he's sprayed the cumbersome construction, he hands me a mirror so that I can look at myself from all angles.

I have to stand tall and keep my head straight at all times, otherwise the nest will fall. I feel silly. Again, I think about those ladies in medieval times who wore elaborate hairstyles and hats. So elaborate mice and rats nested in them, I have read.

On prom night, a corsage arrives at the door: a single orchid looking so delicate and fragile I am afraid to touch it. It is white with a faint pink hue. It's from Bruce. Tension mounts and I sit sweating as I wait for Lucy and Bob who are going to be picking me up. Bruce will be waiting for us at the school. He lives on the other side of town and will be taking the bus to the school. He doesn't own a car.

Lucy and Bob roll into the driveway. My mother sees them before I do. She has been standing at the front door peering out. Bob honks his horn. My mother wants me to wear my coat but I just throw it over my shoulders before I dash out the door.

'Joe,' I hear my mother call. 'Aren't you even going to say something?'

'I don't know why you two fussed so much if your date's blind,' he says. I know he is trying to be funny.

I welcome the blast of cold air that greets me as I run down the steps. My mother comes out to the car with just a sweater tossed over her and opens the door for me. Shivering in the cold, she lifts my dress and brushes off the snow it has accumulated from sweeping the steps. Then she gently tucks the gold velvet dress into the car and finally she raises her cheek for me to kiss. I give her a perfunctory peck.

'Aren't you going to introduce me?' she says rubbing her frigid hands together.

'Sorry, Mom,' I apologize. And then I go through the formalities. Lucy and Bob stretch their hands towards the back seat.

'You'd better get in before you freeze to death, Mom,' I suggest.

'Okay, okay,' she smiles. And with that she shuts the door and Bob backs out the driveway skidding a little when he makes the turn on to the street. I turn to see my mother still standing there clutching her arms tightly against the cold.

I feel a lump forming in my throat. The dizziness is back. The nausea. 'Are you okay?' Lucy asks turning halfway in the front seat. 'Hey,' says Bob. 'No sweat. Bruce is a nice guy.' That doesn't reassure me.

When we get to the school gym, Bruce is nowhere to be found. I begin to cry. He has stood me up, I am sure of it. I look at Lucy with that forlorn, puppy dog look of mine. 'He isn't coming,' I sob.

'Don't be silly,' Lucy comforts me. Bruce isn't like that. He's probably just been held up. 'Come on,' says Lucy. 'Let's go in and see what's happening.' She is all in a tizzy, prancing around like a mare before a race.

I feel stupid. Everyone is with their date but I am with Lucy and Bob. And then suddenly, a huge grin appears on Lucy's face and I watch her run towards a figure in the gym doorway. The gym is dark because they have dimmed the lights, but outside the main doors, there is light. And there, in the doorway stands Bruce. He looks lit up. There's a glow around him making it look like those holy pictures of saints I have seen. My heart thumps.

And then I see him. Lucy draws him near. 'Margaret, this is Bruce. Bruce, this is Margaret.' Even as she says this I try to figure out if she did it the right way, the way they taught us to introduce people to one another. What a thing to be thinking at a time like this.

As he approaches me and comes out from the glare of the background lights, I see him. I see him for what he is. A loser like me. He is just as nervous as I am.

He isn't bad looking. Not at all. Just sissy looking. Prissy. Now I know what Lucy meant when she said, 'He's just your type.' A Mamma's boy. A wimp. That was my type. I wanted a man. Like hers. Like the football heroes. I wanted broad shoulders and confidence. A man who smoked and had yellow fingers. I wanted to cry.

Bruce has dark hair. You could call him tall, dark and handsome but these words somehow don't suit Bruce even though they are technically accurate. The hair is slicked back all right, but it's too neat. And no ducktail. It is cut square and tidy. No long forelock hanging seductively over an eye. Instead, it is plastered back and up and over into a fake wave giving him that preppy look. That sissified look.

His eyes are pretty. Blue and translucent and sparkling. Too pretty, too blue, too translucent. He is wearing a shiny grey suit. The effect is sickening. The pants fit too snugly and the shine on the fabric allows me to see his bulge, his arsenal where he keeps his weapon. It revolts me. I know what is lurking behind that bulge. I also know he is not purposely putting it on display like some of the guys at school. He isn't the type. It is the suit that's at fault and I can't understand why he would wear something that was meant for a midget, with pants that reveal too much of his white socks, and sleeves that won't let him move.

And his mouth. It can be called a full and voluptuous mouth. It is a mouth that would have done well on its own. But on him it looks preposterous, perverse, odd, silly, unsuitable. Totally incongruous. What was a wimp doing with such a mouth? The thought of those liver lips flopping around me makes me sweat. The lump returns. The dizzyness. The nausea.

I had never vomited before because of a man. That was the first time.

He asks me to dance. I oblige. Isn't this want I want? Am I not at the prom all dressed up and with a date? What more did I want? Miracles?

'Having fun?' Lucy says as she swishes by me.

I run to the girls' washroom just in time. The vomit almost gets my dress. Fortunately, it plunges straight into the toilet. I sweat profusely and yet I am shivering with cold. The vomit has gone up my nose and it is lodged in my palate. I attempt to snuff it out. I have had a lot of practice doing this so I know how to go about it.

I hear Lucy run in. She is in a panic. 'What's up?' she wants to know. She is startled at the sight of me regurgitating into the toilet. I can't answer yet because there is still more that wants to come up. 'Did you get your dress dirty?' she asks, alarmed.

'No,' I manage.

'You're not on your period, are you?'

'No.'

Finally, I come out of the stall shivering and shaking. Tears have run down my cheeks etching two lines into my foundation and rouge. I look like a clown. My nose is running. My hands are trembling. My hair is falling apart. The nest is unsteady. I stick a couple of bobby pins into my scalp to hold it all together. Then I take out a pack of Juicy Fruit gum and I put all five sticks into my mouth. I am glad I bought it. It was meant for bad breath.

Juicy Fruit gum reminds me of Bruce.

It is later in the evening. I am still determined to follow this ritual to the end. I am stubborn. After the prom, Lucy and Bob's agenda, which is also ours, includes a late night dinner at a local restaurant. A lot of the others will be there as well and I see this as an opportunity to show myself worthy of their friendship.

But the thought of food brings the nausea back. That tightness in the throat. That shortness of breath. Waves of sickening sensations pound me.

We walk to Bob's car and Bruce chivalrously opens the back door for me. I get in, but as he goes around to the other side, I quickly swing open my door and vomit into the snow. Bruce comes around to my side to see what's wrong with me. He slips and falls. Fortunately he misses the vomit. He brushes the snow off his shiny grey suit and asks if I'm all right. Lucy is in the front seat. She is holding her head in her hands. I am indeed ruining her evening. I am sure she wishes she had never had anything to do with me.

'She must have the flu or something,' she says reassuredly to Bruce.

'I'm all right,' I say, wiping my mouth with a kleenex. 'Can we stop to get some gum?' My mouth tastes horrible.

'I've got some,' says Bruce. He too had come prepared. He likes peppermint.

Peppermint makes me think of Bruce.

But I persevere. I won't give up now. I have gone too far. I will plunge into this normalcy and enjoy it even if it kills me.

The first whiff of food reaches me the moment Bruce opens the car door in the restaurant parking lot. Now I know I won't make it. We enter the restaurant, a nice enough place. Today it's a dive and I still can't go by there without remembering that night. There was a murder there a few years ago. That's the kind of place it has become.

It is actually a motor hotel. Out back is a string of identical rooms numbered 101, 102, 103. I fear the worst. I have heard of boys who take you to motels.

We are seated at a large table. Lucy and her friends have made reservations. I didn't know. Bruce takes my coat and checks it, handing me the stub. I stand there wondering what to do. I can no longer swallow. My mouth is parched. The lump is climbing in my throat.

He pulls a chair out for me. Everyone is laughing, having a ball, as they say. He asks what I want. I want nothing but to get out of there. But he expects an answer.

'What are you having?' I ask.

'Shish kabob,' he replies.

'That'll be fine for me too,' I tell him.

The waiter arrives. 'Can I get you something to drink?' he asks formally. I am already overflowing inside. I look for signs to the ladies room. I spot a couple of doors at the far end of the dining room. If I hurry, I'll make it. I get up, bruise my thigh on the table's edge, knock over a water goblet, and nearly trip on my heels.

I didn't think there could be anything left in me, but I am wrong. I heave and heave again. My body will not be controlled. It is taking over. Green stuff is coming out now. I feel awful about this. I am ruining everyone's evening. I am gross, sickening, revolting. I feel guilty. I should never have become mixed up in this scheme.

I wish someone would take me home. But I know they won't. They are here to eat, to laugh, to have a good time, to neck maybe later on. I can't bear the thought of such things. Especially the necking. His bulbous lips on mine. He makes me sick. It all makes me sick and I vomit more green stuff.

It isn't until after this round of vomiting is over that I realize I am in the men's room. I have just vomited in a urinal. I look back and gaze at them lined up against the wall.

Lucy shoves the washroom door open and I see her standing there looking disgusted. 'You're in the men's room,' she says.

25

I often wonder about Bruce. I wonder if he felt about me the way I felt about him. Did I make him sick?

I don't think I did. After all he kept calling me regardless. I desperately wanted to rid myself of Bruce but he was a leech, holding on to me for reasons unknown at the time.

His persistence annoyed yet flattered me. And more times than I wish to remember I gave in and tried again. Now I know I did it more for myself than for him. There was always that tiny ray of hope that I wouldn't throw up the next time. But I did. Every time. Without exception. Whenever and wherever we were together. Even thoughts of Bruce eventually triggered waves of nausea; he didn't have to be a physical presence to affect me in this manner.

This goes on all winter. No one knows what to make of it. Lucy keeps pushing me to go out with him and force myself to overcome my problem.

My old gang doesn't understand either. They are having problems of their own. Why should they be worried about me anyway? Didn't I all but abandon them when I changed my allegiance and began hanging around with Lucy ?

And I never tell my mother. My father, of course, lives in a world of his own.

Mother does notice I am losing weight. I have always been as thin as a bean pole but my lankiness is becoming unappealing. Cousin Tino says I look like I have just come out of Buchenwald. I think this is mean of him and my thin veneer cracks and a gush of tears floods my face. He comes to me and offers a hug as reconciliation. I shut my eyes and twist my body away from him in retaliation, but I don't run or walk away because I want to be comforted.

'Oh, come on, Margaret. *Scherzo*. I was just teasing,' he says.

But I know he is lying because I can see myself too. I am not blind.

'I'm just worried about you, that's all,' he continues.

All of this does nothing for my self-esteem which is already at a perilously low level.

My mother has tried to fatten me before. Ever since I was a baby, actually. Home remedies, over the counter fatteners, rich food, frothy beaten egg yolks spiced with sugar and marsala. Nothing worked. Lately, however, I had stabilized and this sudden reversal worries her. I am sent to the doctor.

I tell him I eat but the food won't stay down.

'What do you mean?' he asks scarcely looking at me as he leafs through a pile of papers.

'I throw up,' I tell him.

'You throw up?' he echoes. 'Why do you throw up?' he asks.

If I knew that, I want to say, I wouldn't need you. But all I really say is, 'I don't know, Sir.'

'When do you throw up?' he wants to know.

How can I tell him I throw up whenever I am with Bruce.

'After I eat,' I say.

'Every time you eat?' he asks, a little more concerned now.

'Not every time. Just sometimes.' Which is true. I don't explain further. He's the doctor. Let him figure it out.

He tells me to suck on a lemon before every meal.

Mother goes out immediately when I tell her I have to suck on lemons and buys a dozen. Before every meal, I find a neatly cut wedge on my plate. Mother reminds me I have to do as the doctor says. The thought of the yellow wedge waiting for me on the plate nauseates me further. But I do it. I do as I am told.

The vomiting, of course, continues. I am sure now it really has nothing to do with food. It has everything to do with boys.

I do eventually get rid of Bruce and it is shortly after that I find out what it was he had been after. For although he had never done anything remotely resembling a perverse act, never demanded anything from me, I had always felt pressure from him, a sense of urgency.

Lucy calls one day and says, 'Guess what?' And before I get a chance to answer, she continues. 'Bruce is getting married.'

'What?'

'Isn't that great?'

'Married?' I repeat. The information refuses to sink in.

'Yeah. Right. See that. You lost your chance.'

'Who's he marrying? Do I know her?'

'Maybe. She goes to F.H. Martin. But she comes to our dances.'

'How'd they meet?' I wonder.

'I introduced them, silly. When I saw that you two weren't going anywhere, I told him about Julia. That's her name. They're just perfect for each other.'

I had heard that before.

'When's the wedding?' I ask.

'Next week... I guess you weren't invited.'

'No. Of course not... What's the rush? Is she pregnant or something?'

'No, silly. He's just anxious to tie the knot. You know how it is?'

'No, I don't. Why's he so anxious to get married?'

'Well, you know. With his Dad dying like that and his mother not too well. You know.'

'I don't get it,' I reply.

'Gee, Margaret. Do I have to spell it out for you? He's got six younger brothers and sisters and his mother's a wreck. He really needs someone.'

'So he had to get married? Why didn't he hire a cleaning lady?'

'Oh, Margaret. Sometimes you're impossible,' she says in that huffy tone of hers.

So much for romance, I think to myself.

'Hey, listen,' she says altering her tone of voice. I marvel at how she can do this so quickly and effortlessly. 'Want me to fix you up with this guy I know?'

'No, Lucy. Not right now. I'm not interested. I haven't been feeling too great lately, and besides, I'm on medication,' I inform her. I don't tell her about the lemons.

'Gee, that's too bad,' she says. 'Is it that throwing up stuff?'

'Yeah. Sort of.'

'Well, look, see you on Monday, okay. Bob just drove in. Got to go.' She hangs up.

I am proud of myself when I sign off. Proud of the fact that I have been able to face up to my problem instead of aggravating it by fighting against it. And I meant what I had said. I really wasn't interested in anyone. No one at all.

26

I meet Steve in the spring. I don't have any exams
to write except the compulsories. My grades have
been good. I am out on the front porch leafing
through a fashion magazine wishing I looked like the
girls in the ads. We have recently moved to this house
and I like sitting out there. It is so much nicer than
any of the eleven other places we have lived in since
we came to Canada. I am proud to be in this neighborhood because I know it is one of those places
where years ago Italians weren't welcomed. But
things are changing all the time.

My mother says she still isn't sure we'll be
accepted and, in fact, it is shortly after we move in
that we are welcomed by a fire bomb on the back
porch.

The people around here are what my father calls
Wasps. For a long time I thought he meant the insect
because he'd say, 'Wasps: the insect with the vicious
sting.' There are also Jews a few blocks from here.
This makes it even more valuable in my eyes. I like
being the only Italian on the street.

A car pulls up across the street and I recognize
Steve. Like me, he is a senior at our school but he is
in one of the other forms. I've never talked to him,
but I know he is a Jew. Because of that I know he's
off limits. Not because of any religious restriction and
certainly not because my parents would object. On
the contrary. He is out of bounds because I think he
is too good for me. I still think of myself as an outcast.
I am practically just off the boat even though we've

been here years now. I still feel as if I don't belong. I don't fit in.

The thought of him being a Jew makes me think of wet nurses and starving children. I can see my mother as a child sucking on a wet cloth dipped in sugar water. I think of all the silly things my father used to say about Jews being buried in a sitting position to save space in the cemetery. Of course, now I realize a lot of what he said was nonsense, although I'm not sure I have ever been able to convince him of that. Even when I brought home books to prove my points he'd just scoff at the articles. 'Who wrote that?' he'd say. And I'd mention the author. 'Never heard of him,' he'd say. And that would put a lid on this particular conversation.

Steve doesn't see me. He is going to the house across the street. Another grade thirteen student lives there. He's Steve's friend. They're in the same form. But he's not a Jew. This just strikes me. Steve has friends that aren't Jews.

There is no one home and Steve turns and comes down the steps looking a little dejected. It's a look I will come to recognize because he always puts it on when things don't go his way.

He spots me over on the front porch.

'Hi,' he says. 'So you're the one who moved into the neighborhood.'

This means he must recognize me. He must know I too go to his school.

'We just moved in,' I tell him.

I have asked him many times what it was that made him come over that day. His answers never satisfied me. 'I don't know,' he'll say. 'I saw a cute little *shiksa* and decided to take a chance.'

He sits with me for quite a while, outside on the porch. I don't dare let him in. There is no one home.

I don't throw up. That's what I realize the moment he drives away. I'm sorry school is almost over. I figure I'll never see him again, but I am wrong.

He calls and asks me out and my old fear rises up again and I turn him down. He persists. So do I.

Years later, he tells me it was my persistent refusal that spurred him on. He didn't know anything about my problem back then. He had taken my refusals as a personal affront. Silly man.

Finally, during the summer, I relent. But there are conditions. I won't go to restaurants or movie theatres, or anywhere else where there are confined spaces. I must be out in the open.

'Look,' I tell him. 'I have a problem.'

He doesn't understand.

'Let's just forget it,' I suggest.

'No,' he insists. 'Are you a claustrophobic?' he asks.

'A what?' I say in a bewildered fashion.

'You know... Afraid of confined spaces or something.'

'I don't know. I never thought about it in that way. Maybe you're right. Maybe I am a claustro...what is it again?... So look, let's just forget it, okay?'

'We'll go wherever you want,' he insists.

I am the strangest thing he has ever come up against.

He comes to pick me up in his car. He looks nice. He's big. Husky. Perhaps too husky. But I don't mind. He has sparkling coal black eyes and his hair is straight and blue-black. It is very long in front and he constantly has to brush it out of the way. It is thick and full and I like the way it falls over his face. I don't know yet it will turn prematurely gray and make him look older than he really is.

He has nicely shaped, full lips, and a pleasant round face. Not exactly the athletic type, but he is big and I do like the look of him. He looks like a man, not a boy. He seems to know what he's doing. He has that self-assurance I like. I trust him.

How did I misjudge him for so long? Why didn't I see then what I see now? Or was it myself I had misjudged and deceived?

27

The first time Steve asks me to go all the way, I pretend to be shocked. In reality, I am curious. I want to see what all the fuss is about. I am almost twenty and I breathe a sigh of relief knowing someone has finally asked. I have heard from Marion that men want *it* all the time. Her older brother, for instance, could do it 'morning, noon, and night'. He has told her this. Marion and her brother have a candid sort of relationship; older and more experienced in these matters, he's not at all shy about sharing his exploits with her.

I also know from Marion that it is supposed to be the biggest bang anyone could ask for. Again, it's secondhand information derived from her brother, but I take her word for it.

When I hear her talk this way, I listen intently hoping to glean a few morsels of information which I can perhaps apply to my own relationship with Steve. As it is, there is a constant gnawing sensation within me that refuses to let go. I can't help thinking, if only Marion knew that my sexual encounters with Steve are anything but the delirious ecstasy her brother vividly describes to her where tongues vigorously penetrate their partner's mouths in some sort of primitive sport. This French kissing she so fervently recounts in all its pulpy details, repulses me. I take solace in knowing Steve doesn't subscribe to Marion's brother's antics and yet, at the same time, these queer proceedings entice my inquisitiveness.

My encounters with Steve are more of a nuisance and a bother: sometimes messy affairs that leave me wondering if I have been a participant or simply an accessory.

And every now and then, titillating sensations forewarn that I am indeed alive. But whatever else there is, remains unearthed for me, for now at least, and I begin to wonder if there's any truth to Marion's claim that sex is the essential ingredient in a relationship.

Craving answers, I let Steve entice me into a full scale sexual encounter and not just back seat fondling.

He rents a motel room. He has a bottle of champagne. Asti Spumante, actually, not the real stuff. My father would cringe. But I don't say anything. I am petrified. What if the people at the motel find out we aren't even married? He tells me not to worry and pulls a key from his jacket pocket. He smiles a cunning smile, meant to impress me. His smile says, See, I've thought of everything. Aren't I smart?

He picked the key up earlier in the afternoon. All we have to do now is walk up to the door and go in.

This motel is like the one near the restaurant I went to with Bruce. It has rooms lined up just like jail cells. But this sort of arrangement is convenient since there won't be any need to traipse across a lobby.

He drives the car up to our room door and kills the engine.

'Nervous?' he asks.

'What do you think?'

'Look, Margaret, just say the word. If it's going to bother you, we'll forget it.'

He is so rational and prudent, almost to the point of detachment. Where are his manly needs, his uncontrollable male urges, the ones Marion tells me about? Listening to her, I have concluded men go into fits and rages when the need arises; they lose control and can't be restrained. I look at Steve and see no evidence of such turmoil. He looks more like a salivating dog waiting patiently for his reward, an eager beaver proud of what he's been able to accomplish so far. Certainly he's all geared up, but I am equally certain that he is still in control of his desires.

'Let's just go in, Steve,' I say. 'I don't want to sit out here all night.'

I am afraid of being seen. I hesitate when I get out of the car. Steve comes around and opens the car door. I put on a pair of sunglasses. Fortunately, it's still quite sunny out this warm summer eve and the sunglasses don't look out of place. I walk close behind Steve with my head held low. I try not to look about, but I manage to steal a glance out to the sides. There is no one around.

He inserts the key in the lock and turns the knob. The door opens with a squeak. I am greeted by a dark blue shag carpet, matted and not very attractive, a double bed covered in a geometric print bedspread that matches the curtains, teak night stands bearing cheap lamps, a landscape over the bed, centred but off kilter. I tap the landscape lightly to straighten it. I can't stand seeing things in disorder. At the foot of the bed and just a few feet from it there is a dresser of sorts. Three drawers down one side, the top extending into a desk. A small television set sits on the desk end. I open one of the drawers and a bible stares back at me.

The bathroom is in white tile and clean enough. Steve follows me in to get a couple of glasses. They're wrapped in white paper and sit upside down on a small glass tray. He rips the paper off, uncorks the wine, and pours some into these squat round tumblers that look like they've been in too many dishwashers. The sight of the bubbling wine inside these glasses seems incongruous.

The cork had popped to the ceiling with a thunderous thud. Later, when we are doing it, I will be looking at the mark it has left.

Steve places the drinks on his nightstand then walks over to pull the drapes shut. The room is tomb-like in shadows. He turns on one of the lamps and a soft glow embraces the room. I feel a little better.

He sits on the side of the bed and picks up the drinks offering me mine.

'You'll have to come here if you want it,' he says with a smile.

I smile back and join him on the bed.

His body is a surprise. The softness of the male parts is unexpected. They look so vulnerable. So exposed. I am glad mine are all tucked in neatly between my legs instead of hanging down like this.

I can joke about my observations with Steve. 'How can you walk around with all that hanging between your legs?' I ask.

He says my talk excites him. And I see proof of that. The once soft parts are taking on a more structured shape. He's getting hard. I hadn't meant to do this. My question was an honest one.

I pretend it is all satisfying. What did I expect? Fireworks? I must convince myself to be thankful for what I have. After all, I am not getting sick anymore. With Steve, I feel at ease, comfortable, if not excited. And he has cured me of this despicable disease, this claustrophobia or whatever it is. And I am truly grateful to him. I owe him.

Later, we finish the wine and watch a movie. El Cid.
We are like an old married couple and I envision
myself recreating this scene for the rest of my life.

The next day I tell Steve we must never do that
again. I tell him I cannot live with such guilt. I feel
dirty, unclean. Like a slut. A whore. And what if I get
pregnant? Had he thought of that? I play the virtuous
act. I analyze and rationalize. I convince him I am
devastated by the event. And I am. But not for the reasons he believes. He figures once I have done it, I will
not be able to stop. Like eating potato chips. Once
you start you can't stop. He admires my strength of
character. He respects me. This is what I want to hear.
I want to be respected.

And he abides by my decision. We never do it
again. Not then. Not until later, much later, when I
return from my Italian interlude. We do other things,
but not that.

I don't tell Marion any of this. I don't want her to
know I have done it. If she finds out, she'll ask me
questions. She will want to compare notes with her
brother. And then she'll discover, for she is a thor-
ough researcher, that my version of a total sexual
encounter does not measure up to her brother's
description of his exciting affairs. And that, I fear,
will lead her to conclude I have failed. I wouldn't
even be able to pretend it has been the climax of my
life.

28

Lucy calls and invites me to one of her parties. She no longer lives with her sister, the one who used to sit on the couch next to her boyfriend with his fleshy hand indiscreetly thrust beneath her generously proportioned rump. She and Bob have a place of their own now that Bob has a job, and their once infamous lifestyle has become even more exotic and tempting.

Lucy and I are more apart now than ever. I am in university. Steve and I are a couple. Links to Lucy and high school are all but severed. But not completely. There are still some tough tendons that won't let go. I still do not understand why she invites me nor why I go when she does. Because although this is happening less and less frequently, the fact remains, it is still happening.

Lucy dislikes Steve almost as much as he dislikes her. When I am invited to one of her parties, it is understood that I will go solo.

I wonder if Lucy realizes Steve wouldn't go even if she asked him?

'She's a slut,' he says if I happen to mention her.

'She's just different,' I answer protectively.

It's that difference that entices me. What will she be up to now, I wonder? She lives out my fantasies. She is the flip side of my controlled universe. She is the tiny taunting evil angel perched on my left shoulder forever tossing temptation before me.

'Are you still seeing that Jew?' she asks when she calls me.

'You mean, Steve?' I answer, insulted. After all, I am in love with this man. 'Yes, I am.'

'You shouldn't tie yourself down like that,' she says. Which I find a rather ironic statement coming from her. After all, it is she who is now living with a man.

'Look, won't that prick give you a night off,' she blurts out. That too insults me. I think I am free to do as I please. But, of course, I am not. Steve is already beginning to hem me in.

'Look, we're having a Toga party Saturday night. I'd really like it if you came. There'll be some really neat guys. Friends of Bob.'

Toga party. That was the 'in' thing. Did she think I didn't know? I had heard about them. Wild orgies, that's what they turned out to be. You wore a sheet and nothing else. You wrapped it around and tried to look like a Roman. Disgusting. Humiliating. Is this what my culture had come to represent? Debauchery and sex? Perversity and obscenity? But I go. A secret side of me wants to go. I lie to Steve once again. He is not yet suspicious. It's still too early for that. I don't, however, bring a Toga.

'Margaret,' Lucy greets me at the door. She is the perennial hostess. She looks more and more like her sister. Her toga reveals her cleavage which is more ample than ever. She is still quite stunning: those chiseled features, that lustrous flame red hair that frames her face with a mad tangle of curls and waves that bounce with her every move. Every now and then, she shakes her mane like a young filly, lifting her chin and throwing her head back, forcing the observer to focus on that flamboyant face. And then, with the sweep of a hand, she lifts the fiery hair from her shoulders only to allow it to fall back upon her.

It is with these exaggerated theatrical gestures that she greets me. Bob too comes forward, following directly behind her. He circles her waist with one muscular arm, lifts her hair with the other and plants a moist kiss on her smooth throat.

Bob says, 'Long time no see.' He hardly looks at me. He is so intent on fondling Lucy and I can tell he wants her to return to whatever it was they were doing before I arrived.

'Come on in,' says Lucy, pulling me by the arm. 'There are people here I'd like you to meet.' Then she notices. 'Where's your Toga?'

'No Toga,' I say cheerfully and as fervently as I can muster. 'Never wear the things myself,' I continue, hoping she will get my meaning. I am taking a stand.

'You just march on upstairs,' she says tugging me up the narrow squeaky stairway. She is impervious to the new me. I am like putty in her hands. I feel her molding me and I hate myself. I have silly putty where my spine should be. When she uses that imperious tone of hers, I can not fight her.

She rips a sheet from one of the many beds scattered about upstairs and wraps it around me.

'I like a lot of company,' she says in answer to my startled look as I take in the upstairs. 'We can make room for you too if you like sometime,' she says matter-of-factly. 'Now get your clothes off and do that thing up right,' she says pointing to the sheet.

I feel like a fool in this toga of hers and I am sure I also look like one. Steve would be abhorred. My mother would die. My father would disown me. I feel

Steve will walk in at any moment and catch me in my perversity. I worry that my lie will not work. I have told him I am with my parents. But they are out on their own. I am doing this sort of thing more and more. Lucy is right. About Steve. He does hamper my style.

But this is naughty. This is bad. This is not what a proper young woman should be doing on a Saturday night. I know Steve is right. He is right about Lucy and right about everything.

Lucy introduces me to Bill. Bill is a 'living doll'. This is what Lucy says. 'A living doll.' I think about Bruce. My throat tightens the way it used to, but I fight the feeling. I don't throw up anymore, I have to tell myself.

Bill turns out to be a real doll. He is a stunner. Too good to be true, I will eventually find out. Absolutely gorgeous. A lovely full head of California blond hair settling seductively over a bronzed face. A marvelously tanned body. Slim, yet bulging in all the right places: biceps, thighs. A tight little ass that gyrates to music as effortlessly as a Hawaiian dancer. He is lying on a sofa when I first see him, parts of him peeking out from the toga. He is stretched out in a feline position. Posing, really, now that I think about it. I can see him as a centerfold in one of those male nude magazines Marion and I get from her brother. He is so unlike Steve. It is quite obvious to me that Bill's *raison d'être* is strictly sex.

By the end of the night I am lying on the sofa too. We are entangled in each other's arms not caring about our Togas. No one else notices. They are all tangled up in their own affairs. I look over at Lucy. She's not with Bob. I don't see him. I wonder where he is. Later, I see Bob come down the stairs, another woman with him. This must be sexual freedom.

Bill commits suicide about two years after the Toga party. Lucy calls me one day, crying. 'Remember Bill,' she sobs. 'Beautiful, gorgeous Bill. He's dead,' she cries. 'He hung himself in the garage.' It seems Bill was gay. Lucy had been on a mission again. She was going to reform him. That was why he was always at her parties.

I hate Lucy more and more as I struggle to iron out the creases of our strange relationship. She had attempted to use me once again. This time, she expected me to reform a homosexual. And she didn't even tell me.

I am furious. I am sure I must have repulsed Bill. I must have made him sick. The way Bruce made me sick. Did I contribute unknowingly to his death? I feel guilty. I feel like an accessory to a murder.

Marion does not get asked to Lucy's parties. Lucy must realize Marion wouldn't lower herself. In that way, she's like Steve. I admire Marion for this. I admire her and hate myself. I am weak. I am a jellyfish. A wishywashy spineless jellyfish who flops around at the mercy of the current. I ride the latest wave and inevitably come crashing onto the beach. One of these days I am not going to be so lucky and I will find myself splattered against the rocks.

29

Marion and I become more and more free with our thoughts and feelings about ourselves and those around us. We seem to have developed a symbiotic relationship. We thrive on each other.

'Lucy's a tramp,' she says.

'You're so hard on her. You sound like Steve.'

'She's the one who's hard on men. She gives them hard-on's that nearly bust their pants.'

We giggle. I love it when Marion talks like this.

'Well, she lives with Bob now. It's all semi-legal. What do they call that? Commonlaw?' I try to squelch my snickering.

'Not what they do.'

'What are you talking about?'

'Don't you know what they do, Margaret? Don't tell me you're that naive.'

'What in hell are you talking about?'

'Bob's a pimp.'

'Jesus Christ,' I say. 'You must be kidding. I don't believe you. You're making this all up.'

But I'm not sure she is.

Marion stopped trying to belong a long time ago. She's a free spirit; I am a trapped one. I hide things from her, my best friend. I hide things from Steve and from my family. I am evil. I am a schizo, a multiple personality. I must be. Otherwise I wouldn't be keeping company with such diverse segments of society.

'Have you ever thought about suicide?' Marion asks one day.

'Hasn't everyone?' I answer smugly.

Marion is studying chemistry, biology, physics. She's a science major. I am in arts.

'It's easy, you know. Very easy,' she informs me.

We discuss the merits of the various methods. 'All you need is a sharp razor blade. You lie down and the blood drains from your body and you will die without even knowing it.' That's what she tells me. She then proceeds to pantomime her demise, stretching out her arm, slashing the wrist with an imaginary blade, and finally folding her body on to the floor.

But I am not convinced. 'Are you sure about that? When I used to see my mother kill chickens it wasn't so easy,' I tell her. 'It used to take all my mother's strength to hold the damn bird down while the blood dripped into a pail. If she let go — even just a bit — the bloody thing would go flying madly around the room. Like a chicken with its head cut off. You know the saying.'

'That's different,' she informs me. 'Your mother didn't slash the chicken's scrawny wrists; she slashed their skinny throats,' she says as she grabs the base of her neck with one hand and her head with the other then pulls her own neck as if she were the chicken.

Just watching her antics makes me understand there is a difference between wrists and throats.

'Some people take pills,' she says, changing the method. 'But why spend the money?'

'Because it wouldn't be as messy,' I argue.

'But if you don't do it right and they find you before it's too late, they'll pump out your stomach. The razor blade is much more foolproof, if you ask me.'

'Could we change the subject?' I suggest.

Marion asks what I think about reincarnation.

I tell her I don't.

'Seriously,' she says. 'Have you ever thought about it?'

She makes me think about it.

'The way I see it,' she begins, 'we are all in transit. This is just a way station, a stopover. A recycling station perhaps. There is no heaven or hell, you know,' she says. 'It's just a big recycling plant and we're being transformed from one state to another — hopefully to higher and higher levels all the time — but I'm not too sure about this point.'

She says we go on to infinity, but in altered states. I am puzzled. This is not what I've been taught, although I have heard her ideas about heaven and hell before. My mother, for instance, is a firm believer that the here and now is your own heaven or hell. 'It's what you make it,' she always says. 'I've never met God nor Satan,' I have heard her say.

'If you take deep breaths, really deep breaths,' says Marion, 'nine or ten one right after the other, then hold you nose tight, you can pass out.'

This is about as adventuresome as we get for the moment. Drugs and alcohol are out of the question.

I ask Marion, 'Do you ever wish you could be in more than one place at a time? I mean, don't you hate the fact that so much is happening and we don't have any part in it, no role to play?'

In the paper, we read about pocket wars and revolutions, Cuba and Castro and the Missile Crisis, the Cold War and the threat of nuclear disaster. We see protests and marches and hear tough talk from world leaders. There is so much to fear. We know that, but none of it is within our personal field of vision. We are safe. We only see the reality of the rest of the world through the eyes of others: reporters and cameramen, journalists and writers.

'Imagine,' I say to Marion,' while we were in class discussing chromosomes, Kennedy's brains spilled out on Jackie's lap.'

We saw her in her stylish suit climb over the back seat of the convertible reaching out for a secret service man. Why didn't she duck? What bravery. And we saw the car suddenly veer out of the motorcade and rush to safety. How I would love to know what Jackie was thinking during those moments? Did she know then that all their efforts would be futile? What would I have done if I had been her?

I am trying to tell Marion something. I'm not sure myself what it is I want to say. I want to talk about my sterile life and my obsession with this search for fulfillment. I am almost envious of the violent scenes I witness on the television screen each night and read about in the paper. All I am is a spectator.

I am even envious of Marion. She seems so secure in her goals, as if she is being guided by a point of distant light. I instead feel trapped in a glass labyrinth. I fear taking a step for I know I risk shattering the image.

'We don't know the half of it, do we, Margaret?' says Marion. 'We're just two oddballs floating about oblivious to the multitude of happenings.'

Marion's statement catches me by surprise. It makes me wonder if she too feels disjointed and out of place. Maybe she isn't anchored on *terra firma* either. Maybe she too feels she is drifting on quag-mire.

That's how I feel now. I want to divide and multi-ply. Like cells. The way I've seen them under a micro-scope. Divide and multiply until there is more of me to go around. Then each part can go on its merry way and satisfy the needs of the whole. As a single unit, I am incapable of this. If I please one, I bring grief upon the other. I pulsate with a desire to break out of this constraining enclosure.

30

David slips silently to bed, convinced, I am sure that Steve and I are asleep. Sounds from his room die down and when I am certain he is asleep, I get out of bed and go downstairs grabbing my pillow and a blanket. I can't bear to stay in this bed with Steve tonight. Not after the mesh bikini incident. I fold myself up on the couch shivering with cold. I tuck the blanket around me and wait for the chills to dissipate.

Throughout the night, my subversive behavior grates on my mind and I have trouble falling asleep. When I do manage to lapse into slumber, my dreams torment me and shake me back into reality. I decide to take a sleeping pill. The thought of having this tiny capsule inside my body relieves my tension. This is a bad sign. I must not become dependent upon them. But right now, it feels so good to know the tiny yellow pill is beginning to work its magic deep inside me. I lie still, waiting for my body to begin feeling light and free. I wait for the sounds of night around me to slowly hush and finally disappear altogether.

This waiting for sleep reminds me of when David was young. I would rock him gently, singing my melody, and watch his eyelids grow heavy. Then I would lower my voice until it was but a whisper and when I could hear the smooth even breathing of sleep, I would lay him in his crib.

But now it is myself I am watching as I wait for sleep to take me. Funny how I can never catch the actual moment.

The pill has done its job well. I register a sound and I see a fleeting, blurred figure. David? At noon, I awaken still groggy. I am upset with myself for having taken the sedative so late into the night. It has meant missing David this morning, robbing me of a chance to talk to him. I have decided there are things I want him to do for me.

Steve is busy in his study. He comes out when he hears me in the kitchen. He feels my tension.

'Don't worry,' he says raising his hands as if he were at gunpoint, 'No mesh bikinis.'

I force a laugh and relax slightly. He has been able to diffuse the situation and I am glad of it. It's good that he can say this.

'Just wanted to tell you you've had a couple of phone calls.' When I do not respond, he continues. 'David called.'

'David?' I jump in before he has a chance to finish his sentence. 'When did he call?'

'Just a while ago. You were still asleep.'

Guilt washes over me for having missed his call.

'He said he'd be home for dinner. He's got a few more friends to say goodbye to and a couple of things to pick up... And Tino called.' He slips this in as an afterthought.

'Tino?'

'He wants to see David before he leaves. Wants to know if the two of you can go down to his place tomorrow. I told him I was sure you'd be there.'

I detect the note of sarcasm in his voice.

'It wouldn't kill you to come with us.'

'Margaret, please don't start. You know how I feel about him and that snake infested place of his.'

'Where's your sense of adventure?' I challenge him, making it quite clear I am referring to last night.

'Your cousin is crazy,' he replies. 'He's an animal. He should be arrested for impersonating a human.'

References to Tino sour our conversation. This must annoy Steve since it has thwarted his attempts to make up for last night. I curl up on the couch and turn away from him. He too turns and heads back to his study. But then he stops. 'Margaret, look, I'm sorry about last night. Really I am.'

'I know,' I answer sincerely. And I do believe him. I am certain he is truly sorry. I loll around the house all day reading and pretending to be in control while inside I am in shreds. Steve comes out periodically for a drink or a snack. Whenever he emerges, stretching and yawning on his way to the kitchen, he throws cautious glances my way. I know he wants me to ask him to sit and talk, but I am as cold as ice. Finally, he brews a pot of tea and chances to offer me a cup. He sits by me uninvited, glancing at the book I am reading intently, something I picked up from the library.

'So you're into psychology,' he says looking at the cover. 'Memory,' he reads aloud.

I still don't acknowledge his efforts at conversation.

'Here. Have some tea. Or perhaps you'd prefer something stronger? A drink?'

'Tea is fine,' I assure him as I put my book down.

'David will be home soon. You don't want him to find you still on the couch, do you? Why don't you go out for a walk and get some fresh air. It'll make you feel better I'm sure.'

I hate the way he is talking to me now, his tone of voice. So condescending. As if I were a small child. But it's nearly five o'clock and he's right. I should get up and stop reading. And I don't want David to find me like this.

'Go around the block, Margaret,' he says. 'I'll get the barbecue started and I'll do those steaks. I think they're still hanging around.'

I am wearing no makeup. I haven't even combed my hair and I am still wrapped in my wrinkled robe which looks grubby because I have been sitting around in it all afternoon. I drag myself upstairs and pull on a pair of pants and a top. I wrap a scarf around my tousled mop of hair and slip on one of David's jackets. I like the smell. It'll keep me company.

Fall is approaching. Always a bad time for me. It has been bright and quite warm all day, but there is a chill in the air, cold enough for me to see my breath and to turn my nose red, but it is pleasant outside and the sun is still bright in the western sky. Just a hint of wind blows towards me and even that will disappear when I turn the corner and walk in the other direction.

One foot in front of the other I tell myself. I look down at my two feet. Good, they are listening. My brain's computer is functioning as programmed. It is remarkable to see how truly simple it really is. Each step takes me that much further from the house. Away.

I hate *fall*. Even the word disturbs me. Empires fall. So do stock markets. That is what Steve would say. In my childhood dreams I used to fall from tall buildings, from airplanes, from mountain tops, always waking before I hit the ground. Images of things collapsing come to mind. London bridge falling down. People fall from grace. Right now, leaves are falling.

I try *autumn* but that word doesn't sound much better. It conjures up images of a spent youth, a wasted life. 'She's in the autumn of her life.' People say that. It means *decline.* Not as swift as a fall perhaps, nevertheless a decline. Like going down a steep hill with your foot on the brake.

But of course these words are appropriate. I know this as I look at the ground which is littered with leaves lying by the side of the road like so many corpses. Hundreds of them. Some are curled up in a fetal position. These have been on the ground the longest. Others are relatively flat. Some are yellow gold, some rusty red. Those on the roadway are flattened and brown, nearly disintegrated.

I raise my head and look up at the nearly naked trees. Disrobed like this, they look pitifully scrawny and vulnerable. They remind me of those pictures I have seen of war prisoners. Why did they have to undress them before sending them to their deaths? Why did they have to be naked? Why this ultimate humiliation? The thought makes me shudder. All of these nude trunks and branches bring those images to mind and along with them comes the guilt. How many of Steve's relatives perished in that grisly manner?

I look back down at my feet. They are still in motion. It is as if they have been wound up like one of David's childhood toys and are now propelling themselves effortlessly forward. I look up again to get my bearings, to see where it is I am. My legs have taken over. They don't even feel a part of me. They are robot legs that happen to be attached to my torso, but they aren't getting signals from me.

How easy it would be to escape. To go. To keep walking. Farther and farther. But I check my inner signals. Instead, I turn at the corner and head for home. I have come full circle.

I walk past my house smelling the barbecue. Smoke spews from my backyard. Poor Steve. He is trying. I am evil. Wicked. Not worthy of such devotion. He is right to mistrust me.

Instead of turning into my driveway, I keep walking, going around again as if in orbit, in outer space, round and round I go. I am spaced out. Out of space. Crazy. Didn't spaced out mean crazy? On drugs?

I walk by without looking at the house. If Steve sees me, he'll think I've just decided to go around again. He will take it as a good sign. But the truth is, I don't want to face him. I want to be alone.

No. No. That is not true either. I am afraid of being alone. I do not want to be alone. It is Daniel I want. And David. Oh, yes, David, my son, my only son. Let me at least have him if the other cannot be.

31

Tino's place reminds me of Daniel. Especially the woods around the house. Daniel and I made love in the woods once. He laid me down gently on the soft earth floor. Moss and leaves cushioned me. I remember being surprised at the softness of the forest floor. The air had the luxurious scent of nature: the musty scent of mushrooms and leaves, the occasional whiff of pine through the deciduous forest which filled me with awe. All is quiet and stillness in the woods. Down below the tree tops, peace reigns. The only sounds are those of the forest. I remember opening my eyes and seeing the tall oaks and elms swaying high above us, their leaves rustling merrily like a thousand clapping hands, their canopy a shelter for our quivering bodies. When he lifted me up, he laughed. Red splotches covered my back. We had rolled onto a patch of wild strawberries. Our love-making was magical.

Steve has smudged this image with his talk of snakes. I asked him again this morning if he wanted to come with us but he refused. He and Tino have never seen eye to eye and with the passage of time they have both become more entrenched in their ways. Where once they were content, for my sake, to keep themselves on parallel lines, now they are at right angles. All they have in common is me, their vertex, their pivotal point.

David and I set out alone and I am not altogether unhappy about this since it will give me an opportunity to talk to my son. I have finally come to a decision about Daniel. I will ask my son to look him up. I have absolutely no idea what this will lead to but it is something I must do. I will broach the subject later, after out visit. For now, I will have to juggle images of Daniel and me in the woods with those pictures Steve has painted for me. Places inhabited only by snakes and vile creatures.

I envy snakes. I envy the way they shed their skins and carry on. They have no way of feeling a sense of loss, at least I don't think they do. They do not slither away with a sense of regret or remorse. They do not contemplate the past or the future.

I would not make a good snake. I would slither out of my skin time and time again forever looking back upon it to relive events: the tall grasses it has hidden in, the dark holes it has burrowed into, the narrow escapes.

Cousin Tino does not mind snakes. He certainly is not afraid of them. He finds their marking beautiful, their mannerisms beguiling.

David and I are walking through the woods which surround Tino's property, a large tract of land with a narrow winding stream, a small river really, and plenty of bush. There is even an island on the property and it is in there that he lives. In there he can be anywhere he wants.

This piece of property is known for its profusion of snakes and reptiles. Stories abound about men in bulldozers, those who excavated the original house, finding snake pits and hauling up dozens of them with each bucket of dirt. Snakes supposedly dangled from the dozer buckets. One man is rumoured to have left the place half crazed at the sight. Tino likes it all the more because of these stories.

The river breeds water snakes. It is an old muddy river with stagnant grey water, not water you would want to swim in although it was once inviting. We used to come here with Tino to catch crayfish and frogs and the occasional pike or catfish. But now, by the time it reaches Tino's property, it is in fact just a large open sewer. A toxic dump. It runs out of the city collecting toxins and delivers them to Tino's doorstep before splitting in half to circle the island and then wind its last few miles out to the large recipient river. And yet snakes thrive. How resilient they must be.

The river still manages to breed other species as well. There are frogs and the occasional brave fish can be caught. Along the banks rodents are plentiful. A cornfield on the property attracts them. There is a tiny chicken coop with cackling hens and a surly rooster. The narrow building is partitioned down the middle: chickens on one side, rabbits on the other. There are ducks in the yard as well as guinea hens. Another shelter houses turkeys. Just a couple. Cats abound. And there's a dog. All of this is hemmed in by a tall, chain-link fence. And yet foxes still get in, Tino tells me.

David and I cut through the property and head for the narrow wooden bridge which connects the island to the mainland. A chainsaw is buzzing in the distance.

'He's getting ready for winter,' I say to David.

The sound leads us to Tino and before long we catch a glimpse of him high up on an old decaying elm. David laughs.

'Look at him up there. He'd look like a chimp if it weren't for the chain saw,' says David, a wide smile sweeping his face. He has always approved of this strange, eccentric, second cousin.

Tino is straddling a thick trunk sawing an upper branch. He can't see us yet. We wait for the branch to fall and then we catch his attention.

The branch falls with a few tentative crackling sounds and then one final definitive snap and Tino looks down, pleased. He spots us and waves, turning the saw off.

'That one's for you, Margaret,' he shouts. With one hand on the saw and the other on the rough tree trunk, he climbs down as effortlessly as the frisky grey and black squirrels that populate his property.

'I cut down some old apple trees for you too. But that husband of yours is going to have to flex his muscles and swing an axe to them.'

'Then there'll be no heat from my fireplace this winter, Tino,' I say half jokingly. 'But thanks anyway.'

'Maybe David can chop it before he leaves,' he adds with a wink. 'Look at the arms on you,' he says turning to David.

It is a bright fall day today, unusually warm even for this Indian summer of ours. The sun peeks through the tall trees slanting its rays upon us and sometimes shining them into our eyes. A playful sun today.

We cross back through the bush towards the muddy river. It doesn't sparkle or glimmer even with the brightness. It looks thick, like sludge. It is moving, but just barely. It looks like a slow moving brown creature. A big fat snake. How appropriate.

We have to walk through the tall rushes and grasses and the prickly shrubs to get to the path which runs along the riverbank and leads to the house. The earth beneath our feet feels as if it is going to give way at any moment. I don't like being on such precarious ground. But I go on.

Tino is way out in front now. He cuts through the grasses and shrubs like a scythe. He does not even bother to push the growth aside. He makes a path for us. David flails his hands about. Some of the limbs snap when he comes in contact with them but he continues on. Occasionally he calls to me, to reassure himself, I suppose. Who do I look back to for reassurance?

Tino calls back to me. 'Your son doesn't take after his father.'

I remain silent. But I feel the heat rise to my face and my temples throb. I am glad no one is close enough to see me.

The crispy crackling of twigs encourages me on. The rustling of leaves and the tiny branches underfoot make me feel more at ease. These sounds mask the snake. I do hear a rustling in the grass just beyond, but I think it's the wind. Then I see it slithering in the distance. I freeze. Fear grasps me and I cannot move. I manage a feeble cry. In the quiet of the bush, it is enough to capture my son's attention. He turns to me; he too sees the snake. He calls Tino. 'A snake. A long snake. Over here,' he motions to Tino.

'Where?' Tino shouts back.

David indicates the spot by walking towards it.

Tino turns and begins to trot through the underbrush weaving in and out just like the reptile. The snake attempts to escape but Tino is relentless. He chases it, confusing it by forcing it to run in circles. Finally I see Tino drop. When I see him again, he has grabbed the snake by the neck and is holding it proudly.

'It's okay. Just an old fox snake.'

There are rattlesnakes out here. One can't be too glib about spotting a snake. David is excited. 'You got the sucker,' he says running over to take a closer look. I haven't moved.

The snake is a dull, drab, mottled brown colour. It looks like the river. A yard or more in length and quite thick, it dangles from Tino's hand, wriggling and writhing. Tino examines it, and then notices the bulge in its body.

'Just had lunch, eh?' he says to the reptile. 'Come on,' he says to David. 'Let's go over to the bank by those rocks.'

'Are you going to kill it?' David asks.

'Damn right I am,' Tino replies. 'What would you have me do?'

'How are you going to do it?' David wants to know.

'He'll never know what hit him,' says Tino. He swings the snake up onto a large rock and asks David to get him a smaller one. 'Just enough to do the trick,' he says.

'This one okay?' David want to know picking up a hefty specimen.

'Just perfect,' Tino replies. 'Okay, boy, let him have it.' And David whacks the snake on the head as if it were the most natural thing in the world for him to do.

'What a way to go, eh, David? Never knew what hit him. Now watch,' says Tino. He holds the lifeless reptile up by the tail. Its smashed head is bleeding.

With his left hand Tino squeezes the body from tail to mouth and we see the frog pop out.

'Did you see that?' David calls to me. 'Tino, you're something else,' he adds with a laugh.

'You guys better get back here and escort me out,' I plead. 'And don't you dare bring that thing near me, do you hear?'

'Here I come, Mom,' says David, 'with the snake.'

'He's just teasing, Margaret,' Tino reassures me as I watch him swing the long snake, tossing it back into the muddy river.

32

How was I to know it would be Daniel who would release me from the prison of my emotions, free me from the sterility of my landscape allowing body and soul to flower and bloom with a profusion of new sensations? Daniel brought the sun into my life and with his warmth, he melted my resistance and seared me to him, igniting a perpetual flame of desire. It was Daniel who penetrated to the depths of my heart, who embalmed me in his love. And I soaked up his energy and encased it in my personal tabernacle.

When fate thrust me upon him, I began to give serious credence to Marion's theories: Daniel and I must have been one in another life, in another dimension. I knew I had found the all important missing link who would breathe life into me.

The moment my eyes settled upon him, desires awakened and my heart ripened and burst free. How many times have I replayed the scene, imagining I am still that naive, young girl?

I used to tell Marion it was all her doing. All her fault. Only then I didn't put it quite that way. 'I owe it all to you,' I would say. Or, 'Thanks to you...' It was only later, when my life soured, that I fell back on my less conciliatory accusations.

But, of course, it didn't have anything to do with Marion, and I knew this as well as she did. It was my need to break out of my constraining mould that led me to Daniel. Marion was simply the intermediary, my foil and confidant.

'I need a favor,' Marion pleads. 'I won't take no for an answer.'

'Forever the diplomat,' I reply.

'Actually, it's Carlo who needs the favor.'

Carlo is the fellow she's been seeing, a business-man whose office is in the same building where Marion and I have summer jobs working for the govern-ment. Because of our language skills, she and I are assigned to the Immigration Department where we receive and help settle new immigrants. Carlo is the jovial type whose thick curly hair sits like an unruly mop on top of his big square head. His face is wide and his grey eyes twinkle with perpetual mischief. His thick neck swells when he laughs in his raucous manner, his veins popping out looking like a relief map. He lifts weights. His thick thighs bulge through his pants. Yet, despite his girth, he is agile and quick. He also has a verbal dexterity that Marion adores and he always has a joke at the ready. Rambunctious and unpredictable, he is always good for a laugh.

'Carlo's brother is coming over from Italy next week,' Marion continues. 'He's an architect. Daniel's his name. He's going to be here to oversee that river-front project everybody's fussing about. Anyway, Carlo wants us to double date.'

'Shit, Marion, no more blind dates for me. I've been that route. Besides, there's Steve. What would I say to him?'

'I'm sure you could think of something,' she snips, a touch of sarcasm in her voice. She raises her eyebrows lifting her lids so that her eyes are two round circles. 'For Christ's sake, Margaret, I'm not asking you to commit hari-kari,' she adds, her tone sounding alarmingly annoyed.

I am taken aback by her mood swing. I can't understand why she is prying me from Steve. Could she be jealous of my relationship with him? Hardly. She must be sick and tired of my cushiony safe world.

'Well?' she prods me on.

I hesitate, fearful of the consequences. Bruce springs out of hiding. The fear of losing control of my body grips my innards. It all wells up in me again. After all, it wasn't that long ago. How surprisingly easy it is to relive such misery. I have become comfortable and secure with Steve. And yet, there is still a tiny voice taunting me, telling me, ironically, this security is also binding me.

I allow Marion to talk me into this. 'That was in the past,' she says. 'You no longer orbit in those circles,' she continues, her index finger revolving in the air. 'You have booted yourself from the gravitational pull of adolescence and gone on to other spheres,' she quips in her matter-of-fact manner.

I shake my head and smile despite my ambivalence. 'You have such a way with words. Okay,' I say. 'You win.'

This isn't the first time I have been subversive. Whenever I have fallen into temptation and gone to Lucy's I have been dishonest and disloyal to Steve. But this time the guilt is assuaged by the fact that I am doing it as a favour to my friends. Rationally, I tell myself, my intentions are honorable and Marion's own condemnation of my leech-like attachment to Steve convinces me to submerge some guilt.

'You'd think you two were married,' she says finally.

More and more lately, each incident takes me farther and farther from Steve. I lie to him. I make up an excuse. He is suspicious. Things have been tense between us lately. This is the third year we have been a couple and I know that each time I go out and test the waters, there is a chance I will not surface on the same shore again.

33

The four of us are to meet in an unlikely spot. A dance hall.

'Carlo wants to take him to one of the local Italian clubs,' Marion tells me. 'Seems this Daniel has a passion for dancing. Thus the decision, dear friend.'

We both make gruesome faces and declare how utterly uncouth this is.

'Not the DaVinci Club?' I ask condescendingly. The DaVinci Club has a reputation. We like to think it is not the kind of locale frequented by girls of our calibre. We see it as a local watering hole where thirsty, foreign men, mostly Italian, congregate for the express purpose of satisfying those uncontrollable male urges. We see these as hungry young men, men who have just come from the old country, fresh off the boat, sex starved and fermenting with desire.

'That's the place,' Marion confirms. She looks at me and waits for a response. The glint in her eyes betrays her and I know she wants to go. 'Well?' she asks. 'What's the verdict?'

I mull the thought over for a moment. 'Well, that's where to go for good music,' I admit. 'But really, Marion, I hear it's just a pickup joint.'

'Hell, where else can we go to dance? There's nothing but country music taverns in this city. From what I've seen of Daniel, he wouldn't appreciate being subjected to those plaintive wails.'

'Yeah, neither would I,' I agree.

I don't want to admit it but I have long wanted to experience this much touted DaVinci Club. During the school year I often walk by it cradling a load of books in my arms on my way to and from the library.

If it's a weekend night, I always slow my steps to savor the melodies spilling out of the dance hall into the street below. The club exerts the same sort of pull Lucy had upon me, that dichotomy between rational reasoning and primitive emotional need, that titillating temptation immorality — or at least the sense of impending immorality — presents to me.

'Why not,' I say forthright. 'It'll be an experience. Something we can study. Let's look at it as a sociology project. So what if we bump into some of our clients. Besides, the music there is great stuff. Sexy and romantic,' I add pirouetting around Marion.

We giggle. After all, it is summer and we are out of school. Our sophisticated school mates need never discover our secret.

Marion and I are at the club before Carlo and Daniel. We need to get a feel for the place. It is a huge hall with parquet floors. A gigantic sparkling glass ball is suspended from the ceiling. Hundreds of tiny facets glimmer and shimmer as it revolves. A lively five-piece band, complete with a dark haired, drowsy looking male singer, is on stage. I hear the sax, languid and sexy, as I walk in. I feel it melting my resistance. The drums pound a beat in sync with my own footsteps. My heart thumps to the sound. It is as if the drummer is rolling a drum call introducing me to this audience of males. Guitars twang in the background and an accordion adds a touch of vivacity to the tune. They are playing 'Spanish Eyes'. The vocalist steps up to the microphone caressing it as he croons with suggestively deep tones. He shuts his eyes as he sings the pleading tune:

> *Say you and your Spanish eyes*
> *will wait for me.*

Brown wood benches line the perimeter of the hall. There are no other seats anywhere in this large room. And there are no tables. This is a place for dancing. In a barroom to the right of the stage, stools are filled to capacity and patrons have spilled over to the few tables and chairs. Couples sip drinks and gaze into each other's eyes.

Marion and I glance into the bar, then look at one other saying nothing. We walk back into the main hall.

'I sure hope we don't see anybody we know,' I whisper as I look about.

'Oh, come on, Margaret. We just started in Immigration. What are the chances of meeting someone from work?'

'They probably think we're just like the others. Waiting to get picked up,' I complain.

'Loosen up, dear friend. Who gives a shit what they think.'

We settle on a bench facing the main entrance in order to catch sight of Carlo and Daniel as soon as they appear. In the meantime, our eyes scrutinize the dancers as they circle before us as if on parade.

'Quite an eclectic collection,' says Marion. 'Okay,' she continues. 'Let's have it. Your nomination for nerd of the night followed by prick of the pack.'

'Ummm... let me see,' I giggle as I cross my legs resting my elbow on my knee and my chin in the palm of my hand.

'Did you know their brains are packed tightly between their legs?' she says.

'Who do you mean? The men or the women?'

'Smart question. Probably both.'

I laugh. 'So what's upstairs?' I ask coyly.

'In the men's case, their pricks,' she answers briskly. 'That's the only thing on their minds. Haven't you noticed the way they're constantly checking their crotch? Look, look at that one,' she nudges me, 'see how he's got his hands on his balls as if he were holding the crown jewels? It must be some old Italian tradition. They've always got their hands on the trigger.'

'Stop it, will you. They're going to notice.'

'Exactly. That's the point. They want us to take notice.'

She is about to continue when I nudge her apprehensively. 'Marion, for Christ's sake. Look. Isn't that the guy we just settled last week?'

She follows my eyes and, sure enough, it's a familiar face. It is Salvatore, a young Italian, short but extremely handsome, well-dressed, in a light gray suit and fishnet black shoes.

'What'll we do if he sees us?'

'Easy. Tell him we're on assignment. We're here to assure their integration into our society is as pleasant and smooth as can be. We're here to offer ourselves as vessels of love. To sacrifice our virginity, if it will make them happy.'

'Shit, Marion. Stop it, will you. Vessels of love.'

'Can you think of a better excuse?'

'That darned Carlo. This must be his idea of a joke.'

'Oh, come on. Give the guy a break. He just thought it would be fun. And besides, you said it yourself, where else can you go to hear music like this?' she adds closing her eyes, as if in a trance, swaying her body to the strains of the music.

I nudge her and she pops her eyes open. 'Looks like our friend Salvatore will be occupied for the rest of the night,' I say nodding my head in the direction of the bar where the young fellow struts off with a raven haired beauty.

A strange, silent, robot-like type asks me to dance and I accept. I get up and wink over my shoulder just in time to see Marion being whisked off. We stifle our snickering.

'Come here often?' he asks not even bothering to look at me.

'No,' I answer. 'Never.'

He continues to stare into the distance as if he is reading his lines from cue cards.

'I'm here every weekend,' he informs me, as I feel his arms encircling me vice-like.

And then I feel the force upon me and I begin to panic. I feel that old fear and the nausea. The power of a man. He is breathing heavily on my neck and into my ear, his eyes still riveted to some phantom image before him.

I don't know if he is doing this to impress me or because he is in fact aroused. He holds me tightly. I can hardly breathe. His hand on the small of my back is bruising me.

I attempt to wedge some distance between us but he pulls me even closer to his tense body, and I feel his hardness. I almost laugh. I think of Marion's joke about their brains. I want to say something smart. 'Oh my, but what a hard cerebellum you have, sir.' That's what I want to say. But I am sure he wouldn't understand. He doesn't look like the type who would joke about such things. He takes his sexuality seriously.

But these thoughts alleviate my fears and my queasiness subsides.

'Let me go,' I demand pushing him away forcefully. I figure he can understand that. And I pull away. I am no longer at his mercy.

I run over to Marion giggling yet sweating. She too has left the dance floor.

'You should have felt the size of that one, ' I say to her. 'I bet he stuck a dowel down his pants. No one can be that big and hard.' I laugh but I am still quivering.

Containing her laughter, her eyes with that glint of mischievousness in them, Marion says, 'I saw him holding on to you like a drowning man in the middle of the ocean. I bet he thinks he's got the biggest one around. What an asshole.'

Fuck and *asshole* are words Marion and I use when we're alone. We have recently added them to our repertoire.

'Steve always says it isn't the size that counts but rather what you do with it,' I tell Marion.

'Do you believe everything he tells you? I guess Steve has a reason for saying that,' she answers giggling again.

'Know what else he says?'

'What?'

'Only queers dance.'

'Sour grapes.'

'Christ, Marion, I didn't know cocks came in such sizes,' I admit.

'Oh, hell, Margaret. They come in all sizes. That's what my brother tells me. Some have such big ones they have to wear a contraption to keep them from going in too far when they screw a woman. There are guys so big they hang half way to their knees. And that's when they aren't even erect,' she continues.

'Not Carlo?' I snicker.

'Have you paid any attention to his credentials?' she asks twitching her eyebrows like Groucho Marx. 'You have to look at the nose. The nose is a good barometer.'

'I heard it was the hands and feet,' I say as the incident with the dancer fades.

Marion and I have gone through this conversation dozens of times. We enjoy it nonetheless now. We feel so liberated in our abandon. We talk of men in a statistical manner, the way we know they talk about us.

'Hands and feet aren't bad,' Marion admits plunging into our folly. 'But it's the nose that really gives it away. Short and squat and he's got a ball park frank; long and pointy and he's got a wiener that'll hang out both sides of the bun... Just look at them,' says Marion eyes glinting with tears of mirth. 'They strut like peacocks. Don't you just love that word, Margaret? Peacocks?'

Marion's laughter breaks off suddenly: 'Here they come. Carlo and Daniel to the rescue, galloping in on their white steeds. Change of tactics. Turn on the charm.'

I am still sniffling and wiping my nose when I twirl around and see him. My eyes go directly to Daniel even though there are hundreds in the room, as if the entire hall makes way for his arrival. The Red Sea parting. I see him coming towards us and my entire body quivers inside. All the others in the hall become an entourage of bit players who fade out of view as I focus in unequivocally on Daniel.

He is in a navy suit; a red tie peeks out from his vest. He is holding a cigarette. Steve doesn't smoke, says it's a dirty habit.

As he nears me, I make out the features: the broad shoulders, the tapered body, the slight wave of the blond hair, the limpid blue eyes. He is suave and sophisticated, European but without the gaudiness of these others around the room. He has class, not at all like his brother Carlo. I feel like an ice cube swirling in sweet vermouth. When he nears me, his scent is intoxicating. It lingers on my clothes the remainder of the night.

Marion runs up and throws herself theatrically on Carlo who lunges for her himself, reciprocating her gestures with equal zest.

'Just in the nick of time,' she tells him. 'Margaret and I were about to be gobbled up.'

Then, shoving him away with both her hands on his burly chest, she challenges him affectionately. 'What the hell took you so long?'

'Ah...our tardiness is due to obstacles thrown in our path: a barrier crashed down before our eyes, colored lights blinded us, deafening sounds blared at us...'

'A train,' says Daniel stepping aside and addressing me.

Carlo and Marion are so engrossed in their act, they forget about Daniel and me.

'You'll have to excuse them,' I say. 'They sometimes get carried away.'

'Sorry,' says Marion. 'Where are my manners?'

'Please, allow me,' Carlo interjects. 'Let me introduce the illusive Daniel.' He winks at me suggestively.

'Look who's talking,' says Marion.

'Hey...I'm still young.'

'I hate to disillusion you, darling, but your brother looks younger than you,' Marion taunts.

'It's all that clean living up in those mountains...eh, Daniel? Climbing from one summit to another.' Turning to me, he adds with a wink and a raised eyebrow, 'My brother's a nature freak.'

But I get the gist of his meaning. The sexual innuendo comes through loud and clear.

'I thought you lived in Milan,' I say as I offer Daniel my hand.

'I do,' he informs me. 'But I like to go home as often as possible... Carlo tells me you're from the Alps too.'

'The foothills. I've been back once since we came over. When I was eleven. But I remember seeing the mountains north of us.'

'Oh, Jesus Christ, Margaret. You're going to make him homesick if you go on talking about his mountains. I warned him though. The only peaks and valleys he'll see around here are in these women,' says Carlo. 'But we do have an abundance of fertile flatlands. Don't we, Marion?'

'You are perfectly vulgar, do you know that?'

'And you love it.'

'Are they always like this?' Daniel wonders, smiling at me.

The band strikes up a waltz and Daniel asks if I would like to dance.

'I'm a bit rusty,' I admit.

'Don't worry,' says Carlo. 'My brother will lubricate your hinges.'

'Carlo!' Marion exclaims, smacking him on the chest again.

Daniel takes me into his arms and I offer no resistance. He moves as gracefully as a bird in flight. There is no heaviness to him as we glide on the dance floor twirling round and round as if we were on a sheet of ice. The floor is no longer there to hold us. We are dancing on air. He guides me with gentleness and grace and my body moves and flows with his rhythm.

'You feel the music,' he says.

I manage a smile.

The song seems endless and I begin to sweat and feel a tightening of the muscles in my legs.

'I'm really out of shape,' I tell him as the tune ends. There are beads of perspiration on my upper lip.

'Is anything wrong?' he asks

'I just feel a bit dizzy,' I admit.

'Please, forgive me,' he replies.

'It's not your fault.'

'*Sì*, it is. I have a tendency to keep turning in one direction. An old injury,' he adds fingering his left eye. 'But I have a solution.'

'What?'

'We'll turn the other way.'

I laugh.

'What's wrong with your eye?' I ask.

'Oh, nothing to worry about. It still works,' he says. '*Vedi.* See,' he adds as he winks at me.

I smile again. 'There's a bit of Carlo in you, I see.'

'We are brothers.'

The slow and passionate love song which next fills the hall is a familiar one Marion and I often accompany whenever we hear it on the radio.

The song's rising crescendo builds inside me until I, like the singer, feel I am about to burst with intensity. I glance at the singer and see him, his legs apart, throbbing with the music. The microphone is cradled in his hands now and his eyes are squeezed tightly together. He looks as if he could be in agony or ecstasy. With the final pleading tones of the music pulsating within me, I peel myself away from Daniel, almost reeling at the effort. My dizziness must be apparent to him because he steadies me with his arms, but he says nothing.

The band strikes up a lively samba, probably to make up for for the lusty love song which has left couples entwined on the dance floor.

'Shall we try this one?' Daniel asks offering me his arms once again. 'And don't forget, if you feel dizzy, jab me in the ribs to make me turn. Or better yet, keep your eyes on me. That will also help.'

How do I tell him I am having a hard time keeping my eyes off him?

'Perhaps it's that silvery revolving globe,' he suggests pointing to the ornament above us. 'With it rotating up there in this square room, there's no place to get your bearings, except for that,' he says indicating the stage area.

I look about and see what he means.

'I forgot you're an architect. It must look like a square box from your perspective.'

'Utilitarian. Functional. Easy to erect. It serves a purpose.'

'Not like Italy, is it?'

'No. But then, who said it should be? That's the beauty of America. It's just that, seeing this, I am forced to realize my job here isn't going to be easy. How will I ever convince them to throw in some curves and arches? I'm speaking figuratively, you understand. Function isn't everything, you see.'

His gaze returns to me after surveying the hall. I wonder if he has noticed I haven't taken my eyes from his face.

I think of Steve. What will I do about Steve. Poor dependable Steve who can't do a two-step. He is doomed. I think of the times I have attempted to teach him to dance until I finally gave up and resigned myself to the fact I would never dance again. But now, here is Daniel, floating like an illicit dream before me. Daniel does not use force. His powers are such that he does not have to.

Mentally, I scrutinize my checklist on Steve. Do I dare condemn him for the mere lack of rhythm?

When the band breaks for intermission, we find Carlo ready with drinks.

'Hey, Daniele,' he calls saying Daniel's name in Italian. 'What has this Margherita done to loosen your tongue,' he adds saying my own name in Italian. The mellifluous sounds of our names wraps me in communion with Daniel. 'My brother,' Carlo continues addressing me, 'is not a man of many words. He's the silent type. But tonight, you've worked magic on him.'

A faint blush sweeps over Daniel's face.

'Here, you two. In honour of your name, a Margherita to quench your thirst.'

This time I blush.

34

Thoughts of Daniel awaken me the next morning. Images of him have filled me and I am bursting with a desire to go over the previous evening's events. I phone Marion. I am breathless when she finally answers the phone. I begin to subject her to my contrived cliches and silly analogies. 'He's Prince Charming,' I tell her. 'He has the slipper and it fits... I love his accent...Where did he pick that up?'

'He travels a lot. And Carlo says he studied in England,' she tells me.

Strangely enough, Marion says I should watch myself. She warns me, 'Don't let yourself get carried away,' she cautions. 'I think it's passion you've just discovered.' She reminds me he has someone in Italy. 'And he's a hell of a lot older than you,' she adds for good measure. 'Don't forget that.'

'You're a fine one to be saying this now that you've done the damage,' I retort. 'Wasn't it you who dragged me into this?'

'Sure, sure. I dragged you there screaming at the top of your lungs. But look, Margaret, I didn't think you'd throw caution to the winds and dump Steve.'

'What's that supposed to mean?'

'Nothing. I have no right to tell you what to do. Just be careful, dear friend. This was supposed to be for fun. You know. A lark. Nothing serious.' And then, her tone altering a bit, she adds, 'He must be a fountain of experience.' I can almost see her suggestive smile. She chuckles and snickers into the receiver and I imagine her cupping her hand around the mouthpiece feigning secrecy and mimicking the voice of a crank caller. 'I bet he's great in bed.'

'Is that all you think about?' I add twitching my eyebrows the way she does.

'The root of all pleasure,' she says heavily accenting the words.

I know about the other woman. But she's an ocean away. I am here. And I know he's older, but I don't care about that either.

Daniel phones asking if I'll see him again. Little does he know how the rich tones of his voice penetrate my will and dissolve my resistance. 'I'd like to make up for Saturday night,' he says.

'What do you mean?'

'You were uncomfortable.'

'I had a great time.'

'*Allora,* there's no need for me to make up for it?'

'No, I'm not saying that. I'd ...love to see you again.'

We set a date.

At dinner, my father asks, 'So who's this gallant stallion? This Daniele I'm hearing about?'

'He's Carlo's brother. You know. Marion's friend. And don't call him that. He's a gentleman.'

'I hear he's from Milan,' my father adds.

'He lives there but he's from the Alps. Near the Austrian border actually. Not far from our home town.'

My mother looks at me. 'Steve called,' she says.

My stomach churns. A blitz of adrenalin streaks through my body. Oh, God, Steve. What am I going to do about Steve?

Daniel and I decide to drive along the riverfront tracing the two-lane road that follows the shoreline and matches every turn and indentation of the river.

'Where will this road take us?' he asks.

'All the way around the peninsula and along the other lakeshore.'

'Does it go to your famous Point Pelee?'

I turn to him in amazement. 'Point Pelee, famous?'

'Oh, yes. I've read about it. A friend of mine in Italy, a professor of biology, has been there to study the birds.'

'I can't believe it.'

'*È lontano*?'

'About an hour or so from here.'

'Do you mind if we go?'

'Of course not.'

'Is there somewhere we can stop to eat along the way?'

'I know a place on the water. We can go there.'

I keep my eye out for Tino's murky stream and the clump of bush indicating his island. When I spot them up ahead and inland a bit, I point this out to Daniel.

'*Che fortunato*,' he says. 'Seems he's found paradise.'

'Sometimes I wonder,' I tell him. 'He lives there all alone, hermit-like.'

'Alone?'

'He's not married. Never has been actually. He has his reasons,' I sigh.

'I'm sure he does,' Daniel replies focusing on the road ahead.

I get the feeling Daniel doesn't wish to pursue the topic. It seems I have touched a raw nerve. Undaunted in my efforts to know more about him, I chisel away. 'It was the war,' I continue, even as I realize I am being insensitive.

'Pardon?'

'Tino. Why he lives there alone. My mother told me about it once. It's a sad story.'

'War stories usually are,' he says.

I feel the reticence in his voice.

'You remember the war?'

'*Sì.*'

'Were you in it?'

'I didn't fight in it, if that's what you mean. I was too young. But I did what I could.'

'You mean you helped the Partisans? My father and cousin Tino say a lot of young boys helped them out.'

'That's right. We did.'

I feel his tension. His apprehension. He doesn't want to go on but I am all the more intrigued.

'Tino was a Partisan. So was my Dad. And Tino's girlfriend... My parents named me after her, you know.'

'*Da vero?*'

'They say she was extraordinarily courageous.'

'What happened?' he decides to ask. I guess he has realized I am not about to relent.

'They killed her.'

I can see his knuckles whiten as he grips the steering wheel tightly.

'They killed a lot of people,' he informs me.

'I know. But what I can't understand is why they had to do it the way they did. Dying isn't so bad, I suppose. It's the suffering and torture.'

'What happened?'

'They tricked her. They sent someone to tell her Tino was wounded and hiding up in one of the caves in the mountain. When she went up that night, they ambushed her and killed her. Raped her first. They always do that, don't they? They disfigured her face and...well...they brought her back down to the village and threw her in the town square.'

Daniel's silence mystifies me. I glance at him and he senses I am waiting for a response. Surely he was too young to have had a similar experience?

'They killed my mother,' he tells me. She helped in the resistance too. She used to carry supplies up to the camps. They shot her and a couple of other women from the village as well.'

This is not what I had expected. I am sure he must think me crude and unfeeling to have wrenched this painful memory from him. I had hoped to learn something about the man, about his reasons for being alone, like cousin Tino. My mind had dramatized all sorts of possibilities. Childishly, I had postulated sensational theories and conjectures to explain his situation: Daniel's sensitivity to the topic was due to some past torrid affair which had resulted in a tumultuous eruption on the part of a dark and sultry Italian wench. My wild imagination had construed numerous scenarios, without any evidence to support them.

Our outings take on a familiar pattern. We still go dancing and out for a late meal afterwards. Carlo and Marion often accompany us. But when we're alone, we find enjoyment in our excursions to nearby beaches and marshes or to the woods surrounding cousin Tino's property.

Eventually, I tell Daniel about Steve. He nods but says nothing. He just looks into my eyes. I tell him men used to make me sick and he smiles wanting to know, 'Literally or figuratively?'

I have to chuckle. 'You're always asking that sort of question.'

'Am I?' he answers. 'I'm not always sure how to take these expressions.'

'Well, literally,' I tell him. 'They literally made me sick.'

I tell him about Lucy and that bunch. He laughs when I tell him Marion and I used to call her Juicy Lucy.

'You don't have to explain that to me,' he says.

I tell him about Bruce. I tell him what I remember. I can't tell him what is still lying, decaying and covered with mould, in the cellar of my mind. He looks straight at me. 'They simply weren't for you,' he says. 'That's all. There's nothing wrong with you, Margherita.'

35

September hovers on the horizon. The shortened days, the sun's diminishing potency, the cool night breezes off the water, all of these signals send ripples of despair on my summer landscape. I know the time of reckoning is approaching. Soon, I will be immersed in my books, and Steve's shadow lengthens as the summer passes. I had made a pact with him, and he, naive and trusting as usual, had accepted it and lived up to his side of the bargain.

'Give me some breathing space,' I had begged him.

'Breathing space?' he had remarked. 'What the hell's that supposed to mean?' He was truly bewildered by my request.

'I want the summer off,' I wailed.

'The summer off? What is this? You're not punching a time clock for me, you know.'

The conversation had been tense and filled with a gripping animosity on my part. I clawed him with accusations.

'You stifle me,' I charged.

'I stifle you?' he repeated bobbing his head in his usual manner and continuing to echo every word I said. 'Stifle you?'

'Stop repeating everything I say,' I command him reproachfully through gritted teeth.

'Okay. So what is it you want? Lay it on the line.'

'Freedom. Some freedom.'

'Freedom?'

'Stop it.'

'Stop what?'

'I just told you. Stop repeating everything I say,' I exclaim, exasperated with this habit of his.

'Freedom? From what? Me?'

'No...yes... Just some freedom to...to explore...new experiences...to experience...'

'Some other *shmock*. That's it, isn't it? It's some other guy.'

He was right of course. But I lied. I said no. I said I just wanted a chance to meet others. To test our relationship. To be certain, beyond a shadow of a doubt, that we were meant for each other... I went on and on pontificating in this manner, convincing him I was doing it all in the name of love. 'I have to be sure,' I rationalized. 'I have to be sure about us, that this is going to be a strong and mutually satisfactory relationship.' Even as the words spilled clinically and malevolently from my very own tongue, I hated myself. And yet he agreed.

'All right,' he said. 'The summer off. But don't forget, my little *shiksa,* that goes for me too.'

That was his toughest threat.

And so now, with the prospect of another confrontation with Steve looming before me, I fret over the strategy I should follow. I decide to lay my predicament before Daniel. I will tell him about my pact with Steve and about my ambivalence. I decide, however, not to expose the entire truth; I do not intend to tell Daniel he has been critical in this crisis.

'You do what you must do,' Daniel says.

'But I don't know what to do,' I plead.

'Neither do I, Margherita. I don't know what you should do either.'

What had I expected? That he would interfere with my life? What had I envisioned this time with my vivid imagination? Pleas for a continuation of our relationship? And just exactly what sort of a relationship was this? Daniel hadn't made a single intimate gesture to date. What did that tell me? What had I expected? A challenge to a duel with Steve and Daniel fighting over the spoils: me?

September arrives and it is all rather anti-climactic. The first day of classes I find Steve in the cafeteria, sitting alone and looking desolate, feigning indifference as I walk in.

I approach him cautiously, balancing my tray with one hand while clutching books in the other. He doesn't even look up, but of course he knows I am there. I set my tray down beside his without asking if it's all right. He turns to me and looks longingly into my eyes. His are such expressive eyes. He can't hide anything with those eyes. They reveal all. Always have. Especially to me. He is doing his best to be cool and detached, manly and tough. But I know he is a heap of frustration waiting for the release valve to unfetter his emotions. He is a pressure cooker of sentiments. I can almost see steam spewing from his every pore. Oh, what images he develops in me: pots projecting their contents, valves unable to contain their pressure. Surely there has to be some meaning to all this? My heart goes out to him. I am such a shit, I tell myself. A real shit.

'Well,' he says. 'Are the results in yet?'

I know exactly what he means but I don't take the bait.

'How are you?' I ask instead. And I am truly asking this in all sincerity.

'I missed you,' he says. 'I really missed you.'

I see him begin to crumble. I am flattered and yet it is distasteful to have to witness his weakness. I would have preferred to continue on the violent images of a few moments ago instead of this disintegration.

I begin to cry softly and inadvertently he takes it as a positive sign. He turns to me wrapping an arm around me, kissing my cheek. 'It's okay,' he says. 'It's all over now. It's over. Everything's going to be okay.' My sobs heighten at his words. At him. At myself. At my hypocrisy. And I let him hold me because I haven't got the heart to do anything else.

36

This is our final year, a critical one for all of us. I am in Arts, an open-ended avenue with no specific target. At least Steve knows where he's going. For now he has taken a part-time job as an assistant in an accounting firm. I am thankful for that. With this in addition to his studies, he'll have less time for me.

Daniel is working day and night on his project and I hear from him intermittently. Once in a while I read about the fiery debates in connection with his proposals for the riverfront development; I am angry at the simple-minded mentality of this community.

He calls now and then and we drive along the waterfront. But no luxurious walks through the woods, no lingering in restaurants with after dinner drinks. The shape of our lives has changed with the added responsibilities, and I do not wish to contemplate the implications of these changes. I choose instead to let life ride without direction. All I am doing is stalling for time, vacillating capriciously, unwilling and unable to take a stand. My high wire act continues even though I catch myself teetering whenever I allow myself to think about the future.

When I am with Daniel, the dichotomy I feel within widens like a fissure in the earth. I am a volcano on the verge of an eruption, an earthquake whose tremors forewarn casualties.

For now, the tension is balanced and remains taut. But in the back of my mind I know with the slightest relaxation of this tension, my safe world will collapse.

I tell Marion I am living a Jekyll and Hyde existence.

'What do you mean?' she asks puzzled.

In my attempts to explain it to her, I am mapping out my own arguments.

'It sounds crazy, Marion, but when I'm with Steve, I wish he'd keep his hands off me. Not that we do anything much, mind you,' I add for accuracy. 'When I'm with Daniel it's just the opposite.'

'Hormones are marvelous chemicals, aren't they?' she says as she winks suggestively.

'You're a big help,' I hiss. 'I don't know what to do. I don't trust myself. I swear, Marion, if Daniel were to ask me to go to bed with him, I'd jump at the chance.'

'My, my, aren't we getting horny.'

'Stop it, will you. I'm serious. There's something wrong here. Does this mean I love him? What the hell is love anyway?'

'I'll be damned if I know. Spontaneous combustion perhaps? Hell, Margaret, do you have any idea how many people have been asking themselves that very question since time immemorial?' And then narrowing her eyes and peering at me closely she asks, 'Do you mean to tell me he hasn't tried anything yet?'

'Nothing,' I admit. 'Nothing serious.'

'Shit, this is serious.'

When winter comes along, we all welcome the reprieve. Marion and Carlo fly off to a warm southern beach to continue their 'scandalous affair', as she put it. I am envious.

Hanukkah keeps Steve superficially occupied. We both know it is a perfunctory attention on his part, but I convince him to play the role and appease his family. I, of course, have no part in any of this. It wasn't long ago I used to resent the way his family had wiped me from their slates, refusing to accept my presence in their son's life. But now, with Daniel, I not only welcome the rejection, I secretly thank them for it.

'Can't you just play along, for once,' I tell Steve. 'Why do you always have to upset your mother?'

Daniel and I drive out to the lakeshore restaurant we went to during the summer. He knows I am sensitive about being seen in the city with him. Someone may report it to Steve and I'll have a lot of explaining to do. Ours is not a large urban metropolis where we can lose ourselves conveniently.

Snow is falling softly in plump flakes that settle soundlessly. The thickening mantle transforms the very timber of the night, all is muffled in cozy harmony. Even the throb of the engine, as Daniel starts the motor, hardly seems to disturb the magic of the night. It resonates without marring the tranquility. The crunch of the tires accompanies us out of the driveway as they break the virgin white sheet of snow. A bright moon casts luminous light upon the snow, igniting the shimmering crystals right before our eyes.

'There's a blue moon, you know,' Daniel tells me.

'A blue moon?'

'Yes.'

'There was a song by that name.'

'Was there?'

'Yes. One of those mushy love songs...'Blue moon...You saw me standing alone...without a dream in my heart, without a love of my own...' Doesn't ring a bell? I guess it wasn't popular in Italy.'

He laughs.

'I wonder why they call it a blue moon?'

'Because it's the second full moon of the month. That doesn't happen very often. Usually there's just one.'

'Really? I never knew that. So that's where they get the expression "once in a blue moon".'

'I suppose so.'

'We don't have that expression in our Italian dialect, do we?'

'No.'

'What do we say for something that happens rarely?'

'In Italy? In our region? Let's see. Sometimes we say, "*Ogni muart di pàpe.* Whenever a Pope dies." But it sounds silly in English, doesn't it?'

I laugh because it does sound silly in English and yet so right in our native tongue.

My desire flares up and I feel I cannot control myself any longer. I lay my head on his strong shoulder and I dare to kiss him on the neck nuzzling puppy-like into him. He returns my show of affection by holding me closer.

We drive like this in silence until we reach the restaurant, perched on the edge of a cliff overlooking the now frozen lake.

'It looks different in the winter, doesn't it?' I remark.

'I think it's more tranquil. You can't hear the sound of the waves.'

The parking lot has been ploughed, there is a ridge of snow piled along the cliff concealing the wood fence. Daniel parks up against this and I look out at the field of ice. The sight is mesmerizing; the moon, suspended directly above us, big and round, extends a highway of light across the frozen lake. I breathe in deeply and sigh. 'Oh, Daniel, it's so beautiful.'

'And so are you,' he says turning to me. He leans over taking me into his arms and kisses my waiting lips with his warm moist mouth. I offer no resistance. I am faint with desire. He pulls away leaving me aching for more. He says nothing about our state of excitement. He lifts my coat's collar up to protect me from the chill. 'Come,' he says, '*Andiamo,* before we both freeze to death. Let's go and eat.'

His teasing is a prelude and I nibble at my meal wondering if anything will come of this.

After dinner, as I sip an *amaretto,* he pulls out a small heart shaped box of red velvet.

'It's Christmas,' he says. 'For you.'

I am embarrassed

'Oh, Daniel. I have nothing for you. I didn't...'

'Margherita,' he says. 'Please.'

'But I'm so ashamed.'

'Come on, open it.'

I open the box and there, sitting in white satin, is a gold broach in the shape of a daisy, a *margherita* with a sparkling diamond at its centre. My first reaction is one of foreboding and I try to mask this uncalled-for response. How can I tell him that things lying in white satin always remind me of my dead friend, David?

'It's magnificent.'

'I had it made for you.'

Closing the tiny box, he leans across the table and kisses me. His luminous eyes and wonderful smile breaks the spell and I regret that I have allowed my silly notions to interfere. His warm lips summon my previous desire and I kiss him back. But there are people in the room and I control myself.

'*Andiamo?* Shall we go?' he says. We drive back to the city listening to Christmas carols on the car radio. He points out the Big Dipper along the way. 'Back home *in Italia,'* Daniel tells me, 'in the mountains, you can see it so clearly. That was one of the first things I noticed when I came here. The stars seem so far away. There, they seem so close you can almost touch them.'

The glare of the city awaits us ahead. The glow of lights creates a nighttime aurora more intense than usual because of the yuletide feast. As we approach the city, these electric stars twinkle and blink brightly, replacing nature's own diamonds. I crane my head looking for the Big Dipper but it's no use. We are too close to the city. Daniel looks at me and smiles.

'Sometimes you need darkness to see light,' he says.

And then suddenly, without looking at me for my reaction, perhaps fearing what it might be, he says, 'I've got a room.'

I turn and look at him, not comprehending his statement.

'Up in the Skyview Tower Hotel. You don't have to come. I'm not forcing you.'

I smile but he can't see this because he is keeping his eyes straight ahead. I say, 'You want compensation for your expenditures.' I am only joking, but I know immediately he has taken offence. I should never have said this.

'Don't ever say such a thing to me,' he says 'I would never take advantage of you, Margherita.'

'I was just joking. I'm sorry.'

There is a short uneasy pause in our dialogue and then he seems in control once again.

'I'm not afraid of heights,' I tell him.

37

Memories lie simmering or festering in the cauldron of reality until finally they are dredged up. The trick is in finding the implements suitable for the task. They come wrapped in different coverings. Some are cleverly disguised by our conscious mind, so well camouflaged we may not know of their existence. The warning sign may be an underlying malaise of the body, but so few of us are adept at recognizing such symptoms. The spirit may suffer, unable to comprehend the malaise thus leaving voids and blank spaces to litter our lives.

I think of new discoveries being made in our universe. Scientists regularly report new findings: a black hole no one knew existed, moons never before seen by the human eye orbiting familiar planets. Recently, they claimed to have discovered a new planet, although no one has seen it yet. The farther we probe, the more we unveil.

These moons or planets were there; they were there before we detected them, before we developed the means to bring them to light. They were there even as scientists and astronomers stalked the universe in search of other bodies of knowledge. They existed. They did not begin to exist the moment our earthly probes disturbed their tranquility and unveiled their anonymity.

The first time Daniel and I attempt to make love, a multitude of images flash before me. They spring out of hiding and ambush me, planting themselves like unmovable sentinels. A senseless scene is illuminated for my viewing. At first, the images come in short rapid scenes, as if someone is turning a spotlight on and off. They then change to mimic the frames of a television set whose vertical hold has gone off kilter. I am haunted by the image of a man from my past. The dark haired cousin from my great-aunt's house leaps from my memory chamber. I shut my eyes to block the view but it is no use, for the sight is inside me; I tremble with fear.

Daniel senses something is wrong.

'What is it, Margherita?' he asks feeling the tension within me as he releases his grasp.

My body quivers and shakes as terror grips me. I open my eyes to stare straight ahead and watch myself as if on a screen. I see the little girl rubbing the burly, hairy chest and I hear the gruff voice commanding her to 'go down, farther down'. I see him unzip his pants and I feel the hot throbbing organ in my tiny frigid hand. It brands me like a hot poker and I can feel the fiery heat scorching me now.

'Margherita,' Daniel calls shaking me gently. 'Are you all right?'

Trancelike, I shift my eyes from the screen and look at Daniel. I take in his clear blue eyes, so different from the coal black orbs of the cousin. I see Daniel's rumpled blond hair and the wide sweep of his broad shoulders. His compassion swathes me. I realize I am safe, truly safe, there is nothing to fear when I am with Daniel.

'I can't,' I whisper to him.

'Then you won't,' he consoles me, holding me now against his warm body.

'It isn't you,' I attempt to explain.

'I should never have taken you to this place,' he says rising from the bed. He pulls on the clothes he shed just moments before and walks to the window.

He draws the curtains open to let in the night and stands gazing at the city below.

'Do you want to go home?' he asks.

'No. I want to be with you.'

'But this is no good. It's wrong,' he says turning to look at me. 'You're trembling.' He pulls the covers over me to bring some warmth to my naked body. 'Would you like a drink? We can go up to the bar if you like.'

'Yes,' I say. 'Yes. Let's do that.'

As I dress, I know I have been transformed. I will never be the same again. I have discovered my own black hole, my own abyss, and now I fear I will never be able to conceal it again.

I do not yet understand what forces have unleashed these memories on me. They have come like a tornado that swirls out of nowhere without warning, suddenly sweeping into my world and leaving behind wreckage and devastation. But, is it not also true, I console myself, that there is a corollary to this? Is it not true that a peaceful calm may embalm the land after a fierce pounding from the elements, birds will come out to chirp merrily rejoicing in their survival, and the earth will appear fresh, vibrant and rejuvenated? How often have I seen the very winds of destruction change into the soft breezes that caress the night? Nature is a chameleon. We marvel at the wreckage it has left behind and, when the storm passes, we marvel at the calm it leaves in its wake.

Memories are like this: some horrific, some beautiful. They are like ocean waves empowered by the forces of nature to be equally capable of unleashing treachery and even death, or transforming into the soothing and playful laps on a sandy beach.

Daniel and I take the elevator to the top floor of the hotel emerging onto a spectacular, glass enclosed, circular room. The bar forms a smaller circle in the very centre of the restaurant. There are stools around it and a few quaint tables as well. Daniel chooses a table and orders drinks.

When the waitress leaves, he encourages me to speak. 'Tell me about it.'

The need to confess and release myself from these demons overrules my shyness. I feel guilty, as if I have deserved such a fate, but I know this is totally irrational.

I tell Daniel what I remember.

'My God, how long have you been harboring these hideous crimes and remaining silent?'

'No, Daniel. It isn't like that,' I explain. They've just come into my head now. Just now. But I remember it as if it were yesterday.'

In my own mind, I envision them as a jack-in-the-box, a frightening little toy I have always found repulsive; the tiny clown head hiding inside the box and then springing out, leaping at a bewildered child. More often than not, it brings tears of fear to the victim.

Daniel listens to my outpouring reassuring me with his patience and composure. I look out at the city, searching for words which will make sense, when I realize this revolving restaurant has come full circle. It strikes me that this must be a sign — a signal I am compelled to obey. 'Look, Daniel,' I point out, 'we're back where we started.'

Finishing his drink, he stands, and extends his hand to me. I take it and follow his lead.

And when the storm of my telling subsides and the burden of truth is lifted from me, I feel light and free and able to give myself completely to him. I surrender, and he takes me gently, leading me into an enchanted land.

38

Throughout my youth, the same scenes played over and over again, night after night after night, like a broken record. There were three that became hauntingly familiar and regular the way bullies in a school yard become familiar and inescapable sources of terror. They were simply fearful images, nightmares that would not go away. My mother always reassured me in the morning that it was 'just a nightmare'. Even though I don't think I ever told her about them — at least I can't remember ever telling her — she always seemed to know when I had had one.

The most terrifying of these dreams was the one with the dark, sinister looking devil, as devils tend to be. My child's eye concocted a hairy man with glossy black hair and eyes equally shiny and dark. He wore a black cloak, and his dagger was long, sharp, shiny and hot. It seemed to sizzle. He poked it at the fire which roared in a pit somewhere in the recesses of the room. He ran it through the flames before swishing it before my face, like Zorro. This dream always took place in the same dark room, hidden away in a dingy basement. He tied me to a wooden table with ropes which cut into my wrists and ankles, and then he would start the buzz saw whose blade could slice me in half. All the while I would be watching the devil man's smile, and I would see contentment and satisfaction beaming from him as he witnessed my suffering and fear. Just as the blade whizzed and whirred, skimming the top of my head, I would awake.

In the second dream, there are people everywhere, like ants in an ant colony, scrambling furiously to climb and climb and climb in order to reach the top of the most gigantic skyscraper I have ever seen. It stretches up piercing the clouds, its pinnacle hidden by the white masses of fluff. Up and up they climb. I am one of them. Up and up we go, covering the building with our exhausted bodies as we strive to gain the summit. And then suddenly, I slip on a loose brick and lose my grip. Down I go. What horrors await me below? I never reach the earth to consummate the plunge. I always awaken just before final impact.

The third dream is the one I could never comprehend. Not until now. For it was not one of terror or fear. There was never anyone in this dream. No one at all. No protagonist. Not even myself. It was a dream of utter loneliness and despair, so unlike the other two which were teeming with life, with sound, with action. This one was a void and vacant dream.

This third dream has never been completely submerged. Life's silt has not been able to cover it over entirely. I recall dreaming it even in recent times. What has caused it to lift up out of the sand to stare back at me now, is a picture — an illustration — in this book I am holding in my hands, this book on psychology which so puzzled Steve when he noticed it.

The turning of the page blows away tiny granules of loose memory and I am confronted with a startling image: The author of the article has chosen to illustrate his theories on memory by representing our brain with the image of a labyrinth. Using coloured yarn, he shows how one may attempt to extricate oneself from the maze. Blue yarn, green and yellow yarn all lead to nowhere. They are lost, possibly because the ball of yarn had been too short, or perhaps they had become entangled. The red ball of yarn has prevailed. This is obvious as I see it at the bottom of the page, completely out of the labyrinth as though it were suspended. I can trace the path it has taken.

The sight of this red ball is stupefying. This is what I used to see in my dream, although my ball of yarn did not have these realistic proportions. It was on a much larger scale and it wasn't red; it was grey. In my dream, the ball revolves round and round the dark abyss of the heavens, growing in dimension as more and more yarn is wound about it.

Where had the image come from? How had my child's mind come up with such a symbol? Could it have been my mother's yarn? How many times had I seen her do this? With deft fingers, round and round went the yarn and she magically caused the ball to grow and grow. Her hands worked so feverishly at times that my little eyes could hardly keep up with her endeavour.

Next to this picture, the article is entitled: 'Memory: A Molecular Maze'. I read on, trembling in fear of the words I am about to read. But they appear so very innocuous as I look at them: 'Remember the legend of the Minotaur — the half man, half bull monster of ancient Crete that lived at the heart of a vast labyrinth?'

Yes, I do remember. I had relished the study of ancient mythology in my youth.

'Every year,' the article continues, 'seven youths and seven maidens were sent as sacrifice into the labyrinth, which was so full of twisting passages and blind alleys that none were able to find their way back out. But one year the hero Theseus fought and killed the beast. Having killed the Minotaur, Theseus was faced with the additional problem of extricating himself from the depths of the labyrinth. Fortunately, his lover, Ariadne, had given him a ball of thread to unwind as he descended into the maze, thus providing him a way of retracing his steps.'

I marvel at the simplicity of the story. I marvel that such simple actions can have such profound effects. How the obvious is so often hidden by our lack of creativity or by our fearful, apprehensive natures. I have to smile, shake my head in disbelief. What does this remind me of? Something else. Something Daniel told me once. About a famous architect. Brunelleschi, was it? No one trusted his plans to construct the dome of the famous cathedral in Florence, Santa Maria del Fiore. His concept was a secret he would not divulge, so they suspected it was a radical design too complicated to build. But he claimed it was 'simple'; just as simple as making an egg stand upright.

The memory of Daniel telling the hilarious story brings joy to my heart. I remember giggling with anticipation, waiting for some great technical feat to be divulged which would explain how to cause an egg to stand upright.

'So, what happened?' I begged to know.

'Well, according to what I've read, all these great men fiddled with the eggs and, of course, none of them could get these little oval rascals to stand at attention. When they finally all gave up, they challenged Brunelleschi and he proceeded to take an egg and smack it onto the table, thus breaking the shell and allowing it to stand upright.'

'Oh, no,' I cried in astonishment. 'Is that how he did it?'

'*Certo*. It was the only way. It was the simplest way.'

'What did the others say?'

'They all accused him of cheating. "You didn't say we could crack it," they cried. "I didn't say you couldn't," he retorted. Then they cried foul play and claimed his way was too easy. He told them, if it was so easy why hadn't they thought of it?'

'Did he ever tell them his secret about the dome?'

'Brunelleschi was an evasive man who believed it wasn't wise to divulge his inventions and ideas. He was like a fish out of water in his time, and I'm sure a lot of his contemporaries wouldn't have understood even if he had explained... You should see what he was up against,' he said.

'What, Daniel? Tell me.'

'One plan called for the dome to be built over a huge mound of earth piled on the floor of the cathedral. Silver coins were to be mixed in with the dirt.'

'Silver coins?'

'Right. Silver coins. They were supposed to be an incentive for the workers who would have to be called in to remove the dirt once the dome was built.'

'That's preposterous,' I laugh.

'Exactly. It was just a highly innovative technique he developed from his study of ancient Greek and Roman architecture. He believed in looking back in order to go forward, I guess you could say.'

'But do you understand how he did it?'

'I couldn't explain it to you off the top of my head.'

'Ha! Finally. I have unearthed something you can't do.'

I remember him looking at me, saying, 'If that were my only flaw.'

I wrapped my arms around him, smothering him with a thousand kisses and proclaiming my undying love for him.

I turn back to my book and devour the chapter, searching for answers. I read how memories may be submerged like long forgotten wrecks on the bottom of the ocean to be retrieved later. Memories may form scabs and leave scars like the scar on my great-uncle's belly. I read how scientists postulate that a reverberating circuit is established in randomly connected neurons, and that the nerve impulse must circulate many times in a closed, self-exciting circuit until some type of permanent anatomical change has occurred in the synaptic connections between the neurons.

And then the next line strikes me as prophetic: 'At some later time the same group of cells will fire when stimulated again by the same type of sensory input.'

All of this takes on meaning and suddenly what had once been a dark and muddy realm begins to clear. I have disturbed the murky waters and it will take time for them to settle and clear. Nevertheless, this is the beginning, the dawn of a new understanding.

39

Daniel drives me home, the Skyview Tower Hotel receding from view. When he turns into my street I can clearly see Steve's car parked a block away from my house. I duck under the dashboard. 'Don't stop, Daniel,' I urge him. 'Don't stop at the house. Steve's in that car up ahead.'

'Are you sure?'

'Just drive by. He won't suspect anything. He wouldn't recognize you nor the car.'

Daniel follows my instructions and drives by the house continuing to the end of the street.

'You're right,' he says. 'There was someone in that car.'

I come up from my hiding place when I am sure Daniel has made a complete turn.

'What should we do?' Daniel asks.

'Drive to the end of the block and take the next street parallel to mine. There's an alley in between. I'll go in the back way.'

'Nonsense. I won't let you walk up by yourself.'

'It's all right. I'm not afraid.'

'Well, you should be. I'll park on the street and come with you if you're intent on not having this confrontation with Steve.'

At the back entrance Daniel takes me into his arms and for a moment I forget about Steve. I cling to Daniel. 'I'll call you tomorrow,' he promises. And we share a hurried but sensuous kiss.

I stalk through the house silently like a thief. I don't turn on any lights. I look into the street. From my bedroom window I can see Steve's car. My stomach churns with anxiety.

In the morning I awaken in a confused state, in the middle of a dream? Did I really have Daniel last night? But what is this interference? A doorbell. Voices. A man. A woman. A rush of footsteps approaching. My door opening.

'Margaret?'

'Mom.'

'Steve's here. Seems upset. He wanted to bolt on up here but I told him to wait.'

'I'll be down in a minute.'

Seeing them in the kitchen annoys me. Steve is on a first name basis with my parents and this vexes me right now.

'Morning everyone,' I manage.

'Morning, Sleeping Beauty,' Steve says in a strained and sarcastic tone of voice. 'Your father asked me to stay for breakfast. We're going shopping, remember?'

I had forgotten.

In the car, Steve and I are silent. I decide to break the impasse.

'Did you get frostbite?' I ask.

'Frostbite?'

'Last night. Sitting out in the car. It must have been pretty cold out there.'

His jaw tightens.

'I saw you out there playing private eye. How dare you. How dare you do this to me.'

Still no reaction. He drives on and I notice he isn't going downtown.

Chapter 39

'I thought we were going shopping?'

'I lied. I want to talk to you. You're making me crazy. Crazy, I tell you.'

We pull into the parking lot of a city park and sit staring at the snow covered terrain. A moment of deep depression sets in as I witness the stillness of this winter day. I try to envision the park in summer: the pond, now iced over, teeming with fish, water lilies floating luxuriously on the water's surface, beds of snapdragons waiting to be pinched, marigolds frolicking in the breeze, blue delphinium, pink lupines, cosmos. But today there is only whiteness and cold. Steve and I had once communicated so freely, but now the lines have been snapped.

Going into his pants pocket to retrieve it, Steve pulls out a condom and nonchalantly throws it on the car seat between us.

I stare at it incredulously. 'Aren't we subtle.'

'You know what you need? You need to get laid. You need a good screw. A good old-fashioned fucking. That's what you need, you little shit.' He creeps towards me as he says these words.

'Stop it,' I say. 'Stop talking to me that way.'

He feels me slipping through his fingers and has decided to make demands.

'I've been patient, Margaret. Too patient. Enough's enough.'

'Get away from me.' I push him away. 'What the hell. What do you think you're going to do? Screw me here in the car, like this. Are you nuts?'

'I'm going to have you, Margaret. I'm sick of waiting.'

'Waiting? You always get what you need...one way or another, don't you?' I accuse.

He pounces on me forcing me to kiss him, desperately attempting to part my lips with his quivering mouth. He gropes at me with his hands sending them beneath my skirt. His energy surprises and frightens me.

'No,' I scream. 'No. Stop it, please.'

I manage to squeeze to the side of the car and open the door. I run out, plodding through the snow. I hear him turn the car engine off, and then the slam of his door. He is going to follow me. I am frightened of him, frightened of this entire scene. I run but the snow impedes my progress. I trip over a snow covered object. I turn and see Steve gaining on me. I attempt to get up but it's too late. He throws himself upon me, clutching me in his arms. 'Shit, Margaret. Look what you make me do. I'm sorry.'

40

Each time I see Daniel, my pretense with Steve becomes more difficult. The intimacy Daniel and I share makes me wonder if Steve was right. Could it be that this was what I needed? To get laid. A good screw? A good fucking? His words bounce around in my mind.

'What's eating you anyway? You're such a shit.'

Our arguments ignite with simple insults and inevitably end up in a flourish of bitter words, until I finally spit out my venomous request. 'Maybe we should stop seeing each other for a while.' I have to turn away to avoid seeing the incredulous look on his face.

'What the hell? See if I care.' He turns to Marion, our buffer. 'What the hell's got into her?'

Marion, smart assed as usual, replies, 'Another man maybe?'

Steve looks at the two of us.

He begins stalking me in earnest now, keeps tabs on me. Wherever I go, I feel his eyes upon me. This irks me and makes me want to escape — escape from Steve, from everyone.

I plan my escape. Methodically, I arrange my life. I set a course. I take control. I tell no one about my plans: not my parents, not Marion, not even Daniel. It is my secret project.

At school, I have seen ads advertising opportunities overseas — in Africa, Asia, Europe. I scan the bulletin boards for an escape route. I want to go to Italy. It must be Italy. I search daily and then finally notice a tiny ad: Teaching Opportunities Overseas; certificate not required. Italy is on the list. I send for information.

I am forced to reveal my plans to my parents when a response comes in the mail. It's from a private English language school. Yes, yes, certainly, they are always looking for prospective teachers. No teaching certificate is required. They will train those who qualify.

'Mom, Dad, I'm going to Italy. I'm going to teach there... When I graduate in the spring that's what I'm going to do.'

'Hey,' says my father. 'You've got a job already?'

'Sort of.'

My mother says nothing.

'Mom, I want to go. Please don't stop me. I want to go to Italy.'

My mother remains silent, neither encouraging me nor discouraging me. But her neutrality is a burden to me. My youth, however, shrugs it off.

'You can stay with my aunt Amelia,' says my father. 'She lives in Gallarate, just outside Milan. She'd love to have you.'

'Can you ask her, Dad? Can you write and ask? I wouldn't stay long. Just until I find a place of my own.'

'Nonsense,' says my father. 'You can stay there, period. There's no need for you to look for anything else.'

I remain silent for now on this aspect of my escape. I am sure I will be able to extricate myself from the aunt once I am over there.

Daniel is truly shocked at my decision.

'*Sul serio?* You aren't joking, are you?'

'No, I'm going. No one's going to stop me.'

'Maybe I can help you then.'

'In what way?'

'Well, for one thing, I wouldn't limit myself to this one school,' he says pointing to the envelope I am clutching in my hand. 'There are plenty of these private language schools all over Italy. You'd do best to look into a few others and see what they offer. And if you're set on Milan, then I think you should get to know Jane Blue. She's the Canadian vice-consul there. I'm sure she'd be helpful to you.'

'Do you know her?'

'Yes, of course. My suite is in the same building as her office and I know a lot of people there. That's how I got to know about your riverfront project. As for accommodations, I doubt Gallarate will work out for you. It's outside Milan. These schools are all in the *Centro* and then they send you out to teach a few hours here and there all over the city. You wouldn't always be teaching at the school itself.'

'You seem to know a lot about this.'

'Well, I've always kept my English up in one of these schools.'

I say slyly and smile. 'So which one do you attend when you're in Milan? Maybe I can get a job there and I can make sure you don't lose you're fluency.'

He laughs, then continues on about the accommodations. 'If you decide to stay in Gallarate, you'll have to get used to spending time on the roads during rush hours to get to and from there, you see.'

'I should definitely find a place in Milan then?'

'Yes, I think so. If you want, you can stay at my place. I won't be there for months, it'll be free. I can phone and tell someone in the office to give you the keys.'

'Oh, Daniel, I'd love that. But I don't want to impose. I'm sure I'll be out by the time you get back.'

'Well, no need to rush.'

'I insist. I really want to be on my own.'

Everything falls into place rather smoothly. I suppress the tentacles of reproach whenever they sway before me, accusing me of being dishonest and conniving. Besides, I tell myself, all of what I am saying is true. I truly must see Italy. The Italy of my parents. The Italy of cousin Tino. Daniel's Italy. I want to go back.

Steve is bewildered after I show him a number of job offers. 'What is this shit?' he says tossing them back across the table to me as if they were infested with lice.

I take out my airline tickets and place them in front of him.

He opens the folder and reads, shuts it again and slides it across to me. 'I don't get it.'

He isn't struggling with me as much as I had anticipated and I find this unusual. I must have finally broken his resolve.

'Then what?' he asks.

'I don't know, Steve... I really don't know.'

'We've had our ups and downs this past year, haven't we?'

'Thanks to me,' I admit.

'Right,' he says looking thoughtfully at me. 'I guess you need to do this. To get away.'

'I see it as a trial, really,' I tell him. I try to stop myself. I am treading into areas I should avoid. I

know I should not be offering him any possibilities
that I will later renege on. Cut the bonds, I tell
myself. But I can't. I just can't. Looking at him, I know
I owe him. I owe him much. He was trustworthy and
faithful. I was not.

As my departure approaches, I squelch my inner
happiness when I am with Steve. His own emotions
run in the opposite direction. At home, I contain
myself for my mother's sake. And even with Daniel,
I control my euphoria. It is only with Marion I can be
myself.

'This premeditated plan of yours is working in
your favor,' she says.

'Marion, I don't know what I'm doing, you know.
I just know I have to do it.'

'Don't always underestimate yourself... I think
you know very well what you're doing... Who would
have thought you'd be the one going off into the sunset like this? I always figured it would be me. That
darned Carlo. When he entered my life, not to mention my... well, I won't be crude, it was Sayonara
globetrotting for me. But do you know what we
decided? We're going to come over to see you. When
Daniel leaves, we'll be hopping on that plane with
him.'

My parents and Steve see me off, but there is no sign
of Daniel. I had hoped he would have found a way to
come. When I spot Carlo and Marion running in, my
hopes rise and I search for Daniel somewhere in the
distance but he isn't there. He told me it would be
better if he didn't show. Carlo hands me a bouquet

of fragrant, blood-red roses. The note says, See you in Milan. There is no signature. It wasn't necessary. I know this is Daniel.

41

European cities have had a facelift since I was last here, but beneath it lies the same structure. The first time I saw these churches and palaces, these monuments and castles, many were still draped in the complexion of war, their features ravaged and ruined. I remember poking my finger into the indentations on the bronze doors of the Duomo in Milan. Bullets or shrapnel had left their mark. Many of the buildings looked like defrocked skeletons, and parks were muddy wastelands. They have been refurbished and now stand proudly. The scars of war have been concealed.

Italy is full of smells. It does not smell of bacon and beer and cardboard in grocery stores, but rather of the strong pungent aroma of *espresso, gorgonzola, parmigiano, prosciutto, pizza* and a myriad of other tantalizing scents. I walk along the streets of Milan and whiffs of provocative scents meander out from each tiny cubicle: cafés and bakeries, places that sell only cheese, or only fruit and vegetables. How does one resist such temptation?

I think of our supermarkets back home, neat and orderly and antiseptic, where merchants spend money on advertising. They haven't figured it out yet; instead of piped music they should be using piped smells.

Sweat and perspiration envelop the handsome bodies that prance along the streets and strut to congregate in a square. On buses and streetcars I am assaulted by the hairy armpits of women who stretch

their hands to grab the overhead poles as nonchalantly as butterflies alighting on a flower. They are
totally devoid of shame. I am embarrassed for them,
until I realize, from the stares of onlookers, that it is
I who am different. My closely shaved armpits, whose
natural odors have been camouflaged by anti-
perspirants and perfumed powders, are an oddity
and, in time, I will begin to feel the weight of their
stares.

In my first attempt to blend in, I shed my nylon
hose, another point of contention it seems. Women
here sport bare legs in the summer heat. Once I peel
the constraining nylon from my limbs, I see the sense
of it. How much more natural and unrestraining.

The hairy armpits disappear and the public uri-
nals vanish, not because they are no longer there,
they are, but I do not see them anymore. I grow
impervious to a host of cultural differences.

I stay with my father's old aunt for a few days to
appease her and my family, but I soon tell her I have
found a place in the city. She seems as oblivious to
my departure as she was to my arrival. Old and senile,
not at all the way my father had remembered her, she
continually calls me Lydia, my mother's name, and I
finally give up trying to explain that I am Margherita.

Jane Blue gushes over me when we meet. 'Another
Canadian,' she tells her staff as if I were a trophy in
her collection. Her effervescent and spunky personality reels me in. I can see why Daniel thought I should
get to know her. She takes me under her wing immediately, driving me personally over to Daniel's place

which is in a tree-lined street just off Piazza della Repubblica, a stone's throw from his office and Jane's. 'Get yourself settled,' she commands in her vivacious fashion. 'I'll pick you up tonight at eight. There's a bunch of us having dinner at a great little restaurant over near Porta Romana. We'll talk then. *Ciao*.' As an afterthought, she adds as she opens the door to let herself out, 'You're going to fall in love with Milan, Margaret. Just wait and see.' She is off in a flutter of waving arms and smiles, winking as if we were great bosom buddies with a million events to catch up on.

I meander through Daniel's domain and marvel at the cool simplicity of his surroundings: plush beige sofas on gleaming amber marble that shines my image back at me like a mirror. I wish I could name it but I don't know enough about such things yet. Tawny brown vertical blinds stand beneath panels of faintly embroidered curtains. I draw the curtains and the blinds to let in the subdued light. I unlock and push open the tall French doors and walk out to the balcony. On this third floor, I can look out at the canopy of trees that shield the balcony from the sun's heat and from the neighbors.

I do not yet miss the space of my Canadian backyard with its expanse of grass and its flowered perimeter. I do not miss the silence of home as I stand at the balcony and listen to the constant clanging of street cars and the tooting of horns, the static strains of the *filobus* as its rod runs along the electrical wires that are suspended like a web above the entire city. None of this bothers me in the least. I fit in as if I had lived here forever.

My days are filled with work and the trials of looking for an affordable place to live. Jane and a consortium of her friends take up any slack. We whirl about the city in an ever widening circuit. We take in the countryside stretching farther and farther, as far as the weekends allow. I am introduced to the lake region of Como and Garda, the mountains into Switzerland and, finally, the Mediterranean whose shimmering waters are like a sea of diamonds. I drink it in and become intoxicated by the beauty of it all. The infamous Milan smog has not made its debut yet and I begin to wonder if it had been a hoax.

When it does make an appearance, I am too busy with my new flat to care. I have found a place not far from Daniel's, the top floor in a five floor walk-up. Undaunted, I take the flat immediately. The daily climb will exercise my skinny calves.

It is only a large, bright room with sloping ceilings. A bed is tucked beneath one of the pitched walls and the tiniest of kitchens in the other. The *pièce de résistance* is the oversized balcony that juts out from the room, beyond the wide glass doors. Enclosed by a balustrade of white stone, it is a promontory of tranquility from which I can survey the rooftops of Milan.

I prop up a trellis that I find lying on the balcony and go out to purchase vines that will climb my trellis and insulate me from the curious stares of onlookers who inhabit the apartments beneath me.

I become caught up with my new surroundings and a letter-box full of reprimands awaits me as I skip by the *portineria* where an old couple always seem to be standing vigilantly. I know it is their job to keep a watchful eye on the comings and goings, but to me it is an annoying intrusion. I want to be free. I don't want anyone keeping tabs on me, even if it is for my own good.

'*Signorina*,' the woman calls as I am about to climb the steps, two at a time. 'You have mail.'

'*Oh, grazie, Signora,*' I thank her retrieving the envelopes.

My parents and Marion have written. There is even a note from Steve tucked into my parents' letter. *You have us all worried,* he writes. And I know from this he hasn't relinquished the reins. The following day I receive a lengthy letter from him which validates my theory. *I'm thinking about a trip to Europe,* he writes. *I may stop in Milan.*

In mid December, I panic when a telegram arrives. Its cryptic message simply reads, *Midnight train from Zurich. All my love.*

There is no signature. How uncanny. Did he forget to sign his name? Or was it done purposely? Is this a test like those taken by medieval knights on their tortuous journey towards their quest? Could it be Marion's idea of a joke? I can't dismiss that. The possibilities oscillate until I finally give up. Whoever it is, I will be there. That much I know. It is already too late to write to anyone for an explanation. Letters take weeks to get there and weeks to get back, distorting time in the process. And a phone call wouldn't change anything at this point. Whoever it is has left.

I laugh at myself. What if it's Bruce, or my parents, no one at all. A hoax?

I set out for the central station. The mild winter's eve has persuaded me to walk; my flat is close enough and I have no fear of the night here. Nothing in Milan has given me reason to fear and Piazza della Repubblica as well as the smaller Piazza Duca D'Aosta, directly in front of the station, are so very close and always teeming with traffic, as the great front portico of the station disgorges travellers at all hours.

I walk towards the imposing façade which I hear most Milanese find grotesque and pompous, and I climb a long flight of stairs to the great central hall. I stop and stare at the sea of people lugging suitcases, packages tied with thick rope, metal trunks held fast with thin strips of wire, boxes bulging with their contents. Some are scurrying towards the trains, some descending from them, depending upon what leg of their journey they are on. Milan is not only a destination, it is also a transit point and people are forever rushing to make connections.

I enter the platform area where the trains stand patiently waiting to be delivered of their burdens only to be swamped again with new passengers. They take on a personality as I gaze at them: stoic, mechanical beasts of burden catering to the whims of humanity.

I read the signs, looking for Zurigo/Zurich, and when I see it, I simultaneously hear the announcement informing us of its arrival. In the distance, I can see the bright light at the front of the engine as it rounds a slight curve and heads into the station.

The train hisses to a stop like a tired old woman. An avalanche of bodies in never ending waves step out of the cars, suitcases on shoulders, babies in arms, older children being dragged by the arms sleepy and crying. It's nearly Christmas and everyone comes home from Switzerland and other countries far afield where so many Italians work. I do not know where to look or who to look for. I do not know where to stand so I can be recognized. I decide to position myself under the Zurich sign and let whoever is arriving look for me, because it is dizzying to have to scan such a crowd.

Slowly, the multitude of travelers begins to dwindle and I am able to see individuals instead of masses of faces. When the flood is down to a trickle, I recognize a familiar gait. I am almost afraid to believe it is him, but as he draws nearer and nearer, my heart pumping faster and faster synchronized with his own accelerating steps, I break into a trot. I run towards him the way I have seen actors and actresses do in romantic films, only this is real. It is really happening. Oh, ecstasy! It is Daniel. My darling, Daniel.

We crash into each other's arms and he kisses me fervently with hot, burning lips. We look at each other, scrutinizing one another for changes.

'You look wonderful,' he says. 'Your hair. It suits you.'

It is just a mass of chestnut brown curls framing my face and cascading wildly on to my shoulders. No more closely cropped and neatly trimmed tresses for me.

'I'm into the *zingara* look. The gypsy look is all the rage this season in Milan,' I giggle shaking my locks for him. I pull open my coat to reveal a display of clanking chains. 'See,' I show him. 'Don't I look just like a *zingara*?'

He laughs. 'Oh what has Italy done to you?'

I bombard him with questions. 'Why didn't you sign the telegram?'

'Didn't I sign it?'

'No. And it worried me.'

'Why? Who did you expect?'

How do I tell him I am always expecting the worst, and I fear if I permit myself to expect the best, I will be disappointed and even punished. I ask about Marion and George.

'They're in Paris on their way to Spain or Portugal or Africa. I don't know. They don't know either.

They've decided to tour for a while. They'll get here eventually. But don't ask me when...*Dai, andiamo,*' he leads me out. 'Let's go home.'

'It'll have to be my place,' I tell him. 'The painters are still working on yours.'

'They aren't done yet?'

'No. And it's all my fault. They were supposed to come before I arrived. But they were running behind schedule and your staff told them to hold on. They didn't want to inconvenience me.'

'Then we'll go to that hotel just over there,' he says pointing to an elegant building across the *piazza*.

'What's wrong with my place?'

'Nothing, *amore mio*. I just don't want to ruin your reputation.'

'And what about the hotel? They'll want my passport.'

'Have you got it?'

'Sure. I always lug it around. My albatross. My umbilical cord to Canada.'

'I'll tell them you're a cousin just arrived from America.'

'You mean you're going to lie?'

'Sometimes you have to, my darling.'

42

Daniel came to me during the night. His words echo in my ears this morning as I am rudely awakened by a rumbling and restless sky. 'Sometimes you have to, my darling.' That was what he had said. I didn't give them much weight back then, but they weigh heavy on me now, after all the years.

But his deceptions, if it's fair to call them that, were always innocuous; they were not lavish plots destined to bring calamity to anyone. Who were we hurting when he told the hotel clerk we were cousins? And although my naive North American ways did not condone the Latin's aptitude for trickery and conniving, I did learn to tolerate it. My structured Canadian manner was accustomed to people who take numbers, stand patiently in queues, and exhibit some semblance of politeness to fellow citizens. It was in Italy that I learned one had to sometimes push and shove and plot and scheme in order to survive, let alone achieve some semblance of progress.

Outside, storm clouds are gathering, pregnant with rain, ready to burst forth and anoint the land with their gifts. This is good. It is part of God's plan, but I see the approaching storm as an intrusion. A crack of thunder causes the house to shudder and tremble. The noise threatens to completely disintegrate my dream. Consistent with my behavior nowadays, I choose to construe this natural event symbolically. In reality, all that is really happening is the buildup of a storm. But I decorate my surroundings with symbols.

The neighbors are up early, puttering about in their yard, or maybe I am late. I'm not sure. The clock radio is blinking red numerals at me that make no sense. The actual time is unknown to me. The power must have gone out during the night. I am not even able to estimate accurately because of the darkening sky, but it can't be too early; Steve isn't here.

I recall the spat with him and his mesh bikinis. I recall I took a walk before dinner the other night. We had steak. I remember that. And David and I went to Tino's.

These recollections together with the approaching storm wash my dream away like a rainstorm washing film from a window. My mind is still in a haze, clearing now as I shake sleep from me. More and more my state of wakefulness pushes aside the dream. I remember Steve's attempts at joviality. 'It's the Sabbath, my little *shiksa*...' It had been a standing joke between us for years. Ever since he first told me Jews were supposed to re-consummate their marriage on the Sabbath. I have always meant to verify the validity of his statement, but I never got around to it.

David came home piled high with things for his trip. I remember that.

This is a good sign. I can remember the recent past. It must mean I am not old yet. Old is when you forget the recent past and recall the distant past. Short term memory goes and long term memory consolidates. Aging is like going backwards in time, a return to youth, to childhood, to an embryonic stage. Sometimes those most distant memories in time may return and some come back to haunt us floating to the surface like a bloated, dead corpse. What, I wonder, haunts Steve or Daniel? What could my son be doing now that will surface later? Do they have their own dark secrets?

Chapter 42

My mother used to say, 'You'll know tomorrow how stupid you were today.' She was so right. How many times have I felt I had made it to the threshold of understanding only to have the door slam in my face? Wrong, the blocked entrance admonishes. You were wrong. You have made a mistake.

Any yet, ironically, time passing does indeed bring its own wisdom. Perhaps it is the wisdom that allows us to see our errors more clearly or simply to accept them and go on. Or else to take the plunge and reject what has been and steer a new course.

I have always marvelled at the gall some old people develop. With a devil-may-care attitude towards life, they often spout truths slinging them at the nearest bystander without regrets nor apologies. 'Don't mind her,' my mother would say about some old relative. 'She's old.' As if age conferred privileges and rights.

I remember an old woman I would occasionally see at the hairdresser's. Once, as she sat imperiously on her throne in the seat next to mine, looking bedraggled with her sheet of wet hair dripping about her, she said to me: 'You should let your hair grow, honey. Short hair doesn't suit you.' She said this without turning to look at me but rather directing her words at me through the mirror in front of us. The hairdresser, who was appalled yet wise enough not to ruffle anyone's feathers, turned her back to the old woman and whispered with tight lips like a ventriloquist, 'Don't mind her. She's old.' The truth was, the old woman was right. I did look better with long hair.

I have also seen the other type, the flip side of the coin, those Marion and I used to say had 'flipped'. These chose to remain taciturn to the point of becoming non verbal. I have observed such couples with their spouses. These usually have spouses hanging around, which may account for their behavior. Gestures, glances, cues, like a dumb show, take the place of speech. They invent all manner of communication. Speech, it seems, has become too much of an effort.

I will have to add age to my list of things having a duality and duplicity about them in their natures. Old age will have to take its place alongside memories and fire and water.

43

With David's departure imminent, I am flooded by past memories. They gnaw into my marrow, sucking my life's juices from me. This approaching emptiness begins to fill with thoughts of the past — like sand pits on a beach when the tide rolls in. Or when waves wash up flooding and destroying the little dikes and trenches youngsters have bravely worked on for hours, leveling all traces of the day's activities, except for the most stubborn, some elaborate castle with turrets and towers which may balk at the ocean's audacity. But even these monuments will be leveled by the endless rhythm of the waves, destroyed once and for all until new ones are erected. Will my recollections suffer this same fate? Will they too be leveled, destroyed, forgotten, or pardoned? Or will I descend onto the beach searching for yesterday's ruins in order to reconstruct my towers?

The day of David's departure fills me with dread. I cannot bear to see him go. I steal into his room and watch his sleeping form. My David. A man. No longer a boy. Tino had said it too. He is shirtless and I can see the wide expanse of his back and the strong shoulders. His blond hair is mussed the way it used to be when he was a child. Later, when he gets up, he will gel it back in the style of my youth. I marvel that such things go in cycles. Today, that slick look is all the rage again. I retrace my steps for fear of waking him. He hears me. He is a light sleeper. Always has been. The tiniest sound will break his slumber.

'Mom,' he calls, rubbing sleep from his eyes.

I walk back in and embrace him. I feel his warm, firm body and marvel that this is truly my son.

'Come on, Mom,' he teases. 'It isn't the end of the world.'

'I wish it were,' I say forcing a smile.

'Oh, come on. You and Dad can have the time of your lives now.'

'Sure, sure,' I laugh.

'You're making me feel guilty.'

'I'm sorry, son. I don't want you to feel that way. It's just that I'm going to miss you so much.' Retreating from the room, I excuse myself. 'Look, honey, I'm sorry I woke you. We'll talk later.'

I had meant to broach the subject at Tino's, but the snake incident had distracted us.

'We can talk now,' he says sitting up as he plumps a pillow to lean on.

'Well, there's something I have to ask you. Something I'd like you to do for me.'

'Go ahead. Shoot,' he says motioning for me to sit on the bed.

I accept his invitation.

'This is going to sound funny. And I really don't want to go into it, but I'd like you to do something for me when you get to Milan.'

He looks at me inquisitively and a broad grin sweeps his face. 'Sure, Mom. What do you want me to do? Look up an old flame or something?'

I am flushed and I'm sure he can perceive a faint trembling. 'In a way,' I reply with a wink hoping this will distract him and conceal my feelings.

'You aren't kidding, are you?'

'Just listen... I used to know someone in Milan. Daniel's his name. I've got his old address, but I'm not sure it'll be much help, although people don't move around a lot in Italy the way they do here. Anyway, remember my friend Marion? The one who died recently?'

'Sure. I know who you mean. The one who was into cryonics.'

'Into what?'

'Cyronics. You know. She used to talk about freezing her body when she died so she could be thawed out at some time in the future.'

'Oh, right. I remember.' I have to laugh at the memory of Marion and her splendid eccentricities. 'Well, she used to be in love with Daniel's brother. Carlo was his name. He used to live here, as a matter of fact. I'd like you to find Daniel and tell him about Marion. Tell him she's passed away. If you don't find him at this address, someone at the vice-consul office may be able to help you. He used to have a suite in the same building and someone might remember him and know where he is.'

'Sure, Mom. Do I know this guy? Have I ever met him? You know, will he know who I am?'

'He'll know when you mention Marion and me. And, yes, as a matter of fact, you did meet him once. It was when we went to Italy that year. Remember?'

'I remember the trip, but I'm not sure I remember him.'

'Well, you met him then.'

'That's terrible about Marion, by the way.'

'Yes, it is.'

'What happened to her friend, Carlo?'

'He died a long time ago.'

'He's dead too? This is getting to be a bit morbid. What happened to him?'

'It was in Italy. When I lived there.... Remember?... Oh, how could you?... What am I saying? It was before you were born. Before I married Dad. Daniel had been over here on an assignment. When his contract expired, he returned to Italy and Carlo and Marion followed later. We were in the mountains. Near Austria. In Austria, actually. We were climbing and although you always have to be careful, this was more like hiking, really. The trails were well marked and ropes already in place where they were needed. I guess Carlo had been out of practice since he'd been living in Canada for so many years, and he must have overestimated himself because he suddenly lost his balance. We were walking along a narrow path when he slipped and slid down a grassy incline on the side of the mountain. It was incredible that he couldn't stop himself or grab a bush or something to break his fall, but he just kept rolling down the slant. There was a three hundred metre drop at the end of this and he just went over the side. Daniel tried to help him. He went down the grassy slant himself but he had to stop at the cliff. There was nothing he could do. Nothing at all.'

'You mean he went over the cliff? Just like that?'

'I'm afraid so.'

'Did they ever find him?'

'I don't know exactly. I doubt it. I do know a helicopter was sent in to search. It wasn't something we could talk about. It was too horrible for words. And besides, I really didn't want all the gruesome details... Anyway, that's what I wanted to ask you.'

'Sure, Mom. I'll look up Daniel. And I'll stay away from mountains.'

'Thanks, son,' I say as I rise from the bed. When I reach the door, I turn and add, '...And please don't mention this to your father.'

David winks and I smile. 'You're cheeky, do you know?'

'Cheeky? Is that an expression of the twentieth century?'

'Are you going to be joining us for your last supper?'

'Last supper?'

'Well, it's breakfast, but I thought last supper brings out the symbolism of your departure.'

'Honestly, Mom, I think you'd better cut out some of the reading before you mutate.'

44

Death is a thief. Sometimes it comes unexpectedly like a sudden wind that blows in from no earthly dimension. And sometimes it is even more cruel when it leaves a calling card, as was the case with Marion. This disintegration begins to encroach on me in an ever quickening pace. There is no one for me to turn to anymore. Death has orphaned me. Taken my parents from me first and then my friends.

When my parents died, I remember having to go through their belongings. Because of my mother's compulsion for neatness, her belongings and whatever of my father's she chose to look after, were ordered and tidy, clean and fresh. Opening the door to her linen closet, the freshly-laundered scent of her sheets and towels brought a lump to my throat that swelled until I almost burst with grief. She left nothing in a state of disgrace. All was perfection. She kept only what was necessary or pleasing. She was forever tossing out what she deemed outmoded or had outlived its purpose. She would include herself in this pile of discards saying, '*È ora*. It's time for me to go. I've lived my life.' And it was not unusual for her to toss out perfectly functional objects simply because she wanted to replace them with something new and updated. She didn't hoard and she certainly didn't hold on to many mementoes and things from the past. Just a few, very few. As I fingered her possessions I could hear her words: '*Non voglio essere di peso*. I don't want to leave you with a mess, Margaret. I don't want to give you that burden.'

My father, on the other hand, was her antithesis. A hoarder and collector, a scavenger, really who never came home empty handed: odds and ends picked up from garage sales, broken and inoperative machines from which he could remove potentially useful parts, and it was not beneath him to take the occasional tour of the alley to delve into other people's discards. '*Se sono come te...* If they're anything like you,' he would say to my mother in jest, 'those garbage pails are full of treasure.' He never let her forget the time she threw away his teeth. She, on one of her routine reconnaissance missions, had managed to trash his newly acquired dentures. 'What were they doing wrapped up in a ball of kleenex?' she accused. 'They belong in your mouth.'

'They hurt,' he had retorted. 'I just took them out for a while.'

'And left them on the kitchen counter?'

His domain was the basement and a study on the upper level of the house where he kept his books and what he referred to as '*documenti*' which consisted of numerous brown envelopes stuffed with letters from the old country, titles and deeds to old properties in Italy which had changed hands by then, newspaper clippings of events deemed significant by him, all yellowing and brittle and smelling stale, and a drawer full of photographs which had never been sorted and ordered and placed in albums. There was nothing of material value in this room. All of the important documents pertaining to their present possessions and assets were kept by my mother in a drawer in their bedroom.

I have somehow managed to bridge the two of them, having inherited my father's gift for hoarding and collecting along with my mother's compulsion for order and tidiness. Thus I have the worst of both possible worlds, not being able to let go of anything and always wanting to find a place for it in case I might need it later. It is an unfortunate calamity for me which has encumbered me through the years, no doubt a wasteful and unproductive endeavor since it causes me to sift and sort through layers and layers of 'stuff'.

'Stuff', I like the word. I must look up its etymology when I get a chance. As a verb it relates how my mind feels right now. It is full, stuffed to the gills, as I mentally sift and sort the dead and missing.

When my parents died, each item I touched ignited a memory. Now, as I wait for David's departure, I can feel the little tongues of flame lapping at me. They are like the ones I saw in a picture of the Holy Ghost once. They showed the Apostles with little tongues of flames hovering above their heads. The flames were the Holy Ghost who had come to enlighten the followers of Jesus.

'Where are you when I need you?' I cry silently for Marion, gritting my teeth in anger. 'Why have you abandoned me?'

Plagiarizing Christ's words to the Father, I am angry, so very angry that I am so alone.

I am not sure who or what the anger is directed at: Marion for dying or the Almighty for allowing such torment; or maybe I am angry at myself for my cowardly ways and for using Marion even in death. Yes, even now, she has use for me. She comes in handy. How perverse I am. I can use the dead and buried for my own conniving plots.

'What's up?' I had said when she phoned.

'Tom, Dick, and Harry. When I slither by, they're all up and they give me the twenty-one gun salute.' She never lost that sarcastic sense of humor that I envied.

'News?' I said with anticipation in my voice. I never lost hope she would one day find Mr. Right among all those Tom's, Dick's, and Harry's of hers. Even then, after all those years, I still hoped.

'It's time,' she said flippantly.

'Time?'

'I'm ripe. Ready. Ready to take the plunge.'

She's getting married, I thought... She certainly can't be pregnant, although with modern technology and Marion's sense of adventure even that couldn't be ruled out. 'What are you talking about?'

There was a slight pause.

'Time for me to meet my maker. I told Him I didn't take a number, but He said my number was up. He's beckoning me unto Him. Pulled the cord. Hauling in the line...'

There was an uneasy edge to her voice.

'For God's sake what is it?'

The silence was ominous.

'Margaret, I'm dying.'

'Marion, please, what are you talking about. Stop the theatrics.'

Her tone returned to its former flippancy as if a great burden had been lifted from her now that she had managed to release the words. 'I'm finally going to get some answers from the Bastard. I've got questions stockpiled, Margaret. He'd better be ready with some answers. No more of this shit about Faith, Hope, and Charity. I want concrete, honest-to-goodness answers.'

'Oh, God, Marion, I'm coming right over.'

'Shit, you don't have to rush. He isn't sending the dreaded barge just yet. He's going to let me hang around a few more months, just to make sure He lets me have all the agony and torment that goes with the disease. A quick death would be too easy.'

I could hear her sobbing now. 'Oh, Margaret, why couldn't I go the way Carlo did? Fast. Why this? I can't stand the thought of this cancer eating away my insides. The futility of it. The humiliation. The loss of control. My body, Margaret, my body is being eaten by pestilence.'

I could feel her anger gripping me.

'Look, Margaret. I want a Jewish ceremony,' she continued. 'No flowers. I hate their smell in those funeral parlors. I want it to be just like the one we went to — you know, when Steve's uncle died. A simple wood casket, maybe two ferns on either side. That's all. And a short eulogy. Something funny. Remember the story the Rabbi told that time? Remember how he made everybody laugh? I want it to be like that. That was the only time I ever came home from a funeral parlor, and I didn't feel I had to scrub my hands. And a closed casket, do you understand? Just like you people. Well, Steve's people. I don't want anybody looking at me if I can't look back at them. And you do the eulogy, okay? ...What was that story about? Do you remember?'

'The Jew taken slave.'

'Right. That smart assed little Jew and how he managed to con his captors and kill them all. I like that. I couldn't see the connection to the deceased mind you, but it was a good story. Remember how later, with Steve, we talked about it for hours? Steve kept trying to explain it to us over and over again so seriously, and you and I wanted to burst out laughing, and then when he noticed he got pissed off and he stomped off in a rage and we were in hysterics...'

'I remember.'

In the end, she decided on cremation, 'even though you people don't believe in it,' she said. 'I'll pick and choose what I like from where I like.' We laughed.

'I've been looking into ancient burial rites,' she said. 'There are so many ways to go, Margaret. You can be thrown into a lake, a river, or an ocean, launched on a raft, roasted on a pyre, or you can be left on the ground for scavengers...When I read that in Tibet cremation is reserved for the most exalted, I knew that was for me...'

I didn't try to stop her. I let her attempt to shock me to the very end.

'Did you know that in Indonesia they used to collect the liquids from decomposing bodies, mix them with rice if they wanted to splurge, and then ingest them? ...I vetoed that one, for your sake. Just have a shot of brandy instead... And you can have sex with Steve, or anybody else. It's my party; I'll make the rules.'

45

When David leaves, the floodgates open. Steve is sympathetic, I must admit. He calls it the 'empty nest syndrome'. I hate being categorized this way. I hate his lumping me into a group and labelling me. My pain, I prefer to think, is unique.

I know it is only fair that David should pursue his career and Italy was a logical choice, with Milan unquestionably the city most suitable. '*Signora,*' the gentleman from the Embassy in Toronto had replied, in that recognizable tone of superiority David would have to learn to tolerate, 'Milan has one of the finest — if not *the* finest — schools of architecture in the country.' I do not attempt to block his way. Did I not, myself, go off to Europe?

My pain, on my son's departure, is a physical one which manifests itself in an all too physical manner, a familiar pain, I feel the way I did when I was a young woman. I feel a physical emptiness, a deep void, an empty space. My heart has been wrenched from within the cavity of my body. It is the way I felt when Marion and I used to hold our breath and pass out. Except then, my temporary loss of consciousness was a blessing; with this, my body holds on to its senses; it will not allow me to lose my grip and to fall, much as I wish it would.

David goes first to Rome. He has planned a tour of our sun drenched peninsula before settling in Milan. He follows in my footsteps exactly. My Italy of bygone days is resurrected in me, and I pass my days wandering the streets of the metropolis, my memories as guide. I see David on the *Rapido,* approaching Rome. I see him look upon the foreign landscape with anticipation. The green Tuscan hills will turn pale and straw-colored as he approaches the south. He will see Cypress stand as sentinels atop the distant hills. The *Autostrada del Sole,* with its hedge of pink and white oleander dividing the highway, will cross and cross again the Tiber and he will marvel at what a mediocre run of water it is. If he is like me, he would have imagined it a river of strength and purity; but this will not depress his senses. Not at all. And neither will the myriad of idiosyncrasies he will find in Rome: the constant clatter of vehicles, the shrill sounds of motorists disputing rights of way, their heads protruding from car windows, arms waving madly, true to custom, the tooting of horns, the odour of diesel fuel. Nothing will daunt this fresh new mind, this energetic and optimistic spirit who sees the world through the veil of youth.

With David in Rome, I relive my Italian intermezzo. I am again with Daniel.

We plan to meet in Rome, Daniel and I. The romance of this excites me beyond description.

I phone Daniel in the evening and tell him I'll be going to the capital. I am being sent for a refresher course on 'teaching English to the educated Italian', or something along those lines.

'Ah, *sì,*' says Daniel. 'The "educated Italian" must be treated with kid gloves. But never mind. It's a stroke of luck for us. I have to be in Rome myself next week. A conference. I'll be in on Wednesday. The afternoon *Rapido.*'

'I'll be at *Termini* to meet you,' I say brimming with anticipation. I haven't been to Rome yet and I am exuberant at the prospect.

I go to the station well ahead of time. *Termini* in Rome is worlds apart from the Milanese station. My own arrival just a few days earlier had jarred my senses. When I stepped off the train and entered the vast interior of this modern, angular edifice, I felt cheated. Approaching it now from the *piazza*, it again appears eerie and out of place. It is more readily accessible than its Milanese counterpart where one has to contend with long flights of stairs. Nevertheless, it is conspicuously out of place to me. Much more 'utilitarian', Daniel would say.

Flanking the station are the remains of an ancient wall. I dig into my satchel for a faithful guide book, which I carry at all times for moments such as this. *The fourth century B.C. Servian wall,* the book informs me. The clash of past and present has never been more vivid for me. I must look up the station's background. It has to be linked to Mussolini who, as my father used to tell me, vowed Italy's trains would run on schedule. Apparently, he succeeded, but at what cost?

I parade up and down the great cavernous hall, agitated with excitement. I hear the familiar gong which signals the impending announcement of an arrival or departure. I listen for Daniel's. When I hear it, I run to meet the train as it pulls into the station, right on schedule. Mussolini would have swaggered with puffed up conceit, I can't help thinking as I glance at my watch. My eyes scan the passengers. There is always that fear he won't be there, the suspicion that good things can't last. I don't know why I always felt that way. Even then. But this time he is here.

It is April, and already quite warm in Rome. Daniel has tossed his green *Loden* over one shoulder. It must have been cooler in Milan. He is carrying a small suitcase and a briefcase in one hand; beneath his other arm is a large box wrapped in red. It has thin white streamers dangling from a single bow. The ends of the streamers are curled and they bounce gleefully as he approaches me.

Meeting him like this, on new territory, brings out a new excitement. We take a taxi to Daniel's hotel and I hear him tell the driver it's on Via Sistina. I am giddy just thinking about being in Rome with Daniel. My senses are awakened to all of her beguiling traits now that I have Daniel to share in my euphoria.

'Nice planning,' I say smiling at Daniel as we weave through the narrow streets clattering on ancient roads, coming to a stop in front of the hotel. It is situated at the height of the old Spanish Steps where Via Sistina flows into the *piazza* in front of the church, the Trinita dei Monti. My school is on this very street, just a few doors away.

'Where are you staying?' he asks.

'In a *pensione* on Via del Corso.' I had managed to find a reasonably priced room on that renowned street, regretting my decision after I realized it was affordable because it offered few amenities and the bathrooms were communal. 'The walk to and from there is about the only sight seeing I've had a chance to do. They keep us busy all day. And in the evenings, when I try to go out with some of the other teachers, we seem to develop an entourage of male admirers. Or maybe I should call them opportunists?'

Daniel kisses me softly, lifting my face to his. 'Who can blame them,' he teases.

'But it's annoying. The other day, on my way to the *pensione,* a couple of *militari* were following me. I stopped at an intersection and asked a policeman to do something. Do you know what he did?'

'What? I can only imagine.'

'He winked at me and asked if I preferred him. They are bold. I've never had this problem in Milan.'

'Different temperaments, *amore mio.*'

'Well, now you're here, I'll be safe.'

As Daniel pays the taxi driver, I wander to the *piazza* overlooking the Steps. When he has told the porter to take his bags in, he joins me, scooping me into his arms.

'Magnificent,' he says.

'Oh, Daniel, I'm in awe of this city. Do you realize Keats died in that house right over there,' I say pointing to the building directly in front of us. 'I always remembered that because he died on my father's birthday, February 23. To think that Keats once inhabited this mystic domain, that he once looked upon the same churches and palaces and fountains. It's overwhelming. He's buried here in Rome, you know.' As I speak, my words lift me from reality and catapult me into the past. 'Shelley wrote part of "Prometheus Unbound" while in Rome,' I ramble on.

'It is a city that speaks without saying anything,' says Daniel.

'Now that you're here, we'll see Rome?'

'Come,' he says leading me back to the hotel. 'I'll get settled, and then we're off.'

His suite is sumptuous and I gaze childlike when I walk in. This place is worlds apart from my *pensione,* but I don't tell Daniel. He tips the porter who stands anxiously in the doorway. And when the door closes behind him, I rush into his arms and we kiss passionately, as if we hadn't seen each other in weeks. We were together just five days before. It is always this way with us. Each time we come together is like the first time. The excitement never relents.

The anticamera opens onto a spectacular sitting room. A gilded mirror, reflecting our image, is poised above a magnificent fireplace whose mantle is a glossy black marble streaked with veins of gold, like honey. Its beauty is seductive and alluring, I want to caress the stone. The bedroom lies beyond. Its French doors open onto a tiny balcony. Via Sistina is narrow and the balcony reflects this by being narrow itself, just enough room for us to stand.

We throw open the shutters, then the glass doors. The ecru curtains puff into the room. We tie them back. Below, the hustle and bustle of a bar beckons us. We save ourselves for later.

When my course concludes at the end of the week, Daniel and I decide to visit the south since we are already in Rome. He rents a car and we snake our way out of the tangled hub of the city and head for the *Autostrada*. Distances take on new meaning in Italy. The country is compact, teeming with vitality. The eye never ceases to find new focal points. There are no vast, empty spaces here. Before I know it, we are approaching Naples. I anxiously await the sight of Vesuvius, the formidable volcano I have heard so much about. When Daniel points it out, I am disbelieving. 'No,' I say. 'That's Vesuvius?'

'That's the culprit,' Daniel assures me.

'But I thought it would be much more...ominous looking...you know...bigger. It's deceiving.'

Daniel laughs. 'What did you expect?'

'I don't know. That it would look ferocious. That it would be spouting fumes into the air, have horns, or something. I can't imagine such an innocuous looking mountain causing such havoc.'

'The people of Pompeii didn't expect it either. As a matter of fact, they didn't even know Vesuvius was a volcano. It was just a lush green mountain with woods and vineyards,' Daniel tells me.

'Oh, my Lord. They didn't know they were living next to a monster?'

'Not at all. On the contrary. The slopes were rich and fertile, excellent for wine. In Pompeii they've found wine jugs marked *Vesuvium, Lacrima Cristi,* we call it today... They had no way of knowing.'

My eyes are fixed on the mountain. I am amazed to see it has a second peak rising from a depression or valley. 'What's that second hump I see? It seems to have two peaks.'

'It does now, but it didn't before the famous eruption. Then, it only had the one peak.'

I regard Vesuvius with a changed attitude. It takes on a mantle of power and force neatly camouflaged by orchards and vineyards. I look around at the densely populated landscape. I find it remarkable that people persist and live here still. It is as if they are defying the mountain. 'How can they go on living here? Aren't they afraid?'

'You get used to anything, I suppose,' says Daniel. 'What choice have they got?'

'Has it erupted lately?'

'In 1944, I think it was. During the war, as if that wasn't enough,' he laughs. '*Povera Italia.* Poor dear Italy. I think it was the American, Melville, who said the people in these parts have such a *joie de vivre* because they live between God and the Devil.'

When he sights the road sign for Pompeii, he continues. 'Here we go. Pompeii is up ahead. Now you'll see the legacy of Vesuvius.'

On first seeing Pompeii I am reminded of ghost towns in American westerns where tumbleweed rolls haphazardly among dilapidated buildings. Except, of course, these are ancient ruins and not flimsy wooden shacks. I am surprised by the narrowness of the streets and how diminutive the city looks with so much of it destroyed. Surveying it from our vantage point, it looks like a giant labyrinth, a complicated maze. The emptiness is eerie; the silence deafening. As I gaze upon the sun-parched city, exposed in this manner and at the mercy of the elements, it seems so terribly vulnerable. Those few tourists who are here choose to whisper reverently rather than speak in normal tones.

A handful of vendors have set up shop near the entrance to the ruins. Brightly colored awnings shade trinkets and souvenirs, questionable jewelry and travel booklets. A couple of vendors swarm around us as we approach the entrance. They swagger away to sit back upon their chairs under the awnings when they realize Daniel is Italian. Perhaps he feels a sense of remorse at the way this has dismissed them because he asks if I would like a souvenir.

'I wouldn't mind a book,' I admit.

He walks over to the nearest tent and picks up an illustrated guide to Pompeii. The vendor gets up quickly now and excitedly. '*Tre mille,*' he says.

Daniel flips through the book. '*Due,*' he says pointing to the price on the inside back cover. The man insists prices have gone up since the book was printed. Daniel pulls out two thousand lire and places the money on the table, retrieving the book. He shakes his head as he hands it to me. 'It's in their blood,' he says.

I am embarrassed for both of them. I would have given the vendor what he had asked. But another thought wedges into my mind: these once proud and prosperous people have been reduced to this. Daniel must sense my ambivalence. 'Poverty makes thieves,' he says.

When we finally enter the ruins, it is as if I am entering the city of the dead. Once inside, I can feel the pull of antiquity ferrying me farther and farther into the bowels of time. We latch on to a guide who methodically relates the story of the destruction. But his theatrics bore us and Daniel and I slip away from the group and wander the ancient ruins alone. I notice the large, polygon stones used to pave the streets are rutted. 'I didn't know you could wear down stone this way,' I remark in amazement.

'The cart wheels caused that,' Daniel tells me as he bends to touch the smoothed surfaces. There are large raised stones at regular intervals along the road-way and I wonder about their purpose. 'They were for pedestrians to cross from one side of the street to the other,' Daniel tells me. 'That kept their feet dry when the roads flooded. The space on either side of the stones was enough for the cart wheels. Let's take the Via del Abbondanza,' Daniel suggests.

'Via del Abbondanza? That's quite a name.'

'Isn't it. Apparently, when Pompeii was at the height of glory, the name suited it.'

Unassuming exteriors lead into the once sumptu-ous homes of well-to-do merchants and artisans who populated the bustling city. Shops used to occupy these rooms which open onto the street, while the owner's private rooms extended back from there.

The buildings are marked. Those we find most intriguing draw us in. I am incredulous when Daniel points out *un casino*.

'A brothel?' I exclaim.

'Quite routine in those days,' he laughs.

We peek into the house of Giulia Felix, looking past the atrium into the garden, studded with a pool or fish pond. Marble pillars sustain an inviting portico that runs the length of the garden. As we wander through the rooms, I feel we are intruding and trespassing. We are like thieves. But the exquisite splendor I see urges me to explore farther. I can't help myself.

'Oh, Daniel. Did real people actually live in the midst of such beauty?'

'Incredible, isn't it? They were architectural masters.'

We wander at will in and out of these vacant spaces with no one to block our entrance nor to invite us in.

We approach the House of Venus in a Shell. We survey the atrium and the rooms that lead off from it. At the back of the house, we come upon a magnificent garden bordered on two sides by an elegant colonnade of fluted Doric columns. A mural on the far end of the garden wall captures our attention. A nude Venus is sailing the sea in a shell, escorted by two *amoretti* — two cupids. The pearly white Venus stands out against the soft, hazy blue of the sea.

'How sensuous,' I remark.

'Can you imagine the variations in color they would see during the course of a day?' says Daniel. 'How the sun's rays would create various hues?'

I am mesmerized by the sight. We walk around the colonnade and approach the Venus reverently, as if it were the deity the ancients believed her to be.

'*Conosci la storia?* Do you know the story of Venus?' Daniel asks.

'Yes, she sprang from the white foam of the sea.'

'But do you know the origin of the foam?'

'I guess I don't.'

'Well, according to Greek mythology, Earth and Heaven, also known as Gaea and Uranus, by the way, produced several species of unsavory characters. Uranus hated his offspring — who could blame him; some of them were the Cyclopes. Some say he hid them in Gaea's body; others say he hid them in secret places in the earth. Gaea was pretty upset by this. After all, they were her children. And she asked her offspring to do something about it. The only one who did was a Titan named Cronus.'

'I remember this,' I interject. 'But, go on.'

'So, one day, when Uranus approached Gaea, Cronus hacked off his father's testicles — said to have been extraordinarily huge — and the testicles floated on the sea producing the white foam from which she sprang,' he concludes pointing to Venus.

'Well, well, well. I never read that in my texts.'

'No? I suppose it's much too graphic for your North American palates. I'm sure it would have been censored.'

I laugh.

'So what happened to poor Uranus?'

'Uranus? I don't remember. He wasn't of much use to anyone after that, was he?'

I laugh again, squeezing Daniel closer to me. 'I love your stories,' I tell him. 'But they give me ideas,' I wink.

We continue south to Salerno and Amalfi where ancient towns are perched upon craggy summits or embedded into the cliffs along the sea. Their white-washed brilliance is a mirage for the eye. A road sign for Eboli captures my attention.

'That's where my father was during the first war. My grandparents took their entire family down here to escape the occupation.'

'They were refugees?'

'Yes. I remember the stories. My father was very young then. He used to tell me they lived near Eboli. They worked for a wealthy land owner and stayed until the end of the war.'

'There were a lot of people from the north down here at that time.'

'Oh, Daniel, I can't believe all this. The soil I am standing on has seen so much. It's so rich in history I can feel it groping for me. There are ghosts everywhere, Daniel. I can feel their presence. One of my uncles died here during that time. He was buried in Salerno. But after the war, my grandparents returned for his remains. They wanted him in the family tomb in our hometown. They didn't want to leave him down here all alone.'

W e stay the night in Amalfi, taking a large room facing the sea in a hotel that seems to be carved out of the cliffs. I discover in the morning that this is an appropriate description since the hotel is actually anchored to the mountain and a part of it. The room is painted the same soft blue of the sea, and when I open the doors to the balcony, I feel like the Venus in a Shell.

In the morning we head north and back to Milan, just a day's drive. Famous landmarks tug at me and entice me as we drive: Cassino, Assisi, Siena, Firenze, Pisa... 'We'll come back?' I ask.

'We'll return, *amore*. I promise. But we have to get back to Milan.'

As we pass Bologna, Daniel is visibly tired.

'Let me drive,' I suggest.

'I have a better idea,' he says. 'What do you say we veer off course here and go to Verona?'

'Verona? Romeo and Juliet, the ill-fated lovers?'

'One of the castles — I think it's Juliet's — is a hotel. Great food, from what I remember. We can stay there the night. It won't take us long to get to Milan in the morning.'

'So you've been there before?' I tease him playfully, for I have learned my lesson not to pry too deeply.

'A convention a few years ago.'

I settle for his answer, even though I have my doubts. 'Do you suppose it could be true? About Romeo and Juliet?'

'Stranger things have happened,' he tells me.

46

I have not yet had word from David and the counting is beginning to drive me insane. If I look out the window, I count birds at the feeder. One, two, three, four... I will count anything: trees, houses, cars, people. Anything is grist for the mill. Inside the sanctuary of my home, I used to find a reprieve from this obsession. This is no longer the case. This is something I have always done, but it is getting worse. I now count angles in a room, tiles in the bathroom, flowers in the wallpaper, crystal drops on the chandeliers. If I am interrupted, I panic. I am compelled to accelerate the counting because I know I will not be able to leave the room until I have completed the task. The books say this is a symptom: depression waiting in the wings. The counting is an attempt at control, at maintaining law and order in the face of impending disaster.

I also count days. But they crawl by so slowly that I am again forced to occupy my mind with tiles, angles, and corners. They, at least, are tangible and concrete. Time is not.

I am counting the days David has been away, the days I have been waiting for news of Daniel.

Steve must be feeling me slide into this new stage. I am not doing a very good job at camouflaging this sense of despair. I can see him becoming more and more demanding. It is always this way with him. He thinks if he pushes me into a corner, I will have no choice but to comply. I can see the wheels turning in his head tonight. What will it be this time? I hope he is more inventive than the mesh bikini thing. I can tell from his pseudo casual looks at me that he has something up his sleeve. When we're in bed, I decide to break the ice myself. 'Why are you looking at me that way?'

'Didn't think you'd notice,' he says, proud that he has been able to capture my attention. 'You seem distant, Margaret. Far off in that never-never land of yours.'

I do not respond. He tosses a pamphlet across my bed.

'What's this?'

'Your membership to the health club.'

I roll my eyes to the ceiling. So that's his plan. He wants me to join him at the health club. He belongs to one of these bubbly clubs where pen pushers and tongue waggers go to exercise parts of their bodies they never before knew existed. I hold my tongue.

'I want you to come with me. They have a sauna, a jacuzzi. It's great to feel the jets vibrating all around you. It'll relax you. Invigorate you.'

He drones on and on sounding like a commercial for the establishment and I pick up a book and think of Daniel.

'So, you'll come? You've got to get away from all this,' he says pointing to the books. 'They're swallowing you. You have to become more active. It isn't healthy, Margaret.'

I know he is right but my mind is in Rome, in that hotel Daniel and I stayed in on Via Sistina where I came across my first bidet equipped with a jet that spouted icy water at me. How we laughed.

'Well?' he asks, slinking nearer and nearer. I feel his hands groping at me and his breath is heavy on my neck. He kisses my shoulder and slides his lips down towards my breast.

'Please, Steve.'

'Oh, so now you're begging for it?' His attempts at humor frustrate me further and I inch away from him slipping precariously to the edge of the bed.

'You'll love the feeling of coming out of the sauna all sweaty and slimy and sticky. It's so sensual, Margaret.'

'I'm really not in the mood,' I say, referring to his advances.

He persists, refusing to let go, creeping closer and closer. He pulls the covers off, exposing his nakedness. His hand slithers under my nightgown and finds its way between my legs. He attempts to part them.

'Stop it, I tell you, stop it. What the hell's the matter with you?' I fling myself away. 'I've got a suppository up my ass, for God's sake. I'm constipated. Do you expect me to take that on as well?' I say throwing a furtive glance at his erect penis.

'Shit,' he says. 'You're impossible. If you'd get out more, and do something instead of stagnating here fondling these fucking books, you wouldn't have to have a goddamned suppository up your ass.'

'Well, I'm sick and tired of counting thrusts.'

'Counting thrusts?'

'Right. That's what I do.'

'What the hell are you talking about?'

'That I count thrusts. I count. Do you understand? One, two, three, four... I count, on and on and on. I count until I think I'm going to burst. Until I'm sure my mind will explode. I count while I stare at the ceiling and wait for it to be over.'

He sees my frenzy and steadies me.

'Easy,' he says. 'Take it easy. You aren't well.'

I slouch down and cry; he holds me.

'You've got to let go, Margaret. Let him go.'

I pull away, wiping the tears from my eyes, and stare at Steve. Does he know? Could he possibly know of Daniel's hold on me?

No. He doesn't. I can see the answer in his face. In his eyes. He means David... Of course. He means David.

47

I named my son after my friend who died when I was a little girl, the one who used to collect and share bottle caps with me, my sacrificial lamb. That was how I thought of him when I was young. Even though he died while waiting for a bus and holding his mother's hand, guilt grew in me once I understood the risks he had been taking. What if he'd been killed on his way to see me? How would I have felt then? It could have happened this way. My mother had warned me often enough. 'I don't like David crossing the street like that,' she would say. Now I know his death was just life playing one of her sinister tricks.

Steve had liked the name too. For him it summoned thoughts of the biblical David, and that was all right with me. When David was born and I saw him, I almost changed my mind. 'Do you think it'll be bad luck?' I had asked Steve.

'Why should it be?'

'Well, you know. Because of that little boy I told you about. His name was David.'

'Oh, come now, Margaret,' he had assured me. 'Let's not get carried away with superstitions.'

I never gave it much thought after that. Not until that trip to Europe with Steve and David. That was when my superstitions boiled to the surface and I had a hard time blowing away the scum and extinguishing the fire.

Just like the time before, when I had planned my escape from Steve, I had once again masterminded a successful plot allowing me to see Daniel.

I couldn't be sure Daniel would even be in Milan. I had lost track of him. I just took the chance. Steve hadn't been keen on the trip, but, in the end, we compromised. He was on his way to Switzerland for a convention. 'It's so close,' I had said. 'Couldn't David and I come along with you? Then we can go to Italy. You've never been. Remember when I was living over there, you wrote and said you might be coming? You never did.'

But my motives were not honorable. Steve was oblivious to this. I was thankful for it, but resentful as well. Wouldn't he ever notice? He was immersed in his work and it was not an easy task to pry him away from his interests. His accounting firm had been growing. That was what he used to say to people: 'My firm is growing in leaps and bounds.'

We are in my hometown: a sleepy village in the foothills of the Alps. Stone houses act as walls tunnelling us through this maze of timeworn roads. It is also a hilly town. Narrow roads wind up to a summit, then fall down and around a *piazza*. The lack of symmetry bothers Steve.

'What did you expect?' I say. I am annoyed. 'Did you think they would bulldoze the area flat to lay streets in a proper grid?'

He doesn't answer. It is early afternoon. People here rest at this time, but we are not accustomed to the routine. Instead, we decide to stroll to the nearest bar for an ice cream. David thinks it's pretty neat to have a bar where they also sell ice cream. It is a hot August day and the sun is out in full force. We can all use something cold.

There are a few young people in the bar playing the video machines. Steve is surprised to find such modernity in my hometown. 'What did you expect?' I retort. 'Horse drawn carts?' The young people are too boisterous for Steve. When David is finished with his ice cream, we leave.

The motorcycle comes out of nowhere. We hear it in the distance and then suddenly it is there. Both Steve and I are holding David by the hand but the noise of the approaching cycle, or some other inexplicable catalyst, must frighten David. Somehow, he manages to break away from us and he dashes into the narrow street, directly in the path of the motorcycle. I scream. The cyclist swerves and crashes up against the wall on the other side of the street. His bike wraps around and swirls towards us. It comes to a stop a few yards ahead. Miraculously, David is not hit. He stands in the middle of the road, stunned by the events.

When the young cyclist finally looks up I can feel his disdain reaching out for me. What is he thinking? I am a poor excuse for a mother? What sort of mother would let her son dash into the path of an approaching motorcycle? Only an uncaring and undeserving mother. This is surely what he must be thinking. After my friend David's death, I blamed his mother. Why hadn't she been more careful? How could she have let go of his hand? She deserved to be punished for letting my friend die. It took this disaster to make me forgive her.

Steve picks David up and says nothing. He knows he is equally culpable. He goes over to the young man to see if he is all right. 'Margaret,' he calls. 'Don't just stand there. Get over here and ask him is he's okay.'

The cyclist tells us he'll be fine. But he shakes his head as he looks at the bike. He gets up, wipes the dust off his face and notices the blood. His face is cut, but it is only a superficial wound. The blood makes it look a lot worse than it is. He gets his cycle up and walks off, limping slightly.

Steve puts David down. 'You and your bright ideas,' he starts. 'He could have been killed. This place is dangerous. People here don't follow any rules. They just go wherever they want. There aren't any speed limits. No laws. The kid was probably half drunk. They don't have any restrictions on drinking. Anybody can go into a bar and drink. What the hell kind of a country is this? Lawless.'

I say nothing. I am afraid to speak. Afraid God will punish me. I have been dishonest and deceptive. I am deserving of His wrath. And Steve's too. I am afraid my past sins will show and I am going to be held accountable. I pray silently. I ask God to do as he wishes with me, but to please spare our son. Our son must not be hurt. Please, God, I pray, not our son.

Steve wants to leave. He wants to go to a more civilized place. He wants to go back to Switzerland for the duration of our holidays. When we get back to the hotel, I am forced to tell him about the passport.

'Steve,' I call, putting on an expression of disbelief. 'Come here a minute. There's a problem.'

'What is it now?'

'My passport. Look at this. It's expired.'

'What are you talking about? How can it be expired. Let me look at that.' He takes the passport from my hand.

'How could you be so stupid?' he rebukes me.

We decide to leave my hometown the following morning. I can see Steve almost rejoice at the thought. In a way, he is probably glad about my oversight. When our bags are packed and tempers have cooled, I tell Steve there is one thing I want to do before we leave. 'I think you might find it interesting too,' I tell him. I explain about the Jewish cemetery on the outskirts of town. 'I'd like to see it.'

His interest seemed piqued. Or maybe he's sorry he was so rough with me earlier. Whatever it is, he is trying to make up for it now. And so I inquire.

'It's run down but they buried a wealthy industrialist from Trieste there just last year,' a villager informs me.

We leave David with some long lost cousins who are thrilled to have him. They can use him to practice their English.

We snake our way out of town avoiding collisions with oncoming vehicles. Although there are fewer cars on the road at this time of day — three in the afternoon — those that are out, are a threat. They are reckless drivers. Steve is right. And more than once I have to swerve out of their way. I drive past the small lake, which isn't more than a puddle now, and turn into a dusty road. It terminates abruptly in a cornfield. Two other smaller, less travelled roads stretch out like arms.

'Which one?' Steve asks.

'I don't know,' I admit. 'My mother always said the cemetery faced the lake, but I can't tell from here where these roads go. In the old days, you could see all around. But now with all these trees and bushes, it's hard to see.'

We hear a tractor up ahead and ask the farmer for directions. *'Prendete quella,'* he motions towards the one lined with overgrown shrubs and trees. 'Don't try to drive in,' he warns. 'You're better off on foot. Just walk along until you come to a tall cypress. Then you should see the wall.'

Steve and I are sweating. I am not sure he'll agree to the walking. He dislikes discomfort. He may not want to leave his air-conditioned car.

'What do you think?' I ask.

'Let's take a look,' he says.

I am encouraged.

The sun beats down upon us and even I find it oppressive. I can understand why people rest at this time of the day. Anyone with any sense would be doing the same thing right now. We look at the rutted path before us, muddy in spite of the heat. The growth on either side forms a canopy over the path. The light that gets in is filtered through, which accounts for the mud and the small puddles of water.

The foliage, however, also creates shade. A cool, inviting breeze entices us forward.

We walk between the ruts, where the ground is raised and dry. The path becomes less and less muddy and a warmer breeze caresses us. Then the growth stops on one side of the path and the canopy above us looks lopsided. We finally emerge from this tunnel into another cornfield. 'There,' I say when the cypress comes into view. 'There's the tree.' And then we catch sight of the wall, overgrown with a thick blanket of vines and thornbushes.

The wall is crowned with glass shards which have been cemented into the top. Two menacing rows of barbed wire encircle these. The ornate, wrought iron gate is locked and a yellow sign indicates the number to call for information.

We walk up to the gate and stare inside like two children looking at a forbidden scene. There are no wrought iron garlands and strands of pearls and colored beads. Gone are the rose bushes. There are only tall grasses and weeds and crooked headstones.

'Did I ever tell you my uncle once scaled these walls to steal a rosebush for my mother?'

Steve looks at me inquisitively. 'No, never.'

'Well, he did. They used to come by here all the time. They must have followed the same path we did. They had a piece of land out here somewhere. My mother used to stop and look into the cemetery at the beautiful beads that were strung over the headstones, and she used to admire the roses. One day, just before my uncle left for America — he went over before we did — he went in and dug up a bush and took it to her.'

'Maybe that's why they've got the glass and barbed wire,' he says.

We both laugh.

'Too bad we can't get in. I wanted to find that fellow where my grandmother used to work.'

'You're always digging up the past. Come on. Forget it. Let's go back to the hotel and have one of those *apéritif's* before dinner.'

His arms encircle me as he leads me away. I reach up and kiss him on the cheek, then pull away quickly as if I had committed a sacrilege. For a moment, I am in love with him all over again. For a moment, it is as it used to be with us. And with all my heart, I wish this moment to go on, to carry me to infinity.

48

Milan is a veritable graveyard in August. Shops are closed, their metal doors rolled down and locked, covering the windows. Iron bars over these doors and windows for further protection. No one who is anyone stays in Milan in August. The streets are deserted.

'Is there a curfew?' Steve asks.

'Not many people stay in the city during the summer. They all go to the sea or the mountains.'

'How can a city survive like that? It isn't very cost-efficient.'

'Perhaps not,' I say. 'But that's the way it is here.'

The odd car rattles along noisily, its sound echoing between the buildings. As I gaze up at them, I think of Daniel. Could he still be here?

I don't need a map and Steve notices. 'It's as if you never left,' he says. He doesn't know how true this is.

'I know it like the back of my hand,' I smile.

We drive towards the *Centro* and watch for a hotel that will still be open. I know there have to be a few, just as there are a few bars and shops still doing some business. The owners must have taken their vacation earlier, or maybe they'll be taking it later. The only sure thing is that they will be taking it.

'I don't know how people can live in these buildings,' Steve comments.

'It isn't bad once you get used to it,' I tell him. 'Besides, Italians — except for the farmers and the very wealthy — have always lived this way. They're just newer versions of the *insula*.'

I scan the buildings looking for Doric columns, Palladian windows, Travertine facades. I peek into sumptuous courtyards where I know fountains gurgle and statues line colonnades. The balconies, usually vibrant with life, are bare. Their heavy outside-curtains, used during the summer to shield the sun, are pulled back and tied in place to prevent them from whipping about. Shutters are closed tightly. Those with *persiane* look as if they have their eyes closed. We find a place near the central station. 'The consulate office is just down the street,' I tell Steve. 'We can walk to it.'

In my daydreams, I am walking through the *Galleria.* In the distance I see a familiar figure. I recognize the walk. The quick pace, the steady gait. His legs move rhythmically, sensuously. His body is erect; his shoulders do not sway. It is the legs that move briskly causing his alluring buttocks to sway seductively. I used to tease him about this. As I approach him, I make out the mane of blonde hair and I must control an urge to run to him. 'Daniel,' I call out. 'Daniel, it's me.' He turns and I am looking into his cool, blue eyes. His lips curl into a smile. I fall into his arms and kiss his voluptuous lips. They are warm and wet and soft. Familiar. My heart beats wildly as I crush myself against his body. In reality, it does not happen this way at all.

The hotel clerk is not anxious to take us in. '*Signora,*' he tells me. '*Domani partiamo per il mare.*' I tell him we only need a room for the night. We too have to leave tomorrow. I explain my passport has expired and we must get to the vice-consul immediately. He looks at my passport for evidence to support my excuse. He shrugs his shoulders and shakes his head. He'll do us a favour. But we must be out tomorrow.

'I can't believe this,' says Steve. 'A city the size of Milan and we can't even find a room.'

'I told you. Milan is empty in August.'

'So where do all the tourists go?'

'Milan doesn't have that many tourists,' I explain. This is not a total lie. He looks at me, puzzled. 'Those that come are usually with tour groups,' I tell him. 'They stay in the newer hotels on the outskirts of the city. But those places would be filled right now. Besides, we need to be in the *Centro*.'

The proprietor himself takes us to our room. Most of the clerks are on vacation. His wife comes out to see what all the ruckus is about. I hear her tell her husband they don't need the hassle. Get us out. He calms her down, tells her we'll be out tomorrow. She throws her hands up in the air.

We toss our belongings haphazardly into the room and immediately go out again. I promise David a *gelato* in return for his patience. I feel guilty. I am putting my son through this for my own selfish ends.

We walk across the *piazza* and towards Via Pisani. Nothing has changed. We walk in front of the station and I turn to look at it face on, remembering Daniel. 'That's where all the trains come in,' I tell David. 'Big, isn't it?'

I can see the consular building in the distance, a relatively modern edifice with a peach marble facade that shines in the sun. Heavy glass doors lead to more marble and glass. We climb a short flight of stairs. The landing looks over the courtyard. I walk over to the glass and look down. I see Daniel. But this is not the real Daniel. I see the Daniel who used to be mine. I am there with him in the garden.

49

The vice-consul is a man, Geoff Bradbury. He is middleaged, bald, and wearing those half spectacles some men wear instead of bifocals.

'Please, come in,' he says rising for us and offering us his hand. 'I hear you have a problem.'

Steve takes over, explaining our predicament. 'My wife's passport has expired. She didn't realize it until yesterday.'

I feel like a little child who has committed some silly misdemeanor and, like a child, I jump in offering excuses. 'It isn't something I do as a rule. My husband had to be in Switzerland. My son and I decided to join him and then come to Italy. I haven't been back in years.'

'My wife used to live here,' Steve explains. 'She used to teach in Milan.'

'I see,' says Geoff Bradbury. 'You must be thrilled to be back,' he says turning to me. 'You must know Jane Blue, then.'

'Yes, of course,' I reply. I decide to grab this opportunity and ask about her. 'What ever happened to her? Did she ever marry?'

'Yes, as a matter of fact, she did. Married an Italian, actually. Ended up staying on in Italy.' He dials an internal extension as he speaks. 'Gloria, would you ask *la Signora* Brunelli to come in for a moment?'

I get the feeling he has business to attend to and we are taking up too much of his time. But when he places the phone down, he seems eager enough to continue our conversation. 'So, I take it you haven't seen her in a while?'

'It's been years,' I say. 'Was it the architect she married?' I ask this to get a response.

'The architect? Oh, you mean Daniel. No. No. Not him. She married a fellow named Ricardo.'

My heart skips a beat. He knows Daniel. I want desperately to ask about him and decide this is the time. 'Is Daniel still around?' I ask.

'Why, yes. His office is in the building. You knew each other, then?'

'Yes, we did.' I can see Steve is getting impatient with my reminiscing, and so change the subject. 'Can you help me out with this passport?'

'Certainly. I'll need some identification and we'll whip up a passport for you in no time. You'll have to run down to Via Manzoni to get some pictures, however. If they're open, that is. You know how it is in August over here. *Le ferie!* Everyone goes on vacation.' Glancing at his watch, he tells us he'll give them a call. 'No point in you running all the way down if they're closed.'

I stand impatiently waiting and planning my next move. Steve paces near the window feigning some interest in the view.

'*Chiuso?* What a shame. *È aperto domani?*' he asks.

Steve turns to me. 'What'd he say?'

'They're closed for today.'

He lifts his eyes to the ceiling. 'What are we going to do? They want us out of that hotel.'

'Let's take one thing at a time.'

A familiar voice in the doorway interrupts this scene. Turning, I see Jane.

'That's *la signora* Brunelli,' says Geoff Bradbury with a laugh.

'Jane,' I squeal with delight.

'Margaret. For heaven's sake,' she says hugging me.

'You're still here?' I say.

'But of course. Hey, you've heard the saying. "How are you going to keep them down on the farm after they've seen Paris." '

I wish she hadn't said that and I think she regrets it too. But it's too late. I can't help wondering how she ever got to be vice-consul with such undiplomatic gaffes.

'Ricardo Brunelli. Now I remember. That's who it was.'

'Right. He was the one,' she says with a wink. 'Hey, she continues, tickling David. 'What have we got here?'

'This is David.'

'David. I've got one just like him,' she tells us. 'A bit younger. Then we had a girl.'

'You're still working here?' I ask.

'Sure. Old Geoff here usurped my throne when I married, but there's still room for me, right, Geoff?' she quips.

'By the way, Jane,' Geoff Bradbury asks. 'Would Daniel be in?'

'I'll call and see,' she says picking up the phone.

'No, Jane. Please. I don't want to impose.'

'Nonsense,' she says. 'If he's in, he'd be delighted to see you.'

'I'll give him a buzz,' says Geoff Bradbury.

And then it's too late. He is dialing the number.

'Daniele,' he says attempting the Italian pronunciation. 'There's someone here from Canada. Looking down at my passport, he continues, 'a Margaret Croff. She says she used to teach in Milan and you knew each other.'

I can't imagine what Daniel is feeling as he hears this. I concentrate on retaining my composure, directing my attention to David.

'He'll be down in a minute,' he tells me, then turns to Steve and asks about Canada. 'How are things over there?'

'Fruitful. Right now, they're pretty fruitful.'

'What are you in?'

'Accounting. I have my own firm.'

'I see.'

I abhor these conversations. The futility of them. Their only purpose is to boast and flaunt perceived achievements. But at the moment I am thankful for the diversion it offers Steve. He is in his glory when he can discuss economics, business, money.

Their conversation buzzes around me while I listen for a creaking door or a rush of footsteps announcing Daniel's entrance. And then, finally, I hear the quick paced walk echoing in the corridor and I know it is him.

When I see him, I cling to David. I have to hold on to someone or I will collapse. He is still remarkably handsome. He doesn't seem to have gained much weight. His tapered white shirt accentuates his wide muscular shoulders. His pale beige pants drape suggestively accentuating those marvelous buttocks.

He is extremely reserved when he walks in. If he is agitated, no one can tell. But I know him. That's how he would be. We do not embrace nor kiss, even though it is the custom. Instead, he extends his hands taking both of mine and enfolding them into his. 'How nice to see you,' he says. He turns to Steve offering him a firm handshake. 'I'm pleased to meet you,' he tells him. 'I don't think we met when I was in Canada.' And then, crouching to David's level and looking up at me, he asks, 'And who's this?'

'This is *our* son,' I say.

'So, what are your plans?' Jane wants to know.

Steve explains our dilemma. I watch them mouth words but they are mute to me. When Jane announces we must all go to her place for dinner, I tune in again.

'You won't find much else to do in Milan at this time of the year. You know that, Margaret,' she says turning to me. '*Vieni anche tu, Daniele,*' she adds. 'At eight.' Directing her attention back to me, she asks, 'Where are you staying?'

I give the name of the hotel. Daniel glances at me and I can feel the color rising in my face. My temples throb, I am faint.

50

What went wrong? It was certainly nothing to do with former affairs. For although I naively perceived his experience as a threat initially, Daniel was quickly weaned from whatever relationships he had had. Was I just a passing fancy? A mid-life crisis? He was, after all, much older than I. Nearly twenty years separated us. Marion had warned me of this. Had I been too demanding? Not in the physical sense. He was an ardent, fervent lover, a virile, vigorous figure. Oh, Daniel, you raised me from the dungeon of despair and showed me brilliance and light. And then you blinded me forever.

Thinking back now, I see the irony of our final days. I had been reading Hemingway, *A Farewell to Arms,* sobbing bitterly as I ploughed through the final chapters, hoping, praying, yes, always praying, it would be a happy ending, knowing full well it wouldn't be, for I had read the book before.

I remember reverting to childhood theories about the power of the Almighty, of Jesus, to perform miracles. He could change the unhappy ending, obliterate the pages, blank them out and replace them magically, mysteriously, with the ending I wanted for the script. God could do this, I used to believe when I was a child. He was omnipotent. That meant He could do anything.

I was so immersed in the book, I had forgotten to secure my balcony door, and it stood slightly ajar, rain splattering into my sanctuary.

Daniel finds me red-eyed and exhausted this rain-drenched afternoon. The fog and rain had made a tempestuous appearance that day. Ovules of hail had fallen in the mountains to the north. Here in the city, we were shrouded in an oppressive mist.

He took me to one of our favorite haunts that night. The tiny cave-like restaurant Jane and company had introduced me to on my arrival a year ago. He must have thought this underground retreat would offer me some distraction, spare me from the sound of the rain pelleting on windows.

'Can we go there sometime?' I ask, my mind still on the book.

'*Dove, cara?*'

'Lago Maggiore.'

'We've been.'

'Yes, I know. But I'd like to stay for a few days. Right in Stresa. Where the charming *Tenente* Henry meets up with Catherine.'

That weekend, we drove north past Busto Arsizio and Gallarate where I had first stayed with my father's old aunt. We continued to Stresa where a colleague of his had a chalet tucked into the side of the mountain and overlooking the splendid lake.

His reticence to speak did not overly alarm me. I was used to his silences, although they had been increasing with the passage of time. But there was something different that day. No gentle love pats on my thighs, no little kisses on the nape of my neck. And he didn't point things out for me as we drove.

It was true we had traveled the route before. I wanted to blame it on this. But I was only making excuses, knowing one always makes new discoveries even on roads already traveled. It was only when we settled into the chalet that he broached the subject.

'Margaret, I've been thinking.'

I say smiling. 'What deep dark secrets have you been keeping from me? Another woman? A wife, perhaps? Children? Come, come, now, spill the beans.' I had become more liberal in my teasing but beneath my veneer of joviality there was purpose.

'I'll just have to come out with it,' he says rather bluntly. 'I've been offered a contract in Indonesia. Two years, maybe three.'

'Indonesia? How wonderful. How exciting,' I say throwing my arms about him. So that was it.

'But, Margaret, I don't think you should come.'

I let my arms drop from his shoulders and I stand back puzzled. 'You don't want me to come?'

'I didn't say that.'

'You don't want me with you?'

'Nor that.'

'Then what did you say?'

'That I don't think you should come.'

'I'm sorry, Daniel, but I'm confused.'

'So am I, *amore*. That's just it. I think this would be the perfect opportunity to sort things out.'

'What is there to sort out?'

'I want you to go home.'

'But I don't want to go home. I want to be with you. I will follow you to Indonesia, or any other place you go. I will follow you to the end of the earth. *Ti voglio bene*. I adore you.'

'And I love you.'

'You've suddenly developed a strange way of showing it. You aren't making any sense.'

'Margaret, let's face it, darling, I'm much older than you and...'

'You have the nerve to say that now?' I interrupt. 'You knew how old I was when we met.'

'Yes, I did. Of course I did. And I was wrong to lure you away the way I did.'

'Daniel, please. You don't know what you're saying. I have loved you from the moment I set eyes on you.'

'It was the same for me. You know that. I love you, Margaret. I always will.'

I cry hysterically. 'What are you saying? Are you leaving me? Tell me. Tell me the truth.'

'Margaret, please. It's for your own good. You deserve more.'

But I wasn't listening. I was drowning in my own sorrow, oblivious to his. 'Why are you doing this? Why are you being so mysterious all of a sudden? All I want is you. I can't bear to think of life without you. You are everything to me. You know all my secrets.'

'Stop, Margaret. Stop. Listen, please. *Ti prego,* listen.'

'No. No. I won't listen. I won't.'

'You're young. I've been selfish.'

On and on it went until neither of us could bear the pain any longer. 'Oh, Margaret,' he cried. 'I wish I had never met you.' His words were a hot poker through my heart. I knew he couldn't mean them. I knew his pain was every bit as intense as my own and I flung my arms around him. I was confused and bewildered. His lips anointed my body and I returned his fervent kisses with equal intensity. I did not understand anything. How could he make love like this and not want me? And for that brief time I did not care to understand. I had Daniel. He was with me now. And we made love one final time. That was the last time our bodies writhed in ecstasy together. Our grand finale.

51

I leave Milan by train on the first leg of a long and tortuous journey home. In a numbed daze I whisk through the north of Italy into Switzerland, my misery stripping all beauty from my surroundings. France is a blur, I stop in Paris only long enough to connect to a train for Le Havre where I have booked a passage on a ship. I had decided the voyage at sea would be a buffer between Italy and home. I had always promised myself the inconvenience. What better time than now? If I am lucky, I think morbidly, I might even drown this time. Tino isn't around to save me.

I try to distract myself watching the galaxy of passengers. I spend a lot of time in the bar. A handsome, though short Frenchman follows me out one evening, quickening his pace in order not to lose me when he sees me head for the elevator. I find this rather silly considering we are on a ship in the middle of the ocean. He squeezes into the elevator just in the nick of time, and I turn coyly to look at him straight in the eye. 'Is there something I can do for you?'

'I was about to ask *Mademoiselle* the same question,' he says rather suavely as he extends a hand and introduces himself. 'My name is Pierre.'

Ships, like planes and trains, and even hospitals, must have magnetic fields causing the attraction of people in transit. The dubious relationships made when forced to share a confined space usually last the length of the stay. Not everyone understands this.

There are always those cheery effervescent souls who tell you to keep in touch and who might even have the audacity to send postcards from other travels, as if they had become great friends. Pierre and I had no such deceptions.

He has that sensuous French accent most women would kill for. 'I could not help but notice *Mademoiselle* was alone. I was wondering if you would care for a nightcap.'

I find his invitation odd. We have both just come from the bar and I point this out to him. 'I meant in my room,' he says making his intentions clear. His boldness makes me smile. The nerve, I think. But I accept. What have I to lose? I have already lost everything.

'Why not?' I smile.

'Where are you coming from?' he asks, realizing I am on my way home.

'Italy.'

'Italy? I see. And what were you doing in Italy?'

'Making passionate love to an Italian,' I reply.

He laughs. He gradually closes in on me like a male bird in a mating ritual. But my drunken stupor vanishes when I see him naked. Stripped of his clothes, I can now smell the perspiration and I retreat from him. He notices my reaction, but must misinterpret my intentions for he smiles as if he has just gained a victory. 'The male odor is sexually evocative,' he says pulling me to him. 'It is what attracts the female.'

I am repulsed by both his odor and his boastfulness. He must think his body is a sacred shrine capable of gathering worshipers with its secret potions.

When he becomes intimate, I seize as if I were wearing a medieval chastity belt. I shove him away just in time. I turn and vomit. Pierre is aghast. Some men are so fragile, I think.

'It's not you,' I reassure him when I come out of the bathroom. 'It's me'

'But the ship is stable.'

'It isn't the ship. I'm drunk. That's what happens when I'm drunk,' I claim as if this were the most natural thing in the world for me.

He realizes I am truly drunk and finally lets go. I am relieved.

'Then you must stop drinking,' he says. The tension loosens, and we both laugh. We know it's just a game.

Arriving in New York, exhausted from the journey, I descend the gangplank with Pierre, who is helping with my luggage. True to form, I did my share of vomiting, like my mother, and I am surprised the nausea does not relent now that I am on land.

The commotion of the arrival stifles me and we cross the street to hail a taxi. I stumble and look down to see a body lying up against the curb, knees slightly bent towards the chest, his head spilling bright red blood on the pavement. His eyes are closed, I don't know if he is dead or alive.

'*Mon Dieu*,' says Pierre. '*Ça c'est New York.*'

We step over the body just like everyone else, and Pierre whistles for a cab. The body is invisible. No one does anything. Not even us. The cab swerves to avoid the man and brakes just beyond. Pierre and I shake hands. '*Bonne chance*,' he says. 'And remember, no drinking.' We part without the usual formalities. I have a train to catch.

Tunnelling through the city, I feel like an ant in the shadow of the towering skyscrapers. America. This is America, where life takes on a different rhythm.

Like a bird tittering before an earthquake, predicting its arrival, I can sense the difference immediately. In Italy, there was a relaxed fury, a hustle and bustle that is only a charade, an act. Here, it is a true frenzy, not a game at all. Here it is quite serious.

I head for Grand Central Station, for my rendezvous with the train, an all-night run crossing in Buffalo and then into Canada.

Arriving in the early morning, I make out the shapes of my parents in the distance. Standing to their side and slightly behind them, I can see Steve.

52

My body has always been a reliable barometer. And it has its own perverse sense of humor. It has come to the rescue at times, as was the case with Pierre on the ship, and even with Bruce. It was speaking to me.

At first I blame this recent fit of nausea and vomiting on the voyage, but other signals manifest themselves and I am forced to pay attention. My breasts begin to swell voluptuously, the areola darkening. A fine, faint line is marking its presence on my tummy, and abdominal cramps signal distress but fail to bring forth the monthly ritual of blood and pain. The nausea is most uncomfortable in the mornings. I begin to suspect the worse.

I call Marion and explain my symptoms. She makes me laugh immediately.

'Just tell your folks what the girl from my village told hers.'

'What was that?'

'When they discovered she was with child, they asked her what had happened. She said she didn't know. She was asleep at the time.'

'What'll I do, Marion, if I am?'

'Take it easy. Calm down. You'd think you were carrying Jesus Christ himself.'

'That isn't funny. How could you be so callous?'

'Sorry. That was dumb. You can always abort.'

The idea is ludicrous and I know I could never do it. 'No, Marion. I couldn't.'

In the back of my mind I think of the old wives tales about women in the old country giving birth to monsters: babies with the face of an ape, babies with no arms or no legs. I remember the story of Uranus and Gaea and the monsters she produced. I think of that hospital in Italy — the Cotolengo, was it? — where such deformed creatures are kept from the rest of humanity, hidden the way Uranus hid his offspring.

'Well, you'll have to come up with something pretty fast,' Marion says.

'I know.'

'Did I ever tell you Carlo had a kid once?'

'Carlo?'

'Yeah. When he was just a kid himself.'

'Who told you?'

'He did. When we were in Italy. Before the accident...'

'He told you?'

'Well, he told me there were rumors.'

'Wouldn't he have known the truth?'

'No, not really. It's kind of a funny story. We were walking up from the *piazza* towards Daniel's place and we passed that rather large, ornate villa, the one with that balustrade on the top floor and that fancy entrance where the keystone is a cherub. Well, that place used to be a sort of orphanage and home for the mentally unstable, he told me. There was girl there who would do anything for a *golia*. You know, those little black candies. The boys used to ask her to lift her skirts and pull her pants off or display her breasts and sometimes, if she was in the mood, she'd turn and give them a back view bending down until they could see her tits up front. All the while, she'd be smelling her pants.'

'Smelling her pants?'

'Sure. Smelling the crotch. Haven't you ever done that?'

'Smelled my pants?'

'Sure.'

'Well, if I did I wouldn't tell you.'

'Then you do.'

'Stop it, Marion.' Marion is not afraid to ask such questions. She stirs the pot and ladles out the thick dredges of our inner and most private taboos.

'Oh, come on, Margaret. Everybody does it. Anyway, you get the picture. So one day Carlo didn't have any candy and he'd run out of money but looking into a nearby courtyard, he saw a goat. He picked up a bundle of goat droppings, which look just like the tiny *golia,* and wrapped them in paper, twirling the ends like the real thing. He went back to the girl and handed her a fistfull and she went into hysterics. She opened them one after another and ate them smiling at Carlo all the while. So I guess he took advantage of her that night... But a lot of other guys took advantage of her too. So that's why no one could really be sure it was Carlo's kid.'

'Honestly, Marion. I don't know what to believe. Maybe he made up the entire story just for laughs. Or maybe you did. Kid. Goat. Who was he trying to kid? Who are you trying to kid?'

'Maybe he did. I don't know. What does it matter now? ...But back to you my maid in distress. You will definitely have to come up with a good plot this time.'

After my talk with Marion, I convince Steve to take me to the woods. 'They'll be full of blackflies,' he says. He dredges up every excuse he can think of, but eventually gives in.

We drive out of the city leaving behind the overheated buildings and steaming streets. On the road ahead, I see mirages, illusions. The road is as dry as a farmer's field in August, yet it looks wet. I have a habit of pretending to be where I am not whenever I am offered up these illusions by the grace of nature. I have not stopped playing makebelieve even though I am old enough to know better. Clouds, for instance, in certain formations can suggest mountains. This is especially true at dusk. I think of them as such and pretend I am in the Alps.

Steve begrudgingly follows my directions to Tino's. I shouldn't have mentioned him. It has put Steve in a bad mood.

We turn onto a gravel road and Steve swears. The gravel is knocking up against the car. What if a stone hits the body and dents it? He slows almost to a crawl because of the dust. He swears again. I am sorry we're here already. This can't get any worse, I think. But I am wrong. I see the bush up ahead. 'That's it,' I say in relief. 'Just up a few hundred yards.'

At the entrance, I jump out and swing open the decrepit two-by-fours Tino has nailed together to create this makeshift gate.

'That's as far as I'll go,' he says. Ahead of us, the path is bumpy and rutted. I see the sexual innuendo and decide to capitalize on it.

'You don't have to stop,' I say. 'You can go farther,' I wink suggestively.

Tino must have been in here this spring when the ground was wet because the ruts are deep and impassable.

'What the hell are we going to do now?' Steve asks.

'We'll take a walk,' I say.

'Through this shit,' he says pointing to the forest around him.

'You're so romantic,' I say. I am beginning to wear thin on patience. 'You don't have to be afraid.'

'Stop with the lectures.' He is annoyed.

'You're impossible.'

'I'm impossible? Ever since you came back from Europe you've been on my back. You've changed. Do you know that?'

I don't answer. I don't want to get into this argument. My heart is bursting, but I remain silent.

I hear a rustling somewhere in the trees behind us. At first I am excited because I think it might be a deer if I'm lucky. But it isn't.

I see Steve tighten. 'Get in, quick,' he orders me. 'Lock the door.'

A half dozen men in black leather jackets appear from out of nowhere. They are coming towards us at a leisurely pace. They are smiling and leering at me. Steve attempts to start the car, but it fails him. He is perspiring. The men come closer. They are laughing. They are quite near now. I am beginning to feel uneasy. They look threatening. One of them runs up to the car and leers at me through the window. 'Let's have some fun,' he says, then flicks a switchblade into my face.

Steve tries to start the car a second time. It fails again. I sit there immobile and speechless. Three of them have climbed onto the hood. They are looking at us through the windshield. They flick knives at us and laugh. They are grotesque with their dirty beards and greasy hair dangling from big round heads.

Another one comes around and pulls at Steve's door. Finally, the car starts. Steve throws it into reverse and we crash through the rickety gate. They had shut it to keep us in. The car heaves backwards onto the gravel road and the three who are on the hood slip off. I hear their voices. 'After the suckers,' they shout. Steve drives, no longer caring about the dust. He is pale and sickly looking, but I am not. I think of it as an adventure. Tino would have enjoyed this. I think I must be crazy for I know I should be frightened. We are almost killed. Maybe that's what I had hoped for.

I don't say a word to Steve. It is he who finally speaks. 'So much for your goddamned woods,' he snorts. 'I hope you're satisfied. You nearly got us both killed,' he says.

He is scolding me. I have done something wrong. I feel guilty.

'Those goddamned animals,' he says. 'Those fucking animals. They almost killed us.'

'They weren't animals,' I say. Steve glares at me.

When we're a safe distance away, he looks at me, his anger and fear subsiding. My quiet crying raises his sympathy.

'I'm sorry, Margaret. It wasn't your fault.'

'I'm sorry too, Steve. Really I am.'

He places his hand on my knee and I can see he means what he is saying. I am pierced by waves of guilt and so I draw myself closer to him for comfort, or maybe so he can't see me and read my face. He wraps his arm around me drawing me closer to him. 'You look great, you know. Did I tell you that yet?'

He is looking at my full breasts whose roundness he can feel up against him right now. He lets his hand fall from my shoulder and he gently caresses my breast from the side.

I think to myself, perhaps all is not lost, and for a moment I am indeed comforted. Safe. With Steve I can be safe.

As we near the city, we drive by several motels. I snuggle close hoping my plan will work.

'It's been a long time,' he says. I can tell he is getting excited, the way he holds me tighter and tighter. The way he is licking his lips and stumbling over his words.

'Yes, it has.'

'I'm not sure how you feel, Margaret. About us, I mean.'

'I'm here aren't I?' I manage to say.

'Yeah, sure, but you've been away a long time. And you know...'

I decide to turn the tables on him and put him on the spot for a change. 'Remember what you said when I left?'

He turns his head and looks straight ahead. 'I've had my ups and downs while you've been away.'

'Really?' I smile.

'What did you expect? I'm a man, not one of your monks.'

'That was your prerogative,' I say.

'Do you want to stop?' he asks finally.

'If you do.'

And so it is done. We pull into a motel and seal my fate.

53

I have not heard from David about Daniel. I don't know what this means. I am losing the will to fight. My surroundings drag me deeper into despair. The disappearing greenery, the change from color to lack of it, the emergence of greys and browns, geese in formation flying south, black crows swooping down upon the lawn one final time, these natural processes begin to encrust my spirit. The encroachment of despair becomes tangible. Like the buildup of sediment. I see myself becoming smaller and smaller, burrowing deeper and deeper.

Steve does become impatient with me. Who can blame him? His once efficient and congenial wife is becoming a useless appendage. The vomiting returns in all its fury. My stomach will hold nothing. I lose my appetite and Steve attempts to force me to eat. 'Look,' he says. 'I've been through this with you before. You'll get over it.'

I worsen daily. I lie in bed like a corpse. Pale and bedraggled. I wish to see no one. No one but David. Or Daniel. But this I cannot say. I vomit with each smell that mingles with the air I breathe. I retch with pathetic regularity. I can no longer tolerate smells: Steve's coffee brewing, toast, an egg frying, it all makes me sick. Steve insists I see a physician. I am sent in for tests.

In the hospital, the doctors do not know what to make of my ailment. I do not respond. They pierce my white flesh forcing nutrients deep within me, they send rays through my body to detect cancers, anything. Any clue would be welcomed. How can they know that mine is a cancer of the soul? It will not show up on their sophisticated machinery.

'Do you want me to call David?' Steve asks me.
  'No.' I am vehement about this.

54

The hushed clatter of the hospital awakens me this morning. I can hear the rattle of trays as the trolley is rolled down the corridor. When they arrive at my door, a cheery voice calls me by name. 'Here we are, Margaret,' she says. 'Let's see you eat some of this now, do you hear?' I resent her attitude towards me. I resent being treated like a child. Or is this the bedside manner reserved for old people? To her I must seem old. I certainly look it today.

I smelled the disgusting breakfast trays as soon as they emerged from the elevator. But now, with the platters so close, I am hit by a wave of nausea. I turn away from the food, pulling the sheets over my mouth.

The voice says, 'Your husband was up early on his way to work. He dropped off a letter for you. It's right there on your tray.'

I turn, anxious to read David's words. I pick up the lightweight letter with the air mail symbols running along its perimeter, wiping it across the white sheets to decontaminate it from the offensive hospital tray and the repulsive food. My hands shake as I rip open the envelope and lift out the sheet.

Mom, he starts. *I'm settling in, finally. I've had a great time, but it's time to hit the books...* He goes on offering me tidbits of information. *The weather's great, so far. Where's all that* nebbia, *that fog you predicted? ...You were right about the exhaust fumes. I found out they don't have the same emission standards... The food is fabulous... I've gained weight already... There's this great place near* Piazza del Duomo. *I go in for a* panino *now and then... The* galleria *is stupendous*. Favoloso, *as they say. Expensive, but stupendous... I had a Campari for you...* And then at the bottom, as a postscript, he writes: *About your friends... I went to the consulate and managed to track down Jane Brunelli. She doesn't work there anymore but they gave me her number and I called. She was on vacation the first time I tried. When I finally got a hold of her, she was glad to see me. She says hello. She told me to tell you Daniel is ill and in hospital. That explains why there was no answer when I phoned his place. I don't think I should tell him about Marion right now...*

I ring the nursing station and anxiously await a response. But their tardiness annoys me and I am already sitting up on the bed, my legs dangling over the side, when someone finally comes in. 'What can I do for you, dear?' she asks.

'I need some paper and a pen. Would you have any on hand, please?'

'Why certainly, Margaret,' she says amicably. 'How nice to see you sitting up. How about breakfast?' she says lifting the stainless steel lids from the plates.

'I'll have the tea,' I say to appease her.

'Good.'

'Could you take the rest away, please? I'll have my tea and I can write my note on the table top, if you move the tray.'

'I'll get you the pen and paper.'

They must be trained to be agreeable under any and all circumstances, I think to myself as I watch her leave with the tray.

Chapter 54

I must write to David. I must know more about Daniel.

When Steve drops in at lunchtime, he finds me sipping a fresh cup of tea and munching on a dry cracker.

'Well, what a surprise,' he says, kissing me on the forehead. 'David's letter must have cheered you up.'

'Yes,' I tell him. 'It did. It brought back old memories. When I read about him having a drink in the *Galleria* and a sandwich in that bar across from the *Duomo,* I was there with him... And he says he met Jane...you remember Jane, don't you? We went to her place for dinner that time we were in Milan.'

'Sure, I remember.'

I force myself to continue, to tell him about Daniel. I want to shed some of my guilt... 'And you remember Daniel, Carlo's brother?'

'Sure.'

'Apparently he's ill and in hospital.'

'I'm sorry to hear that,' he says the way people mouth such words, even when they don't mean them. 'Say, did you eat anything today?' he asks.

'I had the tea and these biscuits here. Maybe I'll try dinner.'

'Great... I've got to get back to the office. I'll see you tonight.' And with another peck on the forehead, he leaves. I lie back on the bed and begin to formulate a plan. I can no longer procrastinate.

55

In the evening, I go to the patient lounge. The dinner hour news is on. They are doing a special segment on arms control. I watch and listen as an ominously frightening scene unfolds before my eyes. At first, we are shown an expanse of grassy meadow somewhere in middle America. It is punctuated in the distance by a lone, white, clapboard church, its steeple rising into the horizon. A perfectly innocuous, tranquil setting. But the utter calm and beauty of the surroundings is shattered when I hear the commentator tell of the arsenal of weaponry that is stored in bunkers beneath the prairie landscape. It is here that they have pierced the earth and embedded the silos containing destructive forces. I think of the Cyclops and the Titans. I think of Vesuvius. I think of myself. I am that grassy meadow.

Those corny lines Marion and I used to juggle when we sought excuses for our philandering come to mind. 'Carpe diem,' she would quote from the ancient Romans. 'Grab the bull by the balls while he still has them,' she would say. And I, attempting to be more gracious and less crude would quote the non offensive yet equally permissive Herrick:

> Gather ye Rose-buds while ye may,
>   Old Time is still aflying:
> And this same flower that smiles
> today,
>   To-morrow will be dying.

'Ugh,' she'd say.

In my letter to David, I enclose a note for Daniel.

My dearest Daniel,
    With this letter you will have a chance to see our son, David. He is attending the university, as I am sure he will tell you. News of your illness has distressed me. I realize we haven't heard from one another in years, and you must be wondering what would prompt me to seek you out at this stage in our lives. I am doing this because I have a confession to make, but first I must know about you and how you are. Is your illness serious? Please tell me. I must know. There is so much I must know. So much you must know. I will not rest until I hear from you...

As I await a response, my body becomes my ally. It slowly builds resistance and strengthens daily. Steve is pleased with my progress, pleased the test results have all been favorable. When I am finally released, he is sure all will be well.

I am home when Daniel's letter arrives. I clutch the envelope to my breast before opening it.

Mia carissima,
    How can I describe my feelings when your son, David came to see me, delivering your letter? After all these years. You ask if my illness is serious. I am afraid it is if by 'serious' you mean terminal.
    Your letter is filled with questions. It has me concerned... I will be going home soon. The doctors

think that is best. Promise you won't do anything rash until you receive my next letter...

I must see you, Daniel. I must. There is so much I have to tell you. So much I need to know...

His next letter is meant to shock me. To restrain me. But it has the opposite effect. He writes his cryptic message: *This is all you need to know,* and encloses three pictures. The first shows a youthful Daniel, in his prime, crouched proudly on a slab of stone which indicates he is at the top of a mountain. I look intently at the surroundings, trying to pinpoint the location, but it has been too long, and I can't be sure which mountain this is. In the next, Daniel and I are in the Piazza del Duomo, in Milan, feeding the army of pigeons threatening to invade us. The cathedral is our backdrop. In the third photograph, I see a changed Daniel. I know it is him: the same eyes look out at me, the same expression is emitted from the figure, but time has worn the features, thinned the hair, and taken some of the sheen from the eyes. *This is all you need to know,* I read again.

He is telling me to stay away again. He is sending me away. But this time I will not listen.

...Your plan will not work this time, Daniel. You can not keep me from you now. Not even with these photographs which I am returning to you. I simply must have some answers. Why did you leave me, Daniel? Perché?

56

How can I describe the agony that pierced me when I read his reply? How can I paint with words the sorrow that took hold of me?

> *My darling Margaret,*
> *You say you must know and I suppose the time has come for me to cleanse my soul. I was not completely truthful with you, my darling. I did not lie, but I did not reveal all. I wanted to. Oh, yes, how I wanted to. But I decided against it for fear you would make a rash and impetuous decision and decide to stay with me. This would have been detrimental to your happiness. Do you remember when we met? Do you remember when I told you about my eye? That was not all I lost during the war, Margaret. I had also suffered from a severe case of an illness which left me sterile, my darling. Sterile. Do you understand? Had I allowed you to stay, you would not have had the joys of motherhood, of having your wonderful son, David. I could not ask you to pay so dear a price... As for the eye, I was also told I would eventually be blind. Although this has not occurred. The doctors must have made a mistake... When you left and married so quickly, I must admit, I was surprised. I have to be honest and tell you I half expected to find you in Jakarta. But I knew you had made the right decision...*

I make arrangements to leave. When Steve comes home, I tell him I want to go to Italy to see David. I tell him it will change everything if I could go now.

He is taken aback by my quick decision, but is hopeful it will purge me of my despair. 'Maybe that's the best thing to do right now,' he agrees. 'Why not? You're on leave of absence anyway. I'll make the arrangements.'

'I've already booked the flight,' I tell him.

'I see,' he says rather surprised. 'Maybe I should come with you or join you later...take a few weeks off...'

'Oh, no,' I say startled he would even consider this. 'You know how you feel about Italy. Don't you remember?'

'Right. That permissive society where chaos is the norm.'

'I'll be fine. Really, I'm feeling so much stronger.'

'Yes, I can see that.'

57

I write Steve two notes the following morning. The first tells him to go to the bank, to our safety deposit box, and retrieve a second note. In it I write:

Dear Steve,
I am not asking you for mercy, nor for your forgiveness. I am not asking you for anything. I am simply telling you the truth. You may think it rather cowardly of me to tell you in this manner, but I don't have the strength to say it in any other way. Zola has said it for me, actually. I hope he won't mind if I quote him. I read it in one of those books you said were consuming me. I was just looking for answers, Steve.

If you shut up the truth and bury it under the ground, it will but grow, and gather unto itself such explosive power that the day it bursts through it will blow up everything in its way...

It is true that I am going to see David, but this is not the whole truth. I must also see Daniel, David's father. Yes, you've read correctly. I have deceived you.
You will not want to hear how I have loved you too. And I have. You will not want to hear that I have tried to be a good wife because you deserve nothing less. You are a fine and worthy man. But you will not want to hear any of this now...

What do I take with me? What do I leave behind? The burden of my years of accumulating and storing and sorting and filing is ponderous. I pack my father's belongings, the photographs which I have assembled neatly in albums and the old documents of no importance whatsoever. I take my mother's precious heritage: her lace trimmed sheets, her tablecloths and bedspreads and I ship this to myself so it will arrive in Italy to greet me. With me, I take only the necessities and my albums of David. I take these because they are mine.

I drive to Tino's to tell him I am leaving. I find him huddled in front of his fireplace, the wood crackling to keep him company.

'Hey, there,' he says turning to see who has walked in.

'Don't you ever lock your doors?' I say.

'What would anybody want from me? So, what brings you here?'

'I came to say good-bye.'

'Good-bye?'

'I'm off to Italy to see David.'

'You're feeling better then. You're over what ever it is you had.'

'I think so. The doctors said it was some sort of a peculiar virus.'

'They always say that when they don't know what it is.'

'I know,' I say laughing.

'Where's Steve?' he asks looking behind me.

'He's at work. He's not coming. I'm going alone and I'm not sure I'll be back.'

This surprises Tino, but he doesn't delve into it.

Chapter 57

'Why don't you come with me?' I say to him.

'To Italy? Christ, Margaret, it's been so long.'

'I know. Why don't you come?'

'No, I'll pass. *Non c'è niente la per me.* There's nothing for me over there anymore.' He stirs the fire and the flames flicker back to life. 'I'm too old to be gallivanting around the world. But not you, my little Margaret. There's still time for you. Just color that grey hair of yours and go. Seeing you like that makes me feel old.'

'You noticed. I can't say I streak it anymore?'

'Not unless you say you streak it brown.'

'Well, I just may do that, Tino. Color it, I mean. Even though I've always found that deceptive.'

'When are you leaving?'

'Day after tomorrow.'

'This is good-bye?'

'I think so.'

He sits back down facing the fire and I sit next to him. My tears come unrestrained and I hug him. He holds me tenderly and I see his eyes begin to water. 'When you cry,' he says, 'you remind me of when you were a little girl.'

'Do I, Tino? Really? Am I still a little girl to you, Tino?'

'Always, my dear. To me you will always be my little Margherita, grey hair and all.'

58

At the airport I check in, and Steve and I have a drink as we wait for the boarding call. I ask him about his day, how things are going at work, I avoid the truth. When my flight is called, I feel awkward and unreal, as if some phantom Margaret is performing the ritual of departure while another Margaret is leaving. My head throbs in the excitement and fear. I look into Steve's eyes and say good-bye. I am not even crying.

Something in me has snapped. People used to tell me to 'snap out of it' whenever my behaviour made no sense. Or they would say of someone who had lost control, 'She's snapped.' Well, now I have. I have fallen into my share of boobytraps and mines, but I am still here. Life goes on. Or does it? People say that. But it's not true, either. It's a lie. Life ends. Things change. Nothing is constant. North Africa was once a rich and fertile land, Vesuvius once had a single peak, dinosaurs once roamed the earth.

I refuse to continue my penance, saying my ten *Hail Marys, my Our Fathers, and my Act of Contrition* in a rush so no one will know how much I have sinned.

Steve hands me a newspaper he has picked up for me in the terminal. 'Where are your books?' he asks.

'I didn't bring any. I can always pick something up in London,' I say.

I travel into the night. Towards it. I watch the sun sink into the clouds, like a giant fireball. But the night is short on eastbound flights. Morning will come quickly. Soon I will see the purple haze of Ireland, the tapestry of France, and I will soar above the Alps.

I pull out the copy of today's newspaper Steve gave me. I unfold it, appalled at the photograph on the front page. For the passengers sake, not mine.

I fold the picture over so no one can see it.

It shows a jet, like the one we are on, with its top sheared off... Nine people were sucked to a watery grave. It happened over the Pacific. The fuselage split at 22,000 feet. Again, they are saying stress is the culprit. When the plane reached that altitude, its skin peeled, let go, split, taking a chunk of the plane and nine lives with it. The passengers may have died on impact, it says. Or they died when they hit the water. It was a two minute drop.

I can't help but wonder what those two minutes would be like? I try to imagine it. Falling into the giant, open jaws of the sea. I try to sit and stare without blinking for two minutes. I can't. I pinch my flesh and wait for two minutes to go by.

Two minutes is a long time. I wonder if they had time to be afraid? I wonder how many secrets they carried to their graves?

Printed by
Ateliers Graphiques Marc Veilleux Inc.
Cap-Saint-Ignace, Québec
in June 1994.